Beyond the Bridge

The second of the trilogy of stories

1) See you on the other side

2) Beyond the bridge

3) From the River to the Sea

By Kerry Whelan

Foreword

"Beyond the bridge" is a sequel to the novel "See you on the other side"

It follows those who returned from the 'War to end Wars' and the next generation on a journey in life. By the night of Easter Tuesday 1941, twenty-three years later, the Belfast Blitz of the Second World War, would once again see them face new challenges in the townlands of Shaw's Bridge, Drumbeg, Edenderry, Belfast and beyond.

A continuing tale of character, bravery, romance, learning and redemption.

Kerry Whelan

Beyond the bridge

Beyond the bridge

Kerry Whelan

Chapter One

The Promise

On a Spring morning 1919, Davy had slept the first night in his own bed back in the lockkeeper's cottage at Newforge since he went to France in the autumn of 1915. He was awoken with a nudge as he could hear in the dark recess of his brain.

"Wakey, wakey, son. I've a bone to pick with you."

He opened his eyes and raised his head from the pillow. Tom was standing over him with a steaming mug of black tea. Davy raised himself to a sitting position and wondered what he was in for.

"I'm on my first morning home from Hell and my father is going to give me grief. The good mood of last night's dinner at Ballydrain didn't last long," he thought to himself.

"What was it he had done wrong? It had been a great night. He couldn't remember anything that had caused any bother. What could it be?" Davy asked himself.

He sipped the tea and winched as he found out it was hotter than expected. As he raised himself out of bed to face his father, his extra height of three or four inches over him allowed the luxury of looking down at him, hoping that this physical advantage might reduce the imminent tirade.

"Sit down son. you're not in the Army now," rasped Tom, as his stern expression changed to the slightest sign of a grin.

Davy's defence mechanism retreated slightly, as he moved towards the table where Tom had already pulled a chair back and was resting his left hand on the surface.

Davy slumped down in the chair opposite and stared across at his father, with the same expression of innocence he had attempted to portray, like a child about to be given a rude telling off.

Tom stared back at Davy and kept up the silence. Davy could not stand the suspense any longer.

"Did I say something wrong last night then?" was his only response. Tom let out one of his characteristic grunts of irony.

"It's not what you said, son. It's what you didn't say."

Davy continued to look across at Tom in confusion and a certain amount of foreboding. Tom raised his face to the ceiling before he brought it back to eye level with Davy, setting his right hand onto the table as he tossed a small slim box across the worn surface. It skimmed across the table stopping just short of Davy's chest. Davy looked down at the box.

"Oh that!" replied Davy, as he pulled a face dismissing the object, as he moved his head left to right a few times.

"Didn't think it was appropriate. Nothing to brag about. Most of them out there deserved the same and got nothing for their efforts. I was just fortunate. I was noticed. Besides, I didn't want to talk about the war last night; Roger and all that," apologised Davy.

"Aye, that and I told you don't volunteer for anything, the world is full of dead heroes," replied Tom, face as straight as a poker.

"I'm no hero, Da, just found myself in situations that I had to deal with. Bravery didn't come into it." Tom leaned across the table and retrieved the box, and as he prised open the lid, continued.

"It fell out of your kit bag yesterday afternoon. I woke before you after our doze in front of the fire. According to Sir James that's a Distinguished Conduct Medal and that bar attached tells me you earned it twice. I had it in my pocket last night and showed it to Sir James. He reckons the only higher medal is the big one, VC.

Davy shrugged his shoulders and replied "It is what it is. I'm no hero, Da. If you don't mind I don't want to talk about it. It's over now. New challenges to face," as he attempted to rise from the table intent on ending the issue and the uncomfortable sense of embarrassment.

"Don't give me that, son. I've heard the full story from Bill and Jonty. Let's leave it at that."

Tom leaned forward and put both his hands on Davy's forearms in the same way Anna had done to him when she promised him she would bring Davy home. Davy was confused by the action. His father was never one for physical or verbal signs of affection.

"Just one more thing. Listen to me, and listen to me well, because I will not boil my cabbage twice. You see that 'wee girl' up the road. She sat opposite me in your chair before she left for France, and I thought I was looking at your mother. She wasn't that much older than her now, when I brought her to this house as my wife. God help us both, we never knew we would have such a short time together. Promise me one thing Davy, that you will do your best for her, so that if it should all end before its time, you will have no regrets. Regret is a terrible burden, son. You are a lucky young man to have found that one, and if you cause her any distress, it'll be me you'll have to answer, not Sir James."

Tom was already rising from the table as he finished his sentence. Uncomfortable at displaying such emotion.

"Nothing to worry about there, Da," assured Davy, before he continued.

"So, she got to you as well, then? Tom Gibson, my father, the man who is no one's mug. A man made out of the metal he forges every day," staring affectionately into his father's face.

Tom stared back and broke the mood and laughed as he turned to the door.

"A boy left, and a man has returned. That's for sure."

As he started to close the door on his way out, he looked back at Davy again.

"Just remember, don't be her door mat, either. Stick up for yourself when you think it's needed."

Tom stepped back towards Davy, as he lifted the box containing the medal from the table.

"If you haven't any use for it, I have, son, if you don't mind." Tom stood in silence as he tried to force the words out of his mouth.

"I'm proud of you son. You'll have a lot to do to get yourself geared up for that Medical School," as he walked out the door.

Davy waved his hand dismissively.

Tom walked out to the forge, hammered a strong nail in the beam above the fire, took the medal out of the box and hung it over the nail. It would stay there until Tom's death in 1936 when Sir James asked for it to be 'brought home' to Ballydrain.

Chapter two

Coming to terms

Twenty-two years had passed since Davy and Anna had walked up the driveway of Ballydrain, when they returned from the battlefields of France in 1919

Davy had entered The Royal Victoria Hospital to begin his successful career as a surgeon in 1925, the same year he and Anna moved from Mount Charles back up to Ballydrain. Davy had been apprehensive of the idea but as their first child was due in a few months he accepted that it would be best for Anna. It also meant he would be closer to Tom who still tapped his metal hammers, kept the lock open and working, and never missed the chance to let everyone know his son was a doctor.

By the time Tom passed away in 1936, he had the pleasure of sitting in his chair every Sunday with first Roger, then Joseph and finally the apple of his eye, Kathleen, all on his knee reading stories and singing them songs, on more occasions than he ever could have wished.

8

Anna had to come to terms with the demons that invaded her brain. The trauma and emotions, she buried the whole three years on the front by never looking back. Never putting herself in a situation that would allow it to flood back. She refused to go through the doors of any medical facility. For years after the War she made excuses to avoid any reunions, even the Remembrance Day Service at the City Hall in Belfast.

Then, on an Autumn morning, in October 1928, as the leaves of the trees made a carpet of orange on the driveway, the 10th anniversary of the Armistice approached. Anna was walking one of her horses from the stables to the field beside the drive. She saw a figure trying to disguise a slight limp with a determined stride, turn into the gates in the distance and proceed up the driveway towards the house. The figure had a hat pulled over her head and wore an austere coat. Her gait suggested it was someone not lacking in determination..

Anna steadied the horse and stood motionless, apart from containing the reins of the horse, impatient to get back to the field to join his friends.

"It can't be, not her. How do I handle this?" were the thoughts that invaded her brain. Anna was already shaking, as the vision in front of her ripped into her very soul. 1918 flooded back like a dam burst, which failed to hold back the pressure. The determined figure reached the fence beside Anna.

"Nurse Arthur, you haven't changed much, girl. Looks like life is treating you well, my dear."

It was Matron, with the same strong imposing tone of the frontline wards. Anna stood and stared, motionless, not knowing how to respond. She was still in a state of mental disarray.

As Matron got within a few feet of Anna, she looked into Anna's face. She could see her eyes beginning to tear up, her throat flexing as she tried to retain her outward appearance of calm.

"Well I see you are the same strong willed young lady I had the pleasure to work with, my dear. I hear it is Mrs Gibson now, married that young chap, over in Surgical, I hear."

Anna stood rigid, mind still in turmoil. Matron dropped her wardroom manner and stepped forward to embrace Anna and gave Anna a hug of reassurance as she spoke quietly.

"Let it go, Nurse Arthur, Anna." I can see I should have given you warning of my arrival. I am sorry, my dear."

"Oh Matron, I am so sorry. I should be better than this," sighed Anna, as she pulled back from her old boss.

"Just let me put this boy back in the field with his mates, and we'll go up to the house and have tea and the best scones Martha can muster. How does that sound, Matron,." suggested Anna, as she let out a mouthful of air and wiped her face.

"That's more like the young lady I know," smiled Matron.

By the time Anna and Matron sat in the drawing room with a blazing fire warming their faces, Eileen, a fresh-faced girl, came calmly into the room and asked Anna.

"Good Morning, Mam, "Is it scones you'd be wanting then?" "I see you are getting used to the way of things in here then," laughed Anna as she continued. "Would you let Martha know there'll be one extra for lunch today please." smiled Anna.

Matron tried to hold back a smile..

"Oh, and would you nip down to the cellar and bring up a good bottle of sherry for my old boss here," requested Anna, as she gestured towards, Matron.

"Oh my God, is this the lady Martha told me about. Had you and my Auntie Kitty scared to bat an eye!" replied Eileen in surprise. Eileen had a habit of speaking before she engaged her brain. The young naïve fifteen-year-old from Laghy, Donegal, a niece of Kitty, now

Sister Josephine who gave her life to the Poor Claire Hospice in France as she waited to be reunited with Joe who had perished on the first day of the Somme. Eileen had only been working for the family for a few months, and coming from the shores of Donegal Bay, was still getting used to the big bad world beyond, that played by a different set of rules of diplomacy and tack.

When Eileen left the room, Anna looked across at Matron with an embarrassed smile.

"That young lady is Eileen, a niece of Kitty's. She is not long here, Needs a few lessons in etiquette, but I'm working on it," laughed Anna.

"Seems you don't do discipline in a big way here, Anna," smiled Matron.

"No need for it much here. Not interested in ego trips in this house unless they try and take advantage. It's only then they will get 'short shift,' reassured Anna.

"This isn't the Somme. No one is going to die, getting it wrong here, thank goodness," sighed Anna.

Matron, sat rigid, remembering the tight rein she had held in the Nursing Unit.

"Oh Matron, I am sorry, I was not making a snide remark. You were the rock we survived on. You took the pressure from all of us. We would never have gotten through it without you. I still regret never telling you that before we left you. I am glad to have the opportunity to tell you now; even if it is ten years too late."

Matron pulled a grin and waved her hand dismissively.

"We all did what had to be done. We all made our sacrifices, some more than others. Why in the name of God you left the surroundings of this fine place, to face the front line was quite remarkable, my dear."

Anna, embarrassed, smiled softly towards Matron.

"Ah well, some things were worth fighting for," replied Anna.

A brief silence fell between the pair as Matron judged when to address the reason which she had come to visit unannounced. Anna, mind full of uncertainty why her Nemesis had appeared out of the blue, ten years after she last gave her a polite goodbye and a handshake on the morning Davy and Anna began their journey back home.

The awkward silence was broken by Eileen bringing in the tea and scones, still warm, smelling of flour, balanced on a silver tray.

As the two women began negotiating the butter, jam and clotted cream, and cutting the scones, Matron spoke. The situation they found themselves in was unsettling for both. Up to now their relationship had been of mistress and servant. Anna being the servant. Now ten years later, the balance had changed. Both knew it and both were now used to being in control of matters.

"Well Anna, I am sure you are wondering why I am here and that it isn't just to visit this beautiful residence," said Matron, before she continued, as she looked questioningly, into Anna's face.

"Why do you never attend Remembrance Day or have anything to do with the nursing reunions? Your absence has been noted. There are many who would love to see you. You were well thought of Anna. The one with the posh accent. The one the soldiers called the Duchess. Why have you never turned up, my dear?"

A silence returned, as Anna sat, mind turning in knots. She raised her eyes to the ceiling and focused on a crack emerging from a cornice. As she continued to unravel her thoughts, Eileen returned balancing a tray with a bottle of sherry and two crystal glasses.

Without moving her gaze from the crack in the ceiling, Anna instructed,

"Eileen, please go back down to the cellar and bring me up a bottle of Chablis and two large wine glassed. I feel they might be needed rather than the sherry." Anna dropped her eyes from the ceiling, sighed slowly and heavily, as she looked across at Matron.

"Ten years, Matron, ten years I have turned my back on the Somme. It will remain that way for as long as I live. It is the only way I can cope with it; bury it, I look forward and concentrate on each day and the wonderfully fortunate life I have had since. I promised Kitty I would be the best person I could. I have tried to honour that promise. I am afraid to return to all of that. I fear I would not deal with it properly. Fear the fortress I have built since those days would collapse, and me along with it. The nightmares still take over at times, although they are less than the first few years. I cannot cope with the smell of a hospital. I have never visited David at his work. I had my son Roger at home. It will be the same for any more that come along.

Matron, you may see before you a confident women of Belfast's social elite; I believe is what they call us, but I am as fragile and as scarred by the War as anyone. We are not all made of the stuff you are made of Matron."

As Anna finished her admission of weakness, Eileen came back into the room a little quicker than the etiquette required of a good house servant. Even Eileen's innocent brain had picked up that things were not as usual with Mrs Gibson.

As Eileen had rushed through the kitchen, disappeared to the cellar, retrieved the Chablis and straight past Martha, who was rolling dough at the table, she had been met with a shout from Martha.

"Slow up girl! If you drop that bottle I'll have your life!" shouted Martha. As she processed the reason why a bottle of Chablis was needed at ten o'clock in the morning Martha thought to herself.

"Urgent bottle of Chablis at this time of the day, this doesn't sound good," thought Martha to herself, as she stopped rolling the dough, wiped the flour off her hands with her apron, and walked quietly towards the door of the kitchen that Eileen had just passed through.

Anna, thought Martha, had been fond of her wine since she returned from the Somme, but never in the morning. She enjoyed it, no doubt, but it wasn't a crutch, more a calmer, a soother.

As Eileen placed the tray on the table, Anna glared uncharacteristically at Eileen, and raised her voice.

"Open it and fill those glasses, Eileen. Close the door on your way out!"

Eileen closed the door behind her, turned, and almost collided with Martha who loomed over her. Before she got the chance to speak, Martha gestured to her to be silent, before nodding her head in the direction of the kitchen. Eileen took the hint and cleared off.

16

Martha remained silent, shoulder and ear leaning against the heavy door. Inside the drawing room Anna and Matron both sat staring at the wine glasses.

"Matron," sighed Anna, "please come to the point. I do not like to go around in circles. My father has taught me that, and in matters of business he is not often wrong."

Matron leant forward in her chair and adjusted the lapels of her tweed jacket.

"Well if that is the way of it, I would prefer you stop calling me Matron. I haven't been that since I retired last year. I believe we have enough in common for you to call me, Lily. I do feel there is a lack of warmth in being addressed as Matron. Especially to one of my girls of whom I have the highest regard, my dear." replied Matron, before she continued.

"What I came here to say, ask, in fact, is something I had never realised would cause you such distress. I had not understood the level to which you had dug deep and coped with our situation back in the days. I see you have had to cope with it in your own way and I have, to say the least, touch not one raw nerve, but several. For that, my dear Anna, I regret. However, I still have to ask for your understanding and support, just one more time, if I may?" explained Matron, with an expression of compassion Anna had not seen from her since the day Kitty received the news of Joe's demise.

Anna's mind was still spinning, as she lifted one of the glasses of Chablis and threw half of the contents down her throat; hardly stopping on her taste buds. Not the way to drink quality wine, a desecration more like, but the sooner it spread round her system and invaded her brain the better, she thought.

"As you are, I am sure aware," continued Lily, "I have been the Chief Representative of the Nursing Corp at the cenotaph in Belfast since 1919. In addition I have overseen the welfare of all Medical staff veterans who served in the War.

My reason for visiting you today," sighed Lily, "this is the last year I will be taking on the role. I am emigrating to Australia to join my sister and her family. My arthritis is becoming a burden and she has assured me that the weather will be of benefit. I have no close friends or relatives here, so I have nothing to lose." shrugged Matron, as she finally picked up the wine glass and took a lady-like sip.

Anna lifted her glass again and took a more appropriate sip, her hand visibly shaking.

"Keep going Lily, and ?" replied Anna, with a tone of question and irony.

"I need someone to take my place and fill that role. You are the best candidate for the job Anna. I need you on this as much as I needed you to hold down the men dying in agony; calm the ones who needed reassurance," stressed Matron.

Anna said nothing, still trying to regain her composure, all the time thinking "how would father deal with this?"

"Matron, Lily," replied Anna, "I am afraid I am not the person you think I am. I am nothing more than a bird in a gilded cage, who found herself, out of the love of a boy, in a world she had no understanding, who had to raise herself beyond her capabilities. It burnt me out, and only, thanks to the love of my life, and being fortunate enough to have a life such as this, that I have been able to get beyond it. I do not have the strength to relive any of it or anything to do with it." Anna took another sip of her wine before she continued.

"The cenotaph, Remembrance Day, Huuh! David and I always go down to Shaws Bridge that morning and look down the Lagan. Talk to Kitty and Joe in our heads and walk with them up to Minnowburn and Edenderry. That is our Remembrance Day. David does not attend the City Hall cenotaph either. Wild horses would not get him to do it. He never saw the War was worth it. He does not like ceremony. He has a bit too much of his father in him to think otherwise. He might even be right," mused Anna, as she shook her head slowly, before leaning back in her chair, as she searched out the crack in the cornice again.

Another prolonged silence ensued. Anna, hoping she had made her point. Matron calculating when to continue her conversation while attempting to judge Anna's level of brittleness. Anna, still staring at the cornice, broke the silence.

"Lily, while I appreciate your belief that I am worthy of such a position, I regret I am unable to consider your offer. No one knows my weaknesses better than myself. I know I do not have it in me to take on the role," replied Anna, as she dropped her eyes, filled with tears, to look Matron in the face.

Matron concealed her frustration and disappointment by dropping her gaze to the carpet below her feet. A silence invaded the room once again before Matron continued.

"What do you think Nurse Breslin, Kitty, Sister Josephine, would make of all this?

Anna looked in shock at Matron.

"Well," continued Matron, "I believe she would be more than happy to be sitting at home waiting for Joe to return from work, have his dinner ready, if all she had to do was turn up for a ceremony once a year and attend a few meetings."

As Matron slumped back in her chair, Anna returned her gaze. At the same time the heavy door burst open almost taking off the hinges as the handle slamming against the wall, the shudder dislodging one of Sir James's hunting paintings from the wall.

"That's enough, you, Missus whoever you are. Sling your hook and leave our Anna alone. Shift yourself down that driveway or I'll throw you down it!"

Matron sat aghast, but unmoving, as Martha crouched beside Anna, who was now as distraught as the day she and Davy sat opposite the boat club in 1915, deflated by her failed attempt to outwit Sir James on that Autumn Sunday morning.

Martha cradled Anna in her arms like a child and turned again to glare at Matron.

"You still here! Thought I told you to clear off! Think I'm all talk do you!" as she reared up to grab Matron by her tweed jacket. As Martha began to raise Matron from the chair, Anna shouted at Martha.

"Martha, leave her alone. I deserved that!"

Martha released her grip on Matron and let her drop back in the chair. As Martha returned to reassure Anna, Matron adjusted her jacket.

"Sorry, Anna, but I won't let anyone away with talking to you like that!" reassured Martha.

"I know Martha, I know, but just go back to the kitchen and Lily and I will sort this misunderstanding out. Thank you Martha." smiled Anna, as she wiped her eyes, straightened her riding jacket, and stared apologetically at Matron.

Martha glared back at Matron.

"If I hear any more cheek like that out of you, I'll be back!" as she walked in fury out of the door and down the hallway to the kitchen.

Anna raised her eyebrows as she looked across at Matron.

"I do apologise about that, Lily. Martha is a bit overprotective at times."

"No harm done. She was right. I did overstep the mark. It is me who should be apologising. It was low and uncalled for. I am sorry Anna, both for saying it and causing you such hurt," apologised a remorseful Matron. "You clearly dug deeper at the Somme than even I imagined."

Both instinctively lifted their glasses of Chablis, and both took significant gulps, most disrespectfully of the quality of refreshment.

"Right Lily, let's start again. I'm fine now. Surely you can get someone else?" asked Anna.

Matron settled her thoughts and explained, in a lot less assertive manner than earlier.

"You were one of my best nurses, so you have the credibility from your peers. You have the training of how to organise events, organise people, you have the confidence and manner to handle being at the centre of things, and even more importantly, you have standing in this community. You would be listened to, unlike any of the rest of us, myself, included. What's more, from this morning's unfortunate situation, you understand better than most, the feelings that so many of us hold down, buried just below the surface. When veterans approach me every Armistice Day, I see it in their eyes, the haunted look, the trauma. Meeting with old comrades seems to help them."

Lily took a polite sip of the Chablis before she continued.

"I know of no one better suited to the task. I know, Anna, it is a huge ask, but it might help you, as well. You have no idea how many speak to me and ask about you and Kitty. How's the Duchess and her 'wee mate'?' is what most of them say, as they shake their heads in sorrow when I tell them of the fates of Kitty and Joe.

It might do you, and them, a lot of good. The men, who turn up, just want to share a bit of time with people they shared the dreadful experience with. It's not about anything else and it does help to release their demons," explained Matron, as she reached forward to drain the rest of the Chablis.

"Well Lily," Anna sighed, "I think we both need a bit of fresh air after that session. Would you be interested in a walk round our gardens? It will help give you an appetite for lunch," suggested Anna."

"That sounds a lovely idea, Anna," smiled Matron.

Anna showed Lily around the gardens and the mansion courtyard, never mentioning the issue in hand until they reached the mansion steps. Anna spoke first.

"It would just be the cenotaph and a few meetings; no hospital visits. That's still a bridge too far. I know my limits, Lily." suggested Anna.

"No hospital visits, Anna. This post is about aftercare, recovery, healing of the mind. Remembering, comradeship and sharing life. You are as qualified at that as anyone, my dear." reassured Matron.

"Well then, I had better let Martha know to set an extra place for dinner this evening. I presume there will be plenty I will have to learn," assured Anna as she linked Matron's arm and walked her up the steps.

Three weeks later at the cenotaph at Belfast City Hall, Anna stood at the shoulder of Matron with other nursing colleagues she had not seen in ten years, She didn't want any questions, especially about Kitty. It was all too painful. Davy stayed well back in the crowd, keeping well away from fellow veterans as he surveyed the scene.

When formalities ended, the lines of nurses broke up, mingled; handshakes, embraces and greetings, began. All Anna could think of was to scan her eyes for Davy and melt into the background. She had fulfilled her promise to Matron. It was done; she just wanted out of it.

As she searched the crowd for Davy, she felt a persistent tug at her coat. She looked down to see a child, a girl about six years old, and a younger child she assumed was a younger brother, smiling up at her.

"Miss, Miss," shouted the little girl. "Are you the Duchess, Missus? My Daddy says you are!" Anna was taken aback by the child's adulation.

"And who says that I am?" asked Anna, as she placed her hand on the child's face.

"My Daddy, saw you and said, Oh it's the Duchess and told us to go over and give you a hug." Anna's confidence shrunk even further, as she tried to gather her thoughts.

"And where is your Daddy?" asked Anna.

The little girl turned in excitement and pointed in the direction of the crowd of veterans, most sharing lights for their cigarettes, and talking amongst themselves. Anna continued to scan the crowd for a clue, before she spotted one veteran, who was looking at her. He gave her a casual salute and then a cheeky wink.

Anna looked down at the children. "Would you take me over to your Daddy, please?" The two children excitedly dragged Anna over to the veteran.

"Jeez girl. I never thought I'd see you again. If it wasn't for you and the other nurses I'd never be here, and those two wouldn't existed," smiled the veteran, who extended his left hand towards her. He wasn't left-handed; he didn't have a right arm to extend.

"I was in your ward. I have seen a few of the other nurses over the years, but never you or your mate, Kitty. Where have you been girl? There's a lot of us here wondered what happened to you. Thought maybe you hadn't got through it. Oh Jeez, I'm glad you are fine and by the look of you, doing very well. Must have got yourself a rich husband. Living the good life by the look of it."

As he kept hold of her hand he turned to look at some of his mates.

"Hey lads, look whose here. It's the Duchess herself!" he shouted as he attracted the attention of some of the veterans.

Each gave her a hug and spoke to her. Davy, who had watched it all from a distance, decided it was time to get near to Anna. He was unsure how she would continue to handle this situation. As he shuffled his way to Anna's shoulder he heard the one-armed veteran continue.

"Well, where is your mate Kitty then, Duchess?" Anna breathed in, and swallowed, but before she could speak, Davy interrupted.

"She's still working in France, mate. Stayed out there. Still nursing!"

He gave the veteran a look that suggested he didn't ask any more about it. Anna looked over her shoulder at Davy.

"It's fine David, I can deal with this, it's fine." while it was visibly obviously she was anything but fine."

"Kitty stayed in France to be with Joseph," replied Anna, and before the veteran could ask any more, she continued.

"And what about you. How have you been. So glad to see you. Your children are a credit to you. I'm sure you are proud of them."

The Swiss school for young ladies training was coming in handy.

From a distance, Matron, while greeting others, did not miss the engagement between Anna and the veterans.

Matron smiled to herself and thought, "Well that wasn't so hard after all. You'll do girl. Back on the wards, only this time you are the one healing, Nurse Arthur."

As Anna finally managed to extricate herself from the group her last comment was "Well I look forward to seeing you all next year, God bless."

As she turned away, Davy linked her arm. The veteran with the one arm tugged Davy's coat. Davy turned as the veteran whispered,

"Take good care of that girl. One of the best she is, mate." Davy whispered back.

"She takes care of me, more like, boss," assured Davy.

The experience of that morning was a watershed in the healing process Anna had suppressed for over ten years. It was, however, only a stepping-stone. It allowed her to return to the fold of the Nursing Auxiliaries, but a hospital environment was still a step too far and it would remain that way until Easter 1941.

Chapter Three

Ravens in the night

It was a fine Easter Tuesday on the 15th April 1941. The Ulster tradition of celebrating Easter on Monday and Tuesday rather than Friday and Monday meant that everyone at Ballydrain Estate was busy arranging for the annual event that had taken place for fifteen years since 1926. Anna was in her element, flitting around, making sure everyone was carrying out their duties to ensure that the day would pass off without a hitch.

Davy as always, let her get on with it and concentrated on keeping twelve-year-old Joseph, and ten-year-old Kathleen occupied, as they were best kept well away from the organised chaos that was surrounding them. Kitchen staff preparing food, estate volunteers erecting tents and seating. Jonty and his team setting up the gymkhana fences. Some of the best horse people of South Belfast and the Lagan Valley were beginning to arrive in their horse boxes.

Martha, now House Manager, ambled around, sleeves rolled, up keeping a discerning eye on the kitchen staff. Jonty cantered around the estate on his black cob horse. doing the same with the team erecting the fences.

Jonty had become Estate Manager, since McCracken was sadly found slumped against a gate post in the bottom meadow overlooking Edenderry on the far side of the Lagan River some five years earlier. He had suffered a massive heart attack as he checked fences. He had felt the strange pain in his arm all day, felt dizzy, grabbed the gate to steady himself, and then he was gone. Davy and the twins Adam and Allen who both looked after the gardens, farmland and game reserve between them, had gone out to look for him. As they saw him in the distance slumped against the gate, Adam and Allen ran as well as any men in their forties could manage. Davy sighed in sorrow. He knew from the shape of McCracken, there was nothing to be done. It was best he walked. It gave him chance to gather his thoughts and organise McCracken's removal to his cottage on the estate in as respectful way as possible. Best he kept his mind clear to deal with McCracken's widow who herself had been in poor health. 'Concentrate on the living, the dead are someone else's problem' had been drummed into Davy from his early days in medical training, and the nightmare of France.

As Davy dragged his thoughts from the past to the present he remembered he had been allocated the task of keeping Joseph and

Kathleen occupied, well away from the preparations.

"Right, you two, let's go down to the lake and see if Grandpa James has caught any fish." shouted Davy "Last down there is a monkey's uncle,"

Joseph charged ahead, Kathleen running as fast as her little legs could manage. If it had been a case of the winner being the one making the most effort, she would have won with ease.

As the two children reached the water's edge they turned to watch Davy jog towards them. Both made monkey noises, swinging their arms about, pointing and laughing at him. Sir James, who was sitting on his shooting stick, fishing rod in hand, glanced round.

"Shush, be quiet you two. You'll scare the fish," whispered Sir James. The children immediately became silent and stood rigid. Sir James winked at Davy.

"See your man management skills are still intact," smiled Davy, as he stood alongside the elderly and increasingly frail gentleman.

"Right, you two, hold this rod and remember, keep quiet and don't make a sound. If you catch a trout, I'll ask Martha to cook it for your supper. Would you like that?"

"Yes!" shouted the eager pair. Sir James pulled a face and put his finger to his lips.

As the children disputed who should hold which part of the rod Davy spoke quietly to Sir James as they both stared across the lake.

"How are you this morning? Did you get a quiet night?" asked Davy.

"Nothing I couldn't handle David. It is what it is. Seems like today's Easter fete will be my last. I intend to make the best of the day. Watching those two, and us standing here, masters of all we survey is a fine start, don't you think?" pondered, Sir James.

"I think Anna wants that as well. She seems particularly intense with all the preparations. She always wants it done right but she's more focused than usual," replied Davy.

"Yes David, she still has this need to show me she can run things. She really should not bother. She has nothing left to prove; not that she ever did," replied Sir James.

"Well it seems to me it is an inherited trait, the need to be seen to be in control of matters," said Davy, as he flashed an apologetic smile at Sir James.

A silence fell between the two men as they watched the antics of the two anglers. Eventually it was broken by Sir James.

"Does she know? Did you tell her?" asked Sir James with more than a little concern.

No Sir James, I did not," sighed Davy. "I'll let her get Easter over and find the best time to raise it. The war gave her insight in such matters. My guess is she has worked it out and doesn't want to think about it. The event today fills that intent perfectly," reassured Davy.

"Huhh! I wonder where she got that mindset from, David," laughed Sir James under his breathe.

"I wonder," replied Davy in similar manner.

"Hope you have plenty of that morphine stuff when it gets to it. I think it might come in handy, is my guess," mused Sir James.

"If it gets to that stage, I'll have to bring Dr Sinton up to take over. I'm family. It's not ethical practice, James. Anyhow, I believe that stage is still a while off. I'm looking forward to you carving the turkey at Christmas, James."

"Whatever you have to do my boy. Just try and make it as painless as possible for May and Anna. That is all I ask," sighed Sir James, as he turned to look at the two giggling grandchildren.

"My God, will I ever make anglers out of you two. You are not even holding the rod properly. Bring it over here while I teach you a few things about game fishing. Did I tell you about nearly being eaten by a crocodile when I was fishing in Africa?"

"Leave them with you then, James," laughed Davy. "No doubt she'll find me something else to do," sighed Davy.

"Why should you be any different to the rest of us," replied Sir James.

Davy ambled back up the grass towards the House, anticipating the grand day that would be had by all. His mind jumped to the other big event of the day. Linfield were playing Glentoran that afternoon. He had often managed to attend games along with Bill Johnston, who was now on the Committee of the football club, a role he held with pride as much as his position as Master of Edenderry Orange Lodge. You can take the man away from Linfield, but you could not take Linfield from the man; and never would, smiled Davy to himself. On this occasion family loyalty and responsibility took centre stage. Watching Linfield hopefully beat Glentoran would have to wait for another day.

Davy made his way up the grassy slope from the lake to the patio at the side of the mansion house, his eyes scanned the view, trying to pick out Anna. His mind flashed back to the afternoon in 1915 when he and Joe scanned their eyes looking for Anna and Kitty.

Anna appeared, this time, not in an elegant gown, but riding britches, boots and hacking jacket. Anna, was now, like Davy, in her middle forties, but she had lost none of her girlish charm, now added to, by years of experience of dealing with her status in the world of Belfast's power brokers. As she approached, she caught sight of Davy looking in her direction.

"Davy, now you have dumped those two with Dada, I have the very job for you!" teased Anna.

"Now why does that not surprise me, your ladyship," laughed Davy as he tipped his forelock as they shared a short embrace. "Take a break for ten minutes you've been at this since six this morning," urged Davy.

"It's over twenty-six years since Kitty and I strolled down these steps, Davy. I've had twenty-six years of the best life any women could ever hope for. Poor Kitty has not been as fortunate. A life in waiting. She'll be tending German soldiers as we speak. I think I can manage a long day worrying about tent posts, fences and food Davy," sighed Anna, as she raised a thoughtful smile.

"Come with me. I have the very job for you," instructed Anna, as they walked back in the direction of the mansion back door.

"Where is Roger? I haven't seen him all morning?" asked Davy.

"Oh, I sent him down to help with the bottom fences at the far end down by the towpath. He should be with Allen and Adam," replied Anna.

As they negotiated the corridors of the work rooms in the basement of Ballydrain House, they emerged into the kitchen busy with staff preparing roasts, breads and fruit bowls. There was rationing throughout Northern Ireland but the extensive herd of livestock, home grown vegetable and fruit grown on the estate meant that a good day could be had by all.

The afternoon passed with everyone making the best of the day and in good spirits. The only concern Davy had was the lack of cheers coming from Windsor Park were the football match was taking place. On a public holiday, local Belfast derby, crowds of thirty thousand were commonplace. When Linfield scored, the cheers rolled over the city and down the Lagan valley of South Belfast. Today he heard little, except for less noisy, but no less excited celebratory cheers. The sort of sound that away team supporters would muster. Davy had the distinct churning feeling in his stomach that Linfield were not having a good day. He knew he would get a full report of the match from Bill that evening.

By that evening after the Spring sunshine evaporated into a short twilight, and the darkness of night fell upon them, Bill and Davy sat on the steps of the mansion house looking over the lake in the direction of Belfast, Blackmountain, Cavehill and Napoleon's Nose.[1]

As Bill was just about to raise himself from the steps and leave his empty bottle of Guinness and his glass back into the kitchen, he halted his movement as he froze, knees still not straightened. Davy caught his change in demeaner and gave him a confused glance.

"What's that sound?" mused Bill, half asking a question, half talking to himself.

"Don't hear anything, Bill. Are you sure it's not your dodgy ear playing up again?" replied Davy.

"No Davy, my other ear's twice as good to make up. Listen, can you hear it now?" asked Bill.

Davy focus on the night air, trying to cancel out the sound of birds and wildlife.

---

[1] Napoleons Nose. Local name for the Cavehill Escarpment.

"It's like the droning noise of the mill machines, only heavier. But with the Easter holidays, the mills are all closed until the morning. It's not them" replied Davy. Bill looked to the sky, and then southwards.

"Sounds to me it's getting louder," replied Bill, eyes still searching the sky. The drone gained strength as the seconds passed. Bill grimaced.

"I don't like the sound of that, Davy mate. Don't like it at all," whispered Bill, as he let a billow of cigarette smoke slowly flow from his nose and mouth, shaking his head from side to side, as he exhaled.

"Do you reckon it's what 'the powers to be' said couldn't happen?" sighed Davy, as he turned his eyes to look at Bill.

Well Goring[2] sent a few bombers over a week or more ago and did a bit of damage to the Yard[3] but it was only a handful of them. Big boys on the Hill[4] thought it was a token gesture, nothing to get alarmed about. Looks like that was a bit of nonsense to keep us from panicking" replied Bill.

---

[2]Chief of the Luftwaffe
[3] "The Yard" Harland and Wolfe" Belfast shipyard.
[4] "Big boys on the Hill" Parliament building Stormont.

"More likely trying to cover their incompetence," sneered Davy. "Somme, all over again, Bill. Led up the garden path. We got left to deal with the consequences!"

"Jeez, I hope it's not The Somme all over again," sighed Bill, as he began to walk in the direction of the house. As he got to within a few yards of the side kitchen door, Roger, Allen, Adam and Jonty all came out of the door, holding spare chicken legs, left from the afternoon buffet. All, including young Roger, with a glass of beer in the other hand. Jonty spoke first, as always.

"What's up Bill, you've got a face on you like a Lurgan spade. The match wasn't that bad today."

"Shut up Jonty, listen mate," growled Bill.

All four stood silent. Waiting for Bill to explain something. After several seconds Bill still did not speak. Allen was the first to break the silence.

"Bill, what is it you want to say. I'd like to eat my chicken if you don't mind."

"Allen, I said listen. For frig' sake, listen. You're supposed to be the friggin' expert on wildlife. What do you make of that?" snapped Bill, as he pointed to the sky.

Jonty, the twins, and Roger all looked to the sky, as Davy appeared behind Bill. Roger, tried to hide the beer Jonty had given him, as his father caught his eye. Roger was the only one who had no idea what was going on. A combination of youthful innocence and the effect of one of his first drinking sessions fogged his brain.

No sooner had they heard the drone in the distance, air raid sirens started up from Belfast, sending a chill down everyone's spine.

"Not those bastards again!" cursed Adam, as he spat on the ground. The droning noise increased as the boys of 1916, now men in their prime of life, stood searching the black sky southwards. The twins, with their night vision, spotted them first.

It took the rest of the group a few more seconds to focus on what looked like black crows, ravens, gliding through the darkness. Bill, pulled his Gallaher's from his mouth, threw it in frustration on the ground at his feet, and stomped it under his boot.

"So much for they'll never get this far" snarled Bill, in frustration.

Davy took a step back and lodged his frame against the stone wall of the mansion house. As the rest of the group, pointed and considered the consequences, Davy stood in pensive mood. He moved his gaze from the sky to the ground, and back at the sky, as his mind tried to adjust from the relaxed atmosphere of a good day and more than a few glasses of beer, whisky and wine; not the best mix at the best of times. Certainly not for what he knew would be ahead of him long before the morning would break.

As the black crows got level with the mansion, they were to the west.

"Looks as if they're heading right down over the Lisburn Road," advised Bill, who was still the main man among the lads.

The inner mansion front door opened, unnoticed by the group, except for Davy. He knew it was only a matter of time. Davy kept his focus on the door as Anna came out. She looked first at the lads who were all pointing to the sky at the bombers cruising unopposed to Belfast. She could not see Davy amongst them. Then she sensed his presence to her right. He was leaning against the wall beside the entrance, looking at the sky. She knew his focus was not on the night sky. She knew he was plotting and planning. That was his way. Think ahead, no luxury of panic or emotion. She also knew he was as scared and confused as the rest.

She moved over silently beside him, unnoticed by the animated group. They caught each other's eyes as they came together. Nothing was said, they both understood each other's minds. Anna, linked her arm under Davy's as she leant her back against the wall beside him, resting her head against his shoulder.

"Thought I'd seen the last of this," she sighed in a whisper. "You are staying at home this time, girl," whispered Davy, with a similar sigh. Anna just patted his arm and squeezed her arm under his arm.

"That's the end of the long night I was hoping to have, wee girl!" mused Davy, with a glint in his eye before he returned his gaze to the ground."

"The Germans didn't separate us last time. They won't do it this time either. Just have to leave it for another night then, big lad," mimicked Anna, as she slapped him on the chest with her other hand, putting an end to his amorous suggestions, made earlier, as the alcohol kicked in; not that he needed it, as far as his passion for Anna was concerned. The flame in his heart still burned as bright as the first day he met her. Anna felt the same. They were as near to one person as any two people could be. She knew Davy all too well. He always made a joke when he was worried. It was his way of coping.

As the group on the veranda steps searched the sky, other staff and a few remaining guests emerged from the mansion and the Italian garden. Some still holding a glass in their hands. The group swelled in number as the Heinkels, Dorniers and Junkers flew over, almost casually in the direction of the city, increasing in number, in the night sky.

Martha came out of the door, arms on her hips, sleeves rolled up.

"This lot haven't flown over to drop a few in the Lough this time. There must be a hundred or more and they're still coming. Poor sods in the city aren't even going to get time to get under the stairs" exclaimed Martha, as she raised her apron to her face.

Jonty heard her, hobbled away from his mates, and shuffled up beside her.

"Just be thankful we aren't down there with them, Martha." reassured Jonty, as he stroked her shoulder, trying to keep her from the depths of despair. He had been married to Martha for over twenty-years and knew well that her outward formidable image was only her coping mechanism. She was as brittle, loyal, and as easily hurt as the rest. She was already containing her thoughts about their eldest son, Alexander, known by everyone as Alec.

He was, to the last of their knowledge, in North Africa; a Desert Rat, He had signed up at the beginning of the war in the Inniskillings and had been transferred to a Commando unit. Young Alec had

43

inherited his mother's genes and his father's mental resilience. The perfect fit for the role.

As the group strained their eyes on the night sky, Davy separated himself from the mansion wall as he released his grip from Anna's arm.

"I need to go up to the attic and get a better view. Need to get an idea where the casualties are going to be. Get teams set up. It's going to be bad, Anna. It won't be men in uniform this time. It will be families, women and children."

As Davy climbed the stairs two at a time, with Anna moving in a ladylike one step at a time, he turned back to Anna, just behind him.

"You stay down there and find someone sober enough to get me down to the City Hospital," instructed Davy, as if he was giving a ward assistant her orders.

Anna, raised her eyebrows at his superior tone, but in the circumstances, though better of reacting. She knew he had clicked the switch in his head that demanded focus, devoid of feelings. Anna had many characteristics of her father. Davy, was Tom Gibson's son, and had more than enough, at times too much, for his own good, of his father's hard-nosed attitude when hardy came to hardy. Tom Gibson had taken control of Davy's brain.

Anna gave him a look that said, "Watch it big lad," rolled her eyes and retreated down the stairs back out to the sky gazing crowd outside. She did not look for a driver, she had already sorted that task before her foot reached the bottom step.

Anna filtered silently amongst the sky gazers, the first of the bombs were already dropping on their targets. A few at first, then patterns of clusters aimed to fall on specific targets. The onlookers gasped and cursed as the explosions lit up the night sky and made the ground shudder even though they were a good three miles from the centre of the targets.

Bill spotted Anna and casually moved through the crowd until he was on her shoulder. As he lit another Gallaher's Blue and took a long drag, he spoke in almost a whisper to her, as he let the smoke expel from his nostrils.

"It's the North shore and West of the city. Docks and the factories they are after.

Our mills on the Crumlin Road and Percy St, Lower Shankill are in the middle of that," advised Bill.

He had been promoted from Manager of Edenderry Mill to General Manager of the whole Arthur mill empire, since Sir James's health had deteriorated, and Anna put her foot down and told Sir James to retire, promising him that Bill would be their eyes and ears. She and her father would make the business decisions together from the drawing room in Ballydrain.

"Would they have got out before this started?" asked Anna, impassively. She also had gone into 'needs must' mode. She could almost see Matron watching her and the words "The only thing that matters is the patient, If I see any nurse being distracted by anything but the soldier you are attending.........!"

Bill stared ahead, not looking at Anna, as he surveyed the distance carnage.

"Well, we have done fire drills and evacuation drills enough times, but it's when they get outside is the problem. Most of them live in the tight streets around the factories. Air raid shelters, what there are of them, won't do a lot against those bombs. There's a few churches and chapels that have thick walls, basements and crypts. Other than that, it's under the stairs and pray to your God, whoever he may be," sighed Bill, as he expelled another draw of tobacco smoke.

"Dear God!" sighed Anna, as she shook her head slowly from side to side.

Both stood silent, weighing up the situation. Anna was the first to speak.

"Right, Davy is going to have enough on his plate dealing with the consequences. He needs someone to get him to the City Hospital and the Royal, more like.[5] I'll deal with that. No one else is sober enough to do it, Bill.

"Surprised Davy agreed to that" questioned Bill.

Anna gave Bill a look out of the side of her eye and held the stare.

"Oh, right. You haven't told him. Good luck with that then!" replied Bill, holding back a laugh as well as he could, bearing in mind the circumstances.

"Just leave David Gibson to me, Bill. I'll sort it," whispered Anna, as she turned away from Bill.

"Sure you've had him sorted since catching 'spricks' [6] at Minnowburn when you were a 'wee' girl."

"Sure he loves it, Bill," replied Anna, not turning to face him before continuing. "Are you in good enough shape to get there when this stops?"

"No problem Anna, I was at the match this afternoon. Missed most of the drinking today."

---

[5] Royal Victoria Hospital, Grosvenor Road and Falls Road junction.
[6] Gudgeon and Rudd fry - Sticklebacks

"In the meantime I need you to get Jonty to sort as many carts, tractors, anything on wheels that he can, and get them down to the gate lodge ready to go to the factories as soon as it's safe to go up there." Anna instructed. It was not a two-way conversation.

"Get Adam and Allen to put the marquee tents back up. Send someone down to the Scout Hall. Get every tent and ground sheets up here."

Back up in the attic Davy sat impassively, talking to himself, or to be more exactly, Tom Gibson, who had died six years earlier.

"Well Da, you are the man with all the answers. What do I do with this one?" whispered Davy to himself; not that anyone was listening.

As he sat pondering different scenarios and permutations he heard the stamp of female footsteps racing up the wooden attic staircase. As he turned to face the door he saw Anna emerging from the darkness of the landing.

"Transport sorted, ready when you are, Davy," reported Anna, as she disappeared back into the darkness, her boots bouncing down the stairs as she went. Davy sat for a few more minutes as he got a basic sense of what he should do next.

As he descended the stairs and landings back down to the ground floor he passed the drawing room, he sensed movement in the room. It caused him to halt and look in the doorway. Sir James and Lady May were standing at the window looking out over the lake, the illuminated sky and the sound of incessant bombs hitting Belfast.

He stood silently for a few seconds looking at the elderly couple, and as he started to move on towards the hallway, a voice, Sir James's, spoke to him from the darkened room.

"Take care of her, David."

Davy, paused, not sure what that was all about.

"She'll be fine up here, Sir James. Well enough out of it up here. Don't know when I'll be back. You can pour me a stiff one when I do. Think I'll need it."

Davy reached the entrance hall and turned, as he heard Bill from the doorway leading to the back courtyard.

"Your chariot awaits you out back. Anna's got a driver sorted."

Davy walked out to the courtyard and saw the Alfa Romeo sports touring car circle in the yard as it drove up in front of him, its lights causing him to put his Trilby hat down across his eyes and extend his hand beyond the brim for additional protection. He walked round to the front passenger seat, set his bag in the bench back seat and eased himself into the vehicle.

He had hardly settled himself in the soft leather, as a heavily gloved hand put the car in gear and accelerated hard out of the yard and down the two hundred yards drive to the mansion gateway at the Upper Malone Road. The gloves, Sir James's large shooting coat, and the fishing hat did not disguise the identity of the driver. Anna's favourite perfume filled the air.

Davy leant over to the dashboard to try and stop the car. Anna knocked his hand away.

"No Anna. I'll walk it from here if I have to. It's not happening. I've just told your mother and father not to worry about you. I'm getting out here. You are going back up the driveway!"

Anna slammed her foot on the accelerate. The engine growled as she turned the steering wheel hard right just before the automobile was about to collide with the old stone wall on the far side of the road.

"I've already had this conversation with them!" replied impassively. "Hold tight!"

Davy sank back into the car seat; mind turning over as fast as the Alfa engine.

As they sped down the Malone Road towards the junction with Balmoral Avenue and Newforge Lane, Anna, as she concentrated on the road ahead, with no lights on, asked,

"Where am I taking you?"

"Straight down Malone, up the Old Stranmillis Road to Stranmillis Village and pull in just past Chlorine Gardens. It's the highest point around here. I can get a better idea of where it's all happening without us both getting blown to bits. No bloody use to anyone if we are dead," instructed Davy, coldly, without emotion, as he stared ahead at the darkness moving in front of him.

Anna carried out her instructions and a few minute later pulled the roadster into the kerb as they passed Chlorine. She breathed out, sank back into the car seat and sighed as she tried to pull her hands from her gloves that were stuck to her fingers due to the unnatural level of adrenalin running through her system. Matron's voice began haunting her brain once again. She remained silent, knowing Davy needed neither advice nor suggestions to intrude his thought processes.

They sat in silence, the hood pulled down in the cool night air. They could get a better view of what was happening on the ground and in the air. The hood up was going to make no difference if they got caught by a stray shell, so it was best left folded.

The sky was filled with one hundred and fifty bombers circling virtually unopposed. The concentration of bombing was on the North shore. Davy estimated the Belfast Docks, Antrim Road and closer, the lower end of the Shankill and Falls.

As they sat in the silence, they could hear occasional fire from AK-AK guns, all too thinly spread around the city and the lough, manned by terrified, untested, local defence members. Suddenly a heavy explosion came from behind them. The ground shuddered.

"What the hell was that!" gasped Davy.

Anna lifted her head from her arms and survey the darkness that showed flames coming from further back up from where they had driven.

"One's dropped somewhere between the Lisburn Road and Malone Road. Backup about Marlborough, Cadogan I guess," gasped Anna. "Didn't expect that."

Davy stared back and nodded in agreement.

"Either a stray one or more likely trying to put that AK-AK gun at Balmoral out of action!"

"Well that decides it. Might as well try and get down to the City Hospital in the meantime.. There's about the same odds of getting hit down there as here. At least we can get something organised while those bastards run out of their cargo."

Anna had already started the engine, pressed the accelerator and sped down past Friars Bush Graveyard, The Ulster Museum, and opposite the University gates, turned left along Elmwood Avenue; as they saw the blackened stone walls of the hospital come into view ahead. The same building that had been the Belfast Workhouse, back in the days when Kitty and Mary, from the attic of Ballydrain, watched a much younger David and Anna, show their first gesture of defiance against Sir James, in the courtyard of Ballydrain in 1915.

Davy knew the City Hospital like the back of his hand. He was now a Senior Orthopaedic Consultant Surgeon who worked between the Royal Victoria Hospital, City Hospital and The Mater Hospital on the Crumlin Road, but the City had always been his base.

Anna, drove the roadster through the gates and pulled up in front of the entrance. Davy lifted himself from the low seats of the vehicle. It was much too small for his liking, but it was Anna's pride and joy. It was also the fastest way to get Davy to his destination.

As he was about to close the car door, he noticed Anna was still sitting in the driver's seat, arms folded, in an uncharacteristically defensive manner.

"Aren't you getting out, Anna?" quizzed Davy.

"I'll just wait out here. You go on in and do what you have to do. I'm not going in there. Didn't even go near a hospital when I had our three. I cannot do it and you know it." Anna's voice trembled as she spoke the words.

"You can't sit out here by yourself, girl," coaxed Davy, as he added another problem to his list. His brain focused on the immediate problem.

"Right, come with me. I've the very place for you," pleaded Davy again, as he walked round the car and opened the driver's door. Anna hesitated as she stared at Davy before she lifted herself from the comfort of the car. Davy led her round the side of the front building, down an alley between the next building, and hit his shoulder against the unmarked door. As it opened, the damp heat from inside hit them both in the face.

"Look after my driver until I get back please, Sadie," asked Davy, as he looked in the direction of a face, red with the steam of laundry boilers. Sadie, a woman in her fifties, ambled over towards the pair at the door.

Anna gave Davy a look of confusion, while at the same time trying not to offend Sadie.

"Stay here, Anna. We'll not be going anywhere until that lot, clear off. I'll be upstairs sorting things until then," assured Davy as he pointed to the ceiling.

Davy leaned forward to Anna and gave her a lingering hug. Sadie stood, jaw in her chin, not expecting to see the Senior Consultant snogging an impressive looking lady in the hospital laundry in full view of half a dozen other cleaners. Sadie added two and two and made five.

Davy disappeared out of the door as Anna found a small table in the corner surrounded by a few chairs where the staff sat to take a tea break. She sat silently making eye contact with no one.

The drone of large commercial washing boilers, helped to muffle the noise of the five hundred-pound bombs dropping just a mile and a half away.

The sound brought back memories of Anna working with Kitty in the wards, waiting for the anticipated casualties to appear.

"Didn't expect that from him, luv!" shouted Sadie.

"Always heard he was a one-woman man, despite having plenty interested. You must be a bit special to click with him, luv!" taunted Sadie.

Anna smiled to herself as she thought of an appropriate answer to retain the upper hand.

"Ah, you have either got it or you have not," she replied in her best mimicry of Mae West.

Sadie, surprised by the confident, unembarrassed reply, folded a sheet, as she gave herself time for a comment to regain control.

Anna, fully aware of Sadie's tactic, continued.

"So he's a one-woman man is he, then?" she asked with a twinkle in her eye. "That is very reassuring."

Sadie folded the rest of the sheet as she absorbed the conversation. She glanced a few times at the classy face protruding out of the collar of the hunting coat, covered by the fishing hat.

Anna took off her hat and unbuttoned the coat to try and cool down from the tropical heat of the laundry room. As she wiped her forehead and began to settle her thoughts, Sadie continued her inquisition once again.

"Never seen you about here before. Live around here do you, luv?" asked Sadie.

"Few miles up the road, Drumbeg direction," replied Anna, not wanting to embarrass Sadie any further.

"Aye that's where Dr Gibson lives up that way at Ballydrain House. Me and my man, George, took a walk past it one Sunday. Believe he married one of the Arthur family. Some shack that place. Better watch yourself, luv, if his missus catches the pair of you. Never seen her; believe she's a lovely lady, but being an Arthur, she'd be the wrong one to cross from what I hear," advised Sadie.

Anna put her chin briefly into the top of her woollen jumper with the turtleneck, and decided, she had had her fun with Sadie. It had been a few minutes relief from the horror outside.

"Don't worry I'll tell him of your good advice later when we get home, whenever that is," smiled Anna, as she stretched out her hand and continued.

"I apologise for my bad manners. David was in quite a hurry. Allow me to introduce myself. Anna Gibson is the name."

Sadie buried her face in the folded sheet, cursed and laughed at the same time.

"What are you doing down here when you could be well out of it up at Drumbeg, Mrs Gibson? asked Sadie in surprise.

"Only one sober enough to drive and keep that car of mine on the road and between the hedges," replied Anna. "Big day at the House this afternoon. Easter Tuesday."

"Why's he dumped you down here then as if he's hiding you? It looked a bit suspicious," pressed Sadie.

"Aah, No dear, the only one doing the hiding is me," explained Anna, as she shook her head slowly, as she stared towards the stone floor.

"You don't seem the shrinking violet sort, Mrs Gibson, if you don't mind me saying." continued Sadie.

"I vowed in 1919 I would never enter a hospital ward again. Had my fill of it. Afraid I would make a fool of myself. Too many bad memories." mused Anna. "Got through it once; when I was nothing more than a girl. I didn't stop to think about it then. Bit too headstrong for my own good in those days. Three years in a front-line Nursing station at the Somme from 1915. Left my dearest friend there," sighed Anna.

Her throat muscles spasmed as she spoke. The trauma of those years, hidden, quashed and sanitised by time were flooding back in Anna's head.

Sadie was about to lift another heavy sheet to fold, but instead turned to the kettle on the gas ring in the corner.

"Well I think we've both earned a 'wee' cup of tea, Mrs Gibson," suggested Sadie. It was the only thing she could think of to change the mood. "A cup of tea solves everything," thought Sadie.

"That would be lovely," smiled Anna. "But you are the one who needs a break, not me," replied Anna. "Let me make it."

Sadie was about to dispute the idea, but refrained, as she caught on that Anna wanted to do anything that changed the subject.

After Sadie had her tea break, Anna sat alone in the corner for another ten minutes or more, consumed by her own thoughts. She rose from the wooden chair in the corner and shouted over to Sadie above the din of the laundry.

"What direction do I go to find David."

Sadie stared back across the room. "Out the door. Back down the alley you came up. Turn right. Through the big double doors at the far end of the building. Ask someone in there, they'll know!"

Anna nodded, buttoned her coat, pushed her hat back over her head, opened the heavy door, and disappeared into the cold night air. The sound of the bombs reminded her, too much for her liking of the twenty-five pounder shells of some many years before. She could hear Matron's monologue in her head. She was nineteen again.

Back in the laundry room, Sadie laughed too herself.

"Cup of tea sorts everything. I knew it would!"

By the time Anna had woven her way to Davy, she caught sight of him standing in a badly lit corridor, talking to two other medical staff and a nurse of the rank of Sister. As he stopped to listen to one of the group, his eyes wandered over their shoulders. He could see Anna hovering ten feet away. He didn't stop speaking, merely made a gesture with his head, encouraging Anna forward to join the group. As Anna arrived on Davy's side, he continued his conversation with the group. Anna stood silent, a mere observer in this conversation.

"Right then," said Davy, "Sister, you are Senior Nurse in here. Until someone, anyone, higher arrives; if they arrive, you are acting Matron. Understood?

Doctor Young, same applies to you on all A & E issues, you have the reins. It'll be a few hours before any casualties come in here. It won't be before that lot outside stop. In the meantime Doctor Campbell, you get as many operating tables set up as you can. We have no idea how many staff will be able to get in here, or when, but as they do, allocate them to work with any of you three." Davy though for a while. "If any of the surgeons or surgical nursing staff get here, send them straight to me."

"Anna, I have the very job for you. Would you please stand at the entrance over there, and if anyone comes in, establish who they are, and direct them to either Sister O'Neill, Doctor Campbell, or Doctor Young. Make a list of their names and to whom they are allocated."

Anna remained silent and only acknowledged his instruction with a slight dip of the head.

"All we can do now is prepare the facilities, our focus, and hope we do not get a direct hit, which, as thing stand, is unlikely. The Mater Hospital, off the Antrim Road, is much closer to the consequences of the raid. Let's hope it remains operational. Right, get to it folks!"

As Anna turned to carry out her instructions, Davy grabbed her arm. "What happened to staying down in the laundry, girl," whispered.

"It's the 1st of July 1916 all over again David, Matron would have my life if I sat in the corner, feeling sorry for myself. I'll be here when you want me to drive you home," sighed Anna.

"You might be here a long time," replied Davy, as he stared into Anna's eyes and began to bend his head down to instinctively kiss her on the forehead, and caress the back of her neck, but she stopped him in mid action, pushing him away gently.

"No Davy, have to set an example," whispered Anna, as she turned to find paper, pencil and a clip board.

"Anna," continued Davy, "promise me, you won't go off on another of your whims. Don't put yourself in harm's way again. Stay near me. I need to know you are safe here." Anna stopped in her tracks and turned her face back to look into Davy's eyes.

"I promised Tom I would bring you home from France, on an Autumn evening in 1915 and I didn't let him down," in the same determined mood she had shown on that earlier Spring evening she marched Davy up the tree lined driveway, together, in full view of Sir James, full of pride and innocent of the hard years that were ahead of them.

"Anna Arthur, Anna Arthur" sighed Davy, as he smiled and shook his head from side to side.

During the next few hours, staff of all sorts, medical, porters, clerical employees, emerged through the doors of the hospital foyer, all ashen faced, but determined. Those that had arrived had all been fortunate enough to live on the south side of the City. It had only suffered the terrifying sound of the German bombers making repeated runs in the sky above the Lisburn Road, in the direction of the north of the City.

By the middle of the night, a few hours later, the intensity of the bombardment began to slow. There were larger gaps between each explosion, until a brief deathly silence hung over the night air for nothing more than a brief few minutes.

As the first few citizens of North and parts of West Belfast began to emerge from under their staircases, tables, cellars and broken houses, the hospital teams looked at each other. They all knew the talking, planning and estimates had ended. This was it, much different to the Somme, reflected Davy to himself. He had no idea what to expect out there, but this was different. Back in 1916 he was facing bulls, German soldiers. This time it was the lambs that had been slaughtered; left unattended by their shepherds.

Men, women, small children, mothers and fathers, whose only purpose of life was to bring up their families. So many people's lives would be shattered forever.

"Ok folks, deal with it as it comes through the door. I need three A&E nursing staff to come with me and try to get up to the North and West of the City. Try and establish what's the situation with the Mater, RVH[7] and the state of play up there," barked Davy.

---

[7] Royal Victoria Hospital.

As he turned to the door, he passed Anna. "You stay here and keep organising those lists. I'll get back as soon as I can."

Anna glared at him, "No chance. I go where you go!"

"Anna, I'm going up in that ambulance out there. I don't need a driver at the moment, and you'll be safer here. None of your nonsense, girl!" snapped Davy.

"I can get there long before that lump of metal on wheels gets anywhere near where you are going," snapped Anna, not at all impressed by being given a job well below her abilities.

"I know you want me to be safe, and you have lives to save, but I have one, maybe two, factories and my workers, right up in the middle of that mess. It's what has to be. I can get you up there and do something for them at the same time. Jump into the car and tell the ambulances to follow up as soon as they are crewed. I managed the Ards TT[8]. I can manage this event!" scoffed Anna, as she slapped him on the back like a reluctant horse.

"None of your nonsense Davy," demanded Anna. "Father was about to drag himself up to the factories in Belfast. I put my foot down. Bill won't be up there as soon as us. It's my call, Davy. I've had a

---

[8] Annual Road Racing event of the 1930s in Northern Ireland.

wonderful, privileged life being an Arthur. It's payback time. Can't sit up at Ballydrain while all hell is breaking loose on them all. What is it Rab said, "The good shepherd looks after his sheep, or in this case shepherdess?" asked Anna, as they walked out into the night air, already filled with the smell of burnt debris and the glow coming from the North and West sides.

"Well that's sorted then. If Bill is going that's you covered. You can stay here," pleaded Davy, as Anna reached the car door.

"Davy, my love. You should know by now that the Arthurs' give the orders; they don't take them. Now get in the car, we both have our responsibilities!" ordered Anna.

As they both dropped into the roadster, Anna leaned over and grasped Davy around the neck and gave him the same kiss she gave him at Shaws Bridge before the grand entrance to Ballydrain in 1915.

For a few seconds all the mayhem disappeared, until Anna turned to face the dashboard. As they settled back in the seats, Anna slammed the gear stick and the car lurched forward down the hospital driveway as it turned left down the Lisburn Road. As they reached the top of Bradbury Place, Davy pointed to the top of Sandy Row indicating that was the direction he wanted to go. It was a shorter route towards the intense glow on the inner north and west of the city. The centre of

Belfast around the direction of High Street, York St, the Docks and North of the city around the Waterworks would have to be the responsibility of the hospitals in the north of the city. At least that was the plan agreed by the medical teams throughout the city in the weeks before the night the unthinkable had happened.

"See if it's clear to go over Boyne Bridge, down Durham Street, Millfield, over to Brown Square. We should have a better picture of things by then." advised Davy, as he pointed out through the windscreen.

At the same time Anna stabbed her hand against the switch that turned the lights of the roadster to full beam. Davy gave a look as he raised his eyes.

"Black out restrictions, hardly matters now, Davy. Whole bloody place is lit up like the 11th Night!" [9] assured Anna.

As they reached the crest of the steeply arched Boyne Bridge, Anna slowed up to take in the view on the horizon northwards and the City centre to the right. Nothing could have prepared them for what they saw before their eyes. Davy leaned back, face up to the sky and exhaled, his cheeks filled to capacity. Anna gripped the steering wheel

---

[9]Traditional bonfire celebrations in the Unionist communities on the evening before the 12th July Parades.

hard with her gloved hands, her face resting on the steering wheel and said nothing.

"I'll have to go on foot from here. Car will be of little use from here." sighed Davy.

"No Davy, we, will have to walk from here" replied Anna, her face still rested against the steering wheel.

"You get out and wait here a few minutes and I'll leave Alfonso,[10] down at the Linfield Mill back at the bottom of the bridge and I'll be back up. If I leave it down there and tell them it's mine, it'll be safe. Leave it here, and there'll be nothing left but a few nuts and bolts," advised Anna. As she raised her head and opened the car door, she turned to Davy.

"Don't even think of going ahead without me."

Davy returned the stare and let out a grunt of acceptance. A few minutes later Anna was jogging back up to Davy at the top of the bridge.

As Davy watched her he noticed that her right hip was giving her bother as she did her best to attack the steep slope.

---

[10] The name she called her Alfa Romeo.

"Take it a bit slower girl, no point in you making that leg any worse after all the work it had done on it. Few seconds won't make any difference in this mess."

Davy was referring to the old injury she had received from a horse-riding accident, the same injury that turned her attention to the Alfa Romeo, to replaced her competitive edge from eventing and point to point racing. Anna was well known in the local Touring and Hill climb racing events. That was the reason she was confident she was the best one to chauffeur Davy on this night.

Four years earlier, she had been visiting relatives on their estate near Dungannon, a stag had bolted out of trees when she was riding her cousin's horse. Startled, the horse had reared up on it back legs, lost its balance and fallen on its side. Anna was still in the saddle when it hit the ground. Her right leg was the first thing to make contact with the ground. The complication of the large hunter crashing down on to the leg compounding the damage. Davy remembered arriving at Anna's side as she lay screaming in pain and asking if the horse was all right. It took a full year for the upper thigh and hip to mend and be fully functional but the risk of a similar fall off a horse again without a permanent limp, spelt the end of riding horses other than gentle canters. Running up steep hills wasn't a great idea either.

As Anna reached Davy's side, they walked down the far side of the Boyne Bridge across the Grosvenor Road, through Durham St, past the bottom of Albert Street. As they reached the bottom of the Falls Road and looked across to Millfield and Browns Square the smell of cordite and burning buildings hit the back of their throats. The awareness of the smell was then replaced by the piercing screams and shouts that penetrated the night air. The residents of the City's overcrowded and cramped two up two down terrace houses that straddled between the Lower Falls and Lower Shankill had begun emerging from their places of refuge.

People had begun to come out of St Peters Chapel, ashen faced, looking in the direction of the streets around Percy Street. It and the surrounding streets had received direct hits. Davy reckoned they were the early release of the line of bombs dropped in the direct flight path of York Street and the Docks. He drew in breathe and gasped as he imagined the destruction along the north of the city.

It had been agreed between the hospital management weeks earlier that each hospital would look after different sectors. The north of the city would be the Mater Hospitals problem. The City Hospital, south and west, as far as the Shankill, and the Royal Victoria Hospital would spread themselves between the West and North as needed.

Davy decided to concentrate on where he was, the web of streets that wove the Falls and Shankill into an uneasy place of competing views on life. Two communities, who worked together by day and on occasions 'fought the bit out' in the evenings. That night they had a common enemy. One that punched far above both their weights.

As they walked towards the worst area Davy picked out faces of a few RVH staff he knew who were already tending traumatised civilians, who had climbed out from under their staircases and staggered out of their tiny homes, some left only partially standing.

Anna gasped and put her hands over her face.

"Oh my God. It's worse than I could have imagined. Oh My God no!" she swore to herself trying to stifle her words so no one could hear. As Davy turned to speak to her, she was already pushing her way through the crowd of confused locals.

"Anna, stay near me. None of your antics, girl!" shouted Davy.

"I'm just going up to Northumberland Street. I can't leave them to it. Father wouldn't, nor Roger. This is my watch, Davy!" replied Anna as she paused to face him.

"Ok, I understand that, but you can't go up there by yourself. Wait until Bill gets here, and you can go up with him. You said he was coming up to see what the score was up here with the factories when he'd got things organised at Ballydrain.

Anna hesitated, "I'll give him ten minutes, If he's not here by then. I'm going." she shouted as she returned to Davy's side.

They walked up the street, attempting to avoid broken glass, bricks masonry, slates and splintered wood. Both with their hands in the pockets of their opened long coats. Davy had his medical bag slung over his left shoulder.

"Dr Gibson, sir, over here please." shouted a voice from the doorway of a partially collapsed house; one of many in the street. Davy turned to find a young theatre nurse, Gerri Muldoon. He recognised her from the RVH.[11]

"Muldoon, what are you doing down here, kid. Thought you were supposed to get up to surgical, scrubbed and ready for the incoming casualties? That was the plan!" shouted Davy, slightly infuriated that already a well thought out system of operation, was already falling apart at the seams.

"I live down there between the Cullintree Road and Albert St. I was walking home from a friend's house when this all started. I ran into St

---

[11] Royal Victoria Hospital

71

Peter's, because they have a crypt. Seemed better than under the staircase. Didn't expect to be sitting with a couple of hundred Prods singing hymns when all hell let loose," she replied without any emotion, as she helped an elderly lady stagger out of a partly demolished house.

"Anyhow, as soon as the coast was clear I started to make my way up to the Royal but with the state of things down here, I never got the chance. Need your expertise on this one in here." reported Muldoon.

"There's a child, girl about seven years old, trapped leg and arm, caught below a beam. Got the lose rubble out the way but the beam is heavy and part of it is still holding up the gable wall. Don't like the options on this one," whispered Gerri, as she got close to the child. Davy nodded as he listened, before bending his frame to enter the passage to the child in the corner of the broken house.

The child was mercifully, unconscious, but alive. He forced himself to concentrate on what was relevant. On the battlefield, it would have been, amputation to leg and arm get them out and move on to next. This was a seven-year-old child; one of the lambs.

Outside, Anna waited, scanning the smouldering remains of a street, brain racing on the part she would have to play in this mess. As she stood, a voice from behind her barked in her ear.

"Couldn't get here any quicker, had to get a few things moving up home first," apologised Bill.

"How did you get down, Bill?" asked Anna.

Bill nodded to his right. Jonty tipped his cap in Anna's direction, as he tried to hold back a grin from the seat in the horse trap.

"Can't get done for driving a cart with too much drink in you, and he could drive that thing if he was unconscious," advised Bill, as he fumbled in his pocket for a cigarette.

"It's much worse than we could have imagined Bill. Percy Street shelter has had a direct hit. Some of them would have been out before the bombers arrived. Word is some sheltered in St Peters Crypt. The younger ones ran up to Blackmountain and Divis. What worries me more is a lot of our workers live in these streets. Some would have sheltered in the houses. Look at what is left of the houses." sighed Anna, trying to make no facial expression.

Sir James had always told her. Never show weakness and never let anyone know you are not in control. Sir James had told her of Arthur Wellesley, a distant relative, who had spent his summers at Mornington, near Annadale in south Belfast. The Duke of Wellington had sat below a tree during the Battle of Waterloo, newspaper across his face, feigning a quick rest. The face covering was to avoid anyone reading his thoughts. This was the Arthurs' Waterloo.

"Where's Davy?" asked Bill.

"In there," replied Anna, as she pointed in the direction of the crumbling terrace house. Bill disappeared slowly into the darkness of the remains of the house. Davy was leaning forward, knees bent, still trying to work out what might be done to save this poor child, preferably in one piece. Bill stood silently behind him. Drawing on his cigarette.

"Best if you put that out, Bill mate. Few too many fractured gas pipes in here for my liking," whispered Davy, without turning to face Bill who stubbed the cigarette against the ground as he bent forward beside Davy.

"I'll go and find some joiners or scaffolders, might be an idea," suggested Bill, as he backed out of the collapsed room. As he appeared out of the wrecked doorway of the house, he shouted.

"Anyone in the building trade about here?"

"I'm a hod carrier." Came a voice from the crowd milling aimlessly around the broken buildings. Still traumatised by their proximity to the night raid.

"Big Roy McDowell is a joiner and Brian McClure from round the corner is a rigger in the Yard."[12] shouted another voice.

"Well, away and get them, mate. There's a child needs help in there. Away you go, and tell anyone else that's in the trade, to get down here now!" snapped Bill.

Within minutes, several men arrived in front of Bill, all looking confused but available. Bill looked each of them in the eye, weighing them up at the same time.

"Right lads, there's a kid in there with a beam on top of her and the problem is, the beam is keeping the wall and roof up. So I need you lots' expertise in propping that wall up, to allow us to move the beam," asked Bill.

The three men mumbled a few words to each other before the rigger and joiner took the responsibility of securing the gable wall. The hod carrier agreed he was best assisting in lifting the beam. All three enter the crumbling building and stood, hunched behind the crouching theatre nurse and Davy. They didn't speak, just made hand gestures and nods in the direction of the beam, the wall and the stricken child.

---

[12] Harland and Wolfe shipyard.

Bill decided they knew what they were doing and backed out of the area to reunite himself with Anna.

"Well Bill, how is it looking in there?" asked Anna.

"Nothing else I can do in there, Anna," he replied, as he rummaged in his pocket to retrieve a Gallahers Blue,[13] before remembering about the gas risk, withdrew his empty hand, and breathed out, in frustration.

Bill had hardly completed his action before Anna began to walk past him in the direction of the Mill. Bill rolled his eyes to the sky and caught up alongside her.

"Anna, if you don't mind, its best if I do the talking up here. They don't know you. They'd say to themselves 'Who the hell's your woman in the big coat think she is running around telling us what to do'. Let me do the talking. Just don't leave my shoulder, say nothing, please. Your presence will be enough."

Anna kept her determined walk and stifled a grin, her face never leaving the debris covered streets. "I'll try, can't promise anything, Bill."

As they began to make their way forward together, Bill remembered Jonty.

---

[13] Cigarette

"Jonty, you stay where you are mate. Keep an eye on Davy, and wait for us coming back down," yelled Bill to Jonty, who was still sitting on the cart doing his best to keep the horse steady, as it sensed the unease in the air.

Back in the confined space of the crumbling house with the child still wedged, Davy and Muldoon did their best to stabilise the unconscious child while the other three worked at securing the wall.

"That should hold it, mate," advised the rigger, in a whisper.

"Right" whispered Davy. "Let's see if we can lift this off her. Very slowly now, but before we do, if any of you aren't used to what you are about to see, keep it to yourself. I don't need any of you acting 'soft' here. Understood?" Davy looked each one in the eyes.

"One, two, three lift, slowly, carefully now."

He turned his gaze to Gerri Muldoon who needed no instruction. As the beam lifted, Muldoon grabbed the child and began to gently pull her from beneath the beam. The child's once trapped leg, still covered by her nightdress, was thankfully still attached to her body. Her arm was a different matter. As the Shipyard rigger saw the child's arm still lying lifeless on the floor. He turned and faced the wall.

77

"Sweet Lord Almighty," he cursed to himself. He managed to stagger outside as he vomited around the feet of the onlookers.

Muldoon and Davy worked on the little girl and hoped an ambulance would be available soon, very soon.

"I'll have to move on to the next one, Muldoon. Do your best to keep her stable until an ambulance gets here," instructed Davy. Muldoon nodded in silence. Outside, Davy passed the forlorn Shipyard man who gave him a decidedly sheepish grin.

"Sorry about that Sir," he said in embarrassment.

"You did ok, mate. You dealt with it as best you could. You'll be used to it before the night's over," replied Davy, as he gave him a reassuring stare.

"What's your name then?" asked Davy.

"Sammy McBride from Browns Square, what's left of it, "replied the rigger. Still trying to regain his hardman persona.

"Well Sam McBride, are you and your two mates there, up for being my rescue team for as long as this takes," asked Davy as he put both hands deep in his coat pockets.

"I'll try and not let you down," replied the still embarrassed McBride.

"Just do your best. I can ask no more." reassured Davy.

78

"Right, the three of you just shadow me wherever I go," ordered Davy, as he walked away from the demolished building looking for the next casualty in need of his skills.

"How do you not let this take a fizz on you?" asked Sam, as he walked alongside Davy.

"Used to be a butcher, before the Somme. I had a bit of a career change after that," replied Davy. His gaze never leaving the ground, his face expressionless. Sam McBride, looked over at the other two rescuers and gave them a nod of approval.

Davy's thoughts returned to Anna.

"Where is she? I told her not to go running off on one of her missions" he thought to himself.

As he scanned the immediate area a voice shouted at him.

"She's away up to the Mill if it's still there. Bill is with her. They told me to stay her until they get back, Davy!" shouted Jonty, from the trap.

When Bill and Anna turned the corner of the street facing the factory, they met a sight they expected, but did not want to believe. Part of the factory roof was already burnt embers, and some houses near it little more than rubble. Bodies were being pulled out of the gaps in the remains of doorways and holes in walls of houses.

Some staggered out and embraced the nearest to them. Others lay motionless, lifeless, as people tried to cover their faces in an effort to give them some dignity in this madness. As they briefly took in the situation, a voice came from their left.

"Mr Johnston, Mr Johnston. Over here, Sir!"

It was Lizzie Shields, a supervisor in the Finishing Department of the Mill.

"Lizzie, how are you girl?" replied Bill, as he walked over to Lizzie and gave her a supportive hug.

"I'm ok, which is more than can be said for my house, "replied Lizzie, arms folded, as she shook her head in dismay.

"Take it you weren't in it, thank God," said Bill.

"No, most of us got down into St Peters crypt. Never thought I'd see the day I'd be glad to go to chapel," said Lizzie, as she shook her head in disbelief.

Anna stayed back off Bill's shoulder, giving Bill and Lizzie their own space, all the time assessing, thinking, planning. She gave him a bit of time to speak to Lizzie before she walked unnoticed to Bill's shoulder.

"Bill, at word, please!" she whispered before she continued.

"Ask her to get any of our people that live in the houses that's gone, to get them over here to me, as best she can," advised Anna, trying at the same time not to draw attention to herself.

Bill looked at Anna with an expression that said he thought he was running things up here.

"Don't give me that look, Bill. Those people need somewhere to live until this mess settles down. If you get them down here to me I can organise them to go to Ballydrain. When we run out of rooms, outhouses, and the tents from the scout and girl guides hall we will think of something. Other than that, I'll not get in your way," promised Anna, face still devoid of emotion. Matron had invaded her brain once more.

Davy, in the meantime was moving about the streets with his 'three musketeers' at his shoulder. He spent most of his time getting an overview of the level of casualties and directing the medical staff who had arrived. Red Cross, St Johns Ambulance and Knights of Malta medical volunteers seemed to appear out of nowhere. It reminded him of big Rab, now the Reverend Canon Robert Tate, and the tale of the five loaves and two small fish, miraculously feeding five thousand.

Back down amount the ruined streets, Davy decided it was time he should get on up to the Royal Victoria Hospital which was only several hundred yards up the Falls Road, only a few streets from where he was standing. A plan of action had been set up in anticipation of this disaster and he was part of that plan up in the Royal. He turned to look for Gerri Muldoon. She was also part of the plan at the Royal. A good theatre nurse would be more use at an operating table than scavenging around the rubble.

When he spotted Muldoon he waved her over to him. As he turned to look at Jonty to let him know where he was going and get some reassurance that Anna would stick close to Bill, he heard the voice of a young girl shout.

"Hey Mister, would you come over here quick!"

Davy looked in the direction of the request to find a girl about fourteen years of age in a St Johns Ambulance Brigade uniform.

"I can see two people in this house here and they aren't moving. The door's stuck!"

Davy gestured to Sam McBride who strode over to the door and opened it after a few heavy kicks followed by a heavy push with his shoulder. Davy walked, slightly crouched, as he leant in front of the pair huddled together, faces staring up to a hole that was once a ceiling.

They were both unmarked apart from congealed blood from their ears and nostrils that told him they were beyond help. Killed by the pressure of a blast, otherwise there wasn't a scratch on them. No wonder the girl thought they were alive.

He retraced his steps outside and told McBride to get the fourteen -year-old away and find her something to do that was a bit less harrowing. "Girls of fourteen should be playing at being nurses, not scrambling about demolished houses with her neighbours in this state," he thought to himself.

Davy shouted to Muldoon. "We need to get up to the Royal!"

He hitched his grip bag over his shoulder and began his old scout march routine. Twenty paces, twenty running. Time was, he could have ran the seven hundred yards to the Royal at the corner of the Grosvenor Road and Falls Road but approaching mid-forties, heavy coat and grip bag of medical kit, discretion was the better part of valour. Muldoon was matching him stride for stride. As a twenty-two year old feisty Camogie[14] player from the Lower Falls, it was nothing but a light jog, A familiar voice shouted from behind him.

---

[14] Ladies version of Hurling. A hugely popular sport of Irish Nationalism, like hockey, played with a stick and a small hard ball, but without the safety features. By anyone's standards, not a game for the faint hearted.

"Mister, Mister, wait for me. I'm going up with you!" shouted the St Johns Ambulance novice.

Davy turned but kept walking. "Thought I told Sam McBride to find you something a bit safer to do?" shouted Davy.

"He did, sir," said the girl, "but I wasn't having that!" she scorned.

"I'm sure there's something I can do up in the Royal. I'm no child. I've done my badges. I can do light injuries, sir," the girl boasted with pride.

Davy stopped for a brief moment. He knew she was right, but the overriding desire not to destroy a young girl's innocence and childhood was important to him. He leant down towards the girl, who was no more than five foot in height, a good foot below him.

"What is your name?" asked Davy.

"Agnes Miller" she replied. "Well Agnes, I'm needed urgent up at the Royal and you are not ready for what's going to take place up there. It's not your time. You're a brave girl, but it's not going to happen," ordered Davy, in exasperation.

Agnes stared at him, holding back her frustration. Davy though quickly.

"Agnes, so you want to be a nurse, then?" asked Davy, with no emotion in his voice. Agnes nodded her head in agreement.

"Well the first thing a nurse has to learn is how to take orders; even if she doesn't like them. So I am ordering you to go back down where you came. Find the man called Jonty. He'll be sitting on a horse and trap. Tell him, Davy said I have to make sure you stay there, and you are to help with light injuries only." Davy paused as he looked into the face of the confused girl.

"Get back down that road, Nurse Miller. There are people need your help."

Agnes looked over Davy's shoulder at Muldoon, who smiled at the girl and flicked her head in the direction of Millfield. Agnes tried to unravel her thoughts.

"Well, get back down that road and do what I told you," ordered Davy. The disappointment flowed from the girl's face.

Agnes turned on her heels and did not stop until she found Jonty and a casualty with a cut to the head and a bleeding knee. Jonty watched proceedings around him from the comparative safety of the horse and cart. He knew he was best staying there as Bill had told him. The horse needed protecting, and he would only be a nuisance staggering around on one good leg. He had spent over twenty years hobbling around the Estate at Ballydrain and had learnt to get himself round every inch of it with minimum discomfort, but negotiating rubble in the dark did not make any sense. Also, from his vantage point sat up on the front of the cart, he could get a good view of the mayhem, and keep his options open. He had watched Davy's 'musketeers' gather other likeminded volunteers and saw a general state of coordination emerge. He had noticed the young St Johns Ambulance girl was putting on bandages and cleaning blood from head wounds. Then he saw Bill jogging towards him from round the corner of Northumberland St.

"How's it going up there, Bill" shouted Jonty, as Bill approached him.

"How many can you get in that cart and take up to Ballydrain in one go Jonty?"

"One in the front with me, and a 'wean'[15] on their knee. Four at most in the back if you want Bess here to make it home," as he gestured to the edgy horse, which he knew would be only too relieved to get the command. Home!"

"This girl will never let me down and I'll not let her down. Don't care it was the King himself. That's as many as I'll take in one go, Bill!" shouted Jonty.

---

[15] Small child

Bill gave Jonty a knowing stare. "You're the man makes the decisions on the estate. I make them in the factory. It's your call, 'wee man'," replied Bill, as he tapped his forefinger against his eyebrow.

"As soon as I bring you a bunch, get them up to Ballydrain and see if you can get some more transport down. My guess it could be as many as a few hundred camped out for a few weeks. I'll leave that for you to sort. Your problem, Jonty!" shouted Bill, as he disappeared back towards Northumberland St, hoping Anna had not got herself in any difficulty in his absence.

Meanwhile, Anna had been quietly mingling amongst the people who were emerging from the side streets to gaze at what once was their source of employment and homes. Some were devastated, others just stood stone faced, trying to gather their thoughts and emotions.

Anna picked up some bits of conversation. Some of it wasn't overly complimentary about the Arthur family, and how they would be safe and well away from this nightmare. Anna, put her face into her chin. Pulled her hat down and her collar up; not that they would have recognised her, given she rarely went near the factories preferring to leave that to Bill and his managers to report back to her once a week. Since Sir James's health had deteriorated and gotten beyond the stage of making big decisions, Anna had taken upon herself to change the way of operating the Arthur empire. She gave her Managers, who all had to report to Bill, a degree of autonomy, who in turn, had a weekly meeting with Anna at Ballydrain. Decisions were made by Anna. Sir James would nod his head in approval. When he did disapprove he would grimace and make his point short and sweet, leaving it for Anna and Bill to sort it. Otherwise, Sir James would just sit and hide a smile. Sometimes on Friday afternoons Davy would arrive home, cross the hall, and if the door to the reading room was open, would see the three of them Bill, Anna and Sir James sitting round the big table in deep discussion. He would catch Sir James's eye, give a brief nod of the head. Sir James would reply with a discreet wink.

Davy would hang up his coat, leave down his bag and settle himself down at the fireplace in the living room with a glass of Bushmills in his hand. The best way he could find to wind down from his week in Belfast Hospitals. He did not want anything to do with the business end of things, and anyway, his brain had had enough for one week. Jonty, never one to miss a yarn and a drink, often wandered in and joined Davy on his Friday evening wind down.

As Bill arrived back at the Mill he scanned his eyes to find Anna. He picked out the figure in the 'country sports' coat and 'horsey boots.'

He was relieved to find she had kept her word and kept herself to herself.

Bill, being aware most of the onlookers knew him; needed to play this carefully. It was best, he thought, to discreetly angle himself alongside Anna; no need to make a scene.

"Davy's ok, he's on his way up to the Royal. Gave me specific instructions I had to keep an eye on you, girl," whispered Bill, trying not to make it look as if he was muttering a word, staring out at the devastation.

"See the old pair sitting on the wall over there and the other pair to the left. Can we get them down to Jonty?" asked Anna.

"If we can organise a few of their younger ones to send them down to Jonty and walk alongside, for the first run, that's about the best we can manage before the rest of the transport gets down, Anna," replied Bill.

"Looks like that is the way it is then, Bill. I'll go over and sort out the four of them and you gather up the rest of our flock," advised Anna, as she strode over the debris, hands still firmly in her pockets. Hands deep in the pockets helped to disguise the emotions within. Hands flying about would suggest a sense of panic. Arms folded suggested fear. Hands in the pockets gave away nothing. That was the last bit of advice Sir James had given her before she left Ballydrain that evening.

Bill melted into the crowds as they wandered about, uncoordinated, in all directions, to fit their own individual dilemmas. Bill spotted one of the nightshift foremen, who was comforting his wife and two young children who did not really comprehend what was going on around them.

"Jacky, Jacky Patterson, Are you and yours all ok. Did they all get out of the Mill before this started?" asked Bill.

"Aye, as far as I know, Mr Johnston. We got down to St Peter's just in time. Can't say the same for our 'wee' house. Not be worrying about the damp in the walls anymore. No bloody walls!" growled Jacky.

"Aye, well I think we can solve that problem for a while," mused Bill. Jacky looked at Bill as if he was mad.

"Tell your missus to take the kids down to Millfield and make themselves known to a man called Jonty. He'll be sitting in a horse and trap. Tell your Missus she has to do whatever he says. Jonty and me, go a long way back. Now, I need you to find as many of our ones that don't have a roof over their heads to gather themselves up and make themselves known to that lady over there," instructed Bill, as he pointed a finger in the direction of Anna who was bent over an elderly couple.

"Your woman over there, Mr Johnston. The one that's just stood staring at us. Dressed as if she was going to a grouse shoot!" snarled Jacky. "I swear to God, if she stared at us all much longer, I was going to tell her to clear off!"

Bill looked hard at the foreman. Part of him wanted to give Jacky a dig in the mouth, part of him knew his foreman was a bundle of nerves, confused and frightened and not really in control of his senses.

"She's with me, Patterson. Best you change your tune on that one, if you know what's good for you. Save you a bit of embarrassment," advised Bill calmly.

"Is she your Missus, Mr Johnston? Oh I'm sorry boss," pleaded Patterson.

Bill grunted in irony. "No Jacky, son. Never had the pleasure. That privilege was for one of my mates, Davy Gibson."

It took the foreman a few seconds to let his brain unravel Bill's information.

"Sir James's daughter?" winced Patterson, as he dropped his jaw into his chin.

"My boss, and yours, Jacky. Don't be taken in by her appearance. That one's got more backbone than you and me, put together. Just do what she tells you and pass the word around the rest. The only reason she's done nothing but stand there and observe is because I've told her. She'll not let any of us down, old son.

"Now come on Jacky. She pays you to be a Supervisor. Start supervising. Your shift's still on, mate!"

Gerri Muldoon and Davy rushed through the doors of the Royal Emergency Department. Davy could see that at least the basics of the systems he and the other senior medics set up had begun to take shape.

"I'm away in to get scrubbed up," advised Muldoon, as she disappeared down a corridor.

At the same time a junior doctor whom Davy had worked with on several operations came along beside him.

"Things are under control at the moment, but I assume you are going to tell me that's about to change," sighed the young doctor.

"How many casualties have you got in at this stage?" asked Davy, still looking straight ahead, thinking.

"About thirty or forty at present," replied Desmond McCollum, the junior doctor.

"Well, allowing for the hope that the Mater, and the other North Belfast hospitals are operating. There'll be three hundred in here and two hundred in the City within the next few hours." advised Davy, still making no eye contact with McCollum.

"That rather messes up or plans for a hundred." exhaled McCollum.

"Does a bit, young man," grunted Davy in irony. Going to have to work off our instincts on this," advised Davy, as he turned to look McCollum in the face for the first time since their conversation began. McCollum looked back at Davy in confusion.

"As my old friend Rab Tate says, It's five loaves and two small fish time."

McCollum, still looked at Davy, hoping for a more practical solution.

"The fish and the loaves were always there, young Desmond. The crowd had them all the time. It just took someone to get them to admit it and produce the goods. That's what we are going to do here Desmond, young sir. Come with me and we'll see if we can perform a few miracles."

Chapter Four

Shelter

While Davy was preparing for the imminent surge of casualties to flood into the hospital, further down the road at the mill and surrounding streets, bodies were being removed from the rubble and placed in a corner, covered as well as possible under any spare sheets remnants of curtains and table clothes. The badly injured were still being comforted where they had been found. The walking wounded, and those with cuts scrapes and bruises looked ashen faced as they searched for relatives and friends; asking the whereabouts of others. Slowly a group began to form that began to hover near Anna. She called out to Bill who was moving amongst them, pointing instructions to Jacky Patterson.

"Gather them in Bill, please." suggested Anna.

"Best you come over here, Anna. It would be easier," advised Bill. Anna realised that some of the workers where in a state of shock and in no mental state to bite their fingers never mind form an orderly gathering. As she mingled amongst the dispirited bunch, Bill stood alongside her.

"Right folks. Need to get you all somewhere safe to get yourselves sorted. So would you go with this lady beside me here and she'll deal with it," instructed Bill.

Anna said nothing, just gave a nod and started to walk through them in the direction of Jonty down at Millfield. Some didn't move, others trudged alongside her.

"Where are we going, Missus?" came a voice.

Anna finally broke her silence, deliberately trying to tone down her polite accent.

"Malone Road, somewhere a bit safer!" advised Anna, still not making any eye contact.

"How far up the Malone Road? My mother here has bad legs. She'll never make it past the Boyne Bridge!"

"Past Dunmurry Lane, near Drumbeg Bridge. We'll get something sorted for your mother, but you, might have to be patient" reassured Anna, only making the slightest look in the direction of the doubting woman who was linking arms with her mother. The woman asking the questions, who was carrying considerable weight herself. blew out her cheeks.

"Drumbeg! That's halfway to Lisburn, Missus! "

"Well that's the best I can offer, my dear. You are welcome to stay here, and I will get your mother up to Drumbeg, if that is your choice!" retorted Anna, who was not in the mood for soft soaping anyone.

"We all have to make sacrifices in the circumstances, one way or another!" snapped Anna, as she turned and stood in front of the woman.

Anna was back to full Matron mode and in no mood for anyone who could not dig deep. The woman, was taken aback by the sudden reply from the hitherto quiet onlooker. She stared at Anna, trying to weigh up her options. Would she apologise or give her a smack in the face? Anna well aware either scenario was possible, took another step towards the woman, close enough to receive the smack in the face. The woman stared into Anna's eyes and did not like the look of contained rage.

"Who the frig are you, Missus, running round here like Lady Muck!" spluttered the woman.

"That my dear, is for you to wonder, and me to know. Now, I can get your mother to a safe place and it's up to you if you want to share it. We all have to dig deep in these situations!" snapped Anna again.

The woman turned to her mother and started to proceeded to walk her in the direction of Millfield. Anna turned to look for Bill who had stood offside and had missed none of the exchange. Bill just gave her a wink and touched his cap, shook his head, looked to the sky, and laughed to himself. As he got within a few feet of Anna he leant towards her and whispered.

"That'll teach her not to mess with an Arthur," grinned Bill, before he continued.

"I know her. A bit of a mouthy bitch at the best of times. Nice one Anna. Your Da would have been proud of you." continued Bill. Anna closed her eyes and shook her head from side to side.

Just ahead of them, the old lady being helped down the road by her mouthy daughter, gave her a tug with her arm.

"See you, you have about as much brains as a barnacle," snapped the old woman.

"Why, what did I say wrong?" replied the daughter.

She's taking us to Drumbeg, you stupid girl. Now just tell me who lives at Drumbeg? Stupid bitch!" declared the old lady, "and to think I reared you!"

As the dazed group of refugees arrived at Millfield and gathered around Jonty and his cart, Anna waved to the elderly lady with the bad leg and the mouthy daughter.

"Would you help your mother on to the trap," before she turned to the rest of the group who by this time had passed word round each other of Anna's identity.

"There are three more spaces for those that need it. The rest will have to keep walking up to Drumbeg or wait here. Hope to be able to get some more transport on the way. Can't promise anything, but if any of you have any better options for a roof over your heads feel free to take them. Just let Mr Johnston know, so we know you are not missing."

"I'm away back up to the mill to find the rest of our lot, Mrs Gibson," said Bill, conscious that he wanted the onlookers to see his respect to Anna, intending that it would enhance her standing in the situation.

"Yes Bill, Jonty will get the first batch up and I will pick up the car at the Linfield Mill, get on up ahead, and send more transport down," advised Anna."

"Mrs Gibson, best you stay up there. You'll have enough to sort out back home. There's nothing more you can do down here. I've enough foremen here to keep me right. I promised Davy, so please stay up there. Promise."

Anna didn't speak; just gave him a glance of acceptance.

As Jonty was about to negotiate a turn of the horse and trap, the sound of a motorbike engine emerged out of the darkness. The helmetless rider of a Norton motorcycle pulled up and got off, Anna froze, both in concern and anger. A grinning, gangly, fifteen-year-old walked towards her. She wanted to shout at him, but her instinct told her to keep the conversation personal. As he arrived alongside her, she rasped.

"What the hell are you doing down here, Roger. You're only allowed to ride that thing around the estate. You aren't sixteen yet. Get back on that machine and up that road now!" ordered Anna, through gritted teeth, and a facial expression that gave away nothing.

"Doing my bit for the family, mother." replied Roger.

"I'm sure Allen, Adam and Martha can find you something to do at home. We are going to be slightly overcrowded for a while, it would seem. Now get back up home now, young man!" ordered Anna.

Roger gave her a look and held a smile as best he could and stood his ground.

"Roger, I know you mean well but you are going home, now!" insisted Anna. The two stood looking at each other, motionless without speaking.

"He'll be ok with me, Anna. He has to leave the nest sometime," added Bill, from over Roger's shoulder, as he grimaced and waved his head from side to side, looking Anna in the face.

Roger looked at Bill, who ignored his stare, as he brushed past Roger and whispered in Anna's ear.

"He'll never forgive you if you don't. It'll be his mill some day and he might as well start his apprenticeship now. He'll be with me. He'll be fine. He's an Arthur. You weren't that much older when you took yourself to France, Anna."

In the back of Anna's head she immediately remembered Bill tell her he would look after her brother Roger, at the garden party before they went to France in 1915 . She suppressed her desire to remind Bill that he had not managed to bring her brother Roger back home, but stopped herself, knowing that Bill, for over twenty-five years, still lived with that afternoon's failed promise. She closed her eyes, sighed,

"Just this once, and he comes back with you. Don't leave him up here by himself. Promise me, Bill. "

Bill said nothing, just dipped his head and turned to Roger.

"Right kid! First lesson in management coming up. Stick with me and do what you are told!" as he gave Roger a wink and turned him in the direction of the Mill.

Offside of this conversation, the young St Johns Ambulance girl was hovering about in the vicinity, helping with light injuries, as she had been instructed. Jonty looked over at her and shouted.

"Hey Agnes, I have to do a run here, but I'll be back down. In the meantime it's not safe for you here by yourself. See that man talking to the lad with the motor bike, he's a mate of mine. Go with those two and stay with them. They'll have a bit of first aid work up at Arthurs' Mill."

Agnes, looked, slightly confused, at Jonty.

"Yes, Mr Price" she replied, as she turned to walk over to Bill.

Jonty was a bit surprised at her acceptance without question. Then he smiled to himself as it registered in his brain that Agnes had been weighing up the youth on the motor bike.

"Mr Price says you have work for me up at Arthurs Mill, Sir," interrupted Agnes, as Bill continued his conversation with Roger.

"Aye girl, best we keep an eye on you, for your own good. Instructions from Doctor Gibson, no less. He wants a full report," joked Bill.

Agnes nodded her head and made no eye contact with Roger, who like any youth of almost sixteen, was assessing Agnes, and deciding she might be worth chatting up in more appropriate circumstances.

As the team of three disappeared out of Jonty's sight, he gave the reins of the trap a pull as the horse willingly trotted away from the place he was only too glad to leave.

By the time Anna and the walking party reached the Sandy Row end of the Boyne Bridge and the Linfield Mill, she turned to the followers.

"Right, I'm going ahead to get some things sorted and get more transport. Please keep walking up the Malone Road past the Dub, Dunmurry Lane. Hopefully there'll be a lift on the way up before then. If not, I apologise, but things are a bit challenging for us all."

At that, Anna disappeared in the darkness, through the gates of the Linfield Mill.

A few minutes later, she drove out of the gates and turned right, up Sandy Row. By the time she reached the top of Sandy Row near the junction of the Lisburn Road and King William Park she could see the group of refugees. She scanned her eyes for the one that appeared the slowest and most cumbersome, struggling to keep up. Her eyes rolled in her head when she realised it was the overweight daughter with the oversized mouth. She mumbled, speaking under her breath to the two-seater roadster. "I'm sorry about this Alphonso, needs must old boy!"

"Right folks, I can take one along with me, any offers?"

A woman from the group shouted.

"Take her and get her out of my sight. Fed up listening to her moaning!" as she glared at the overweight woman who had confronted Anna earlier. Anna gave the woman a knowing glance, opened the passenger door of the roadster, and did not speak. Neither did the big woman with the big mouth as she plunked herself on the springs of the leather front seat.

By the time Anna and the woman turned into the gates at Ballydrain, neither had spoken. When the car circled the courtyard Martha was already walking down the steps to greet Anna, who got out of the car and met Martha halfway across the courtyard.

"It is quite a mess down there, Martha. I passed Jonty, he'll be at Broomhill by now with a few more who will arrive shortly. Get as many of the older ones as you can into the house. The rest will have to go in the outhouses and tents until we can farm them out to somewhere."

Then, as she finished her request, she leaned close to Martha as if she was giving her an affectionate hug and whispered in her ear.

"Make sure this woman isn't in the house. Needs brought down a peg. It'll serve her right."

Martha, kept her face straight, as she whispered back. "My pleasure Anna, leave that with me. I know the very place to put her up for the night."

"I will leave it in your capable hands Martha. Now, I need to get more transport up to Millfield. There could be quite a crowd here by the morning."

As Anna disappeared into the house, Martha ambled over to the woman who had just managed to separate herself from the tight bucket seats of the sports car.

"Right girl, see that far corner of the back courtyard around there, ask for Allen. He'll get you sorted out. Sorry it's only an outhouse, but it's a roof until we get something better sorted," advised Martha.

As the woman waddled in the direction Martha had pointed, she was increasingly met by a smell. The outhouse was close by the sileage shed. As Martha, ambled back into the house she allowed herself the luxury of a laugh to herself.

"That'll clear your head and let you know you shouldn't get lippy with an Arthur.

Chapter five

Five loaves and two small fish

While all was unravelling at Ballydrain, the scene at the Royal was intensifying. The pressure of the incoming patients was building. The system set up in advance had allowed for the assumption that local General Practitioners from Belfast and beyond would try and get to bombed areas and act as front line medics and triage, prioritising and freeing up hospital and theatre staff to remain at the Hospitals to deal with what arrived. That was the reason Davy had pulled Gerri Muldoon out of the mayhem in around Millfield.

Even so, the numbers were not good, given that the ferocity of the raid had been much more than expected. The 'five loaves and two small fish' had to come into play. Davy, after a conversation with other senior medics made a joint decision. The most important matter was to save lives. How to deal with that, was where the miracle had to come in to play. Shortage of experienced theatre staff would have to be covered by trained nurses who had no operating room experience, the subsequent shortage of accident and emergency nurses would have to be supplemented by someone else; but whom, was the question. The group of senior doctors all agreed it was a 'needs must' situation.

It was agreed by the group that Davy was the best person to undertake the solution to the problem. The organisation of the solution required skills that the other medics with their clipped accents and superior bearing would have been less effective. The next part of the plan required a more appropriate tone.

Davy separated himself from the rest of the senior group; he scanned the reception area. His eyes focused on some porters who were wheeling in patients and some cleaning staff who were mopping up areas of the floor as they tried to limit the blood and vomit regularly scattered about the floor. As two porters left a casualty in the hands of a junior doctor, Davy shouted.

"Right lads, over here a minute," as they moved towards him.

"How long have you boys been porters?"

The older one, about mid-thirties, replied, "I've been doing this for five years. Gabriel here, has been here four years."

"That'll do grand; the very men then," gestured Davy.

"When you've been bringing patients in and pushing them about, you have seen the medical staff checking pulses, stitches, checking for signs?"

"More times than we've had hot dinners," interrupted Gabriel, as he pulled a cigarette from his pocket, glad of the opportunity to light up.

"So you'd know how to check a pulse, have an idea of the signs if someone was not good. Put a bandage on. Maybe a few stitches, not in vital areas; basically minor injuries."

"Yes sir, but we aren't qualified." replied Paul, the other porter.

Davy had to hold back a smile as he remembered himself saying the same words to the junior doctor at the Somme who had told him to grab an apron and cut whatever he was told, some twenty-five years earlier.

"That lads, is my problem. Your responsibility ends with me telling you to do it. Normal rules went out the window a few hours ago. Same as I was told a long time ago."

Both men gave Davy a nod of approval.

"See if you can get the hold of any more of your lads who would be up to doing the same and get them over to that senior nurse at reception.

"But whose going to do the porters' jobs Doc?" asked Paul.

"My problem, lads. You just do what you are told until enough trained medics and student doctors get here. Then you can slide back to your regular job," assured Davy.

The two conscripts turned to each other as Gabriel said,

"Right Sir, leave it with us. We'll find a few more of the boys that know as much as us and get over to the desk there!" as they disappeared amongst the maze of staff and patients moving back and forth.

Davy scanned the area again and walked towards a cleaner who was mopping the floor trying to keep it free from blood and dirt.

"Doing a grand job there, girl. Would you be interested in a change of career for a few hours?"

The woman, in her forties, stopped mopping and leant her elbow against it, glad of the excuse to take a breather, while looking at him as if he was daft.

"If you can push a mop, I take it you could manage a trolley or a chair or a stretcher?" suggested Davy.

"Give it a go, Dr Gibson!" replied the cleaner.

Right, get out to the casualty bay as they come in, and tell them I said you are to do porter work. I'll get some more of your mates here to follow you. Away you go, now!"

As the cleaner disappeared out of the door, Davy thought to himself. "Now how do we solve the cleaner shortage?"

The floors were an accident waiting to happen as they were a mess. He stared at the influx of injured and their able-bodied relatives and neighbours.

Within a few minutes, relatives and neighbours of injured, were moping the floors with a renewed zeal.

"Five loaves and two small fish!" chuckled Davy to himself, as he disappeared into surgical to get involved in heavy duty surgery. David had managed to push everyone slightly above their comfort zones.

After he scrubbed up he went round the operating theatres advising overstretched theatre staff and surgeons, taking over some difficult cases. The night, like the Somme, seemed to pass quickly. His brain too occupied with the here and now.

By midmorning, having removed his surgical gown and mask, he walked out of a side entrance near surgical. He needed a few minutes to clear his head and renew his focus. He found a low wall and dropped himself wearily against it; half sitting, half standing. He had an overwhelming desire for a cigarette, a sense he had not felt since he was a final year student doing a session on postmortems. It was his first introduction to the insides of lungs of deceased chain smokers. He forced the idea from his brain by focusing his thoughts of cradling Anna in his arms when he finally got home.

The Royal appeared to be adjusting with the unexpected influx. Staff levels had coped because every member of medical staff and some retired volunteers, had walked into reception without ever being asked. Hospital staff, like Gerri Muldoon, who had found themselves needed down at the scenes of devastation had been able to return to the posts they had been trained for, courtesy of the local General Practitioners converging from near and far to act as the front-line medics amongst the rubble and fires. Davy decided to get back over to the City Hospital and see what the situation was like. The original plan had been for him to be based at the City. That plan had long been blown out of the water, literally, not to mention the powers to be, assuring everyone it was very unlikely to happen.

His mind turned to Anna, as he wondered what she was up to at this point in time. Bill was supposed to keep an eye on her, Anna had promised him she would behave. He hoped that would be the case. In the circumstances it was out of his control.

His thoughts moved on to what was the quickest way to the City Hospital. While the City was on the south side and the Royal on the west they were not actually far apart. He could walk it by the time transport could be sorted. He grabbed his big coat, hat and bag and headed out of the back gate of the hospital, down Roden Street, turned left on the Donegall Road, then right through the back of the City Hospital, a distance of less than a mile.

As he walked through the side entrance of the City Hospital and through reception he looked a dishevelled figure. The cold night air had been replaced by a mild spring day, which meant his coat was too warm and he had to open it and take his hat off, as the brisk walk had further created excessive heat. He did not have the appearance of a Senior Consultant.

"Can I help you Sir" asked a voice coming from his left. It was a young lady who had volunteered to do the job on reception while the regular was posted to more important duties. Davy was taken aback by the question. It was not something he was used to being asked. He was not in the best of mood.

"Aye, hang my coat and hat up. That would be a start!" rasped Davy in a fit of pique.

"But sir, I have to log everyone in first." appealed the girl.

Davy turned to her in exasperation, while knowing full well it was part of the agreed plan that this would be the function of whoever was on reception.

"Don't worry yourself. I am Doctor Gibson. Senior Consultant of this place. Stick that down on your piece of paper and take my hat and coat like a good girl. I've had quite enough complications for one night. Don't you add to them, please!" snapped Davy, as he almost threw the hat and coat across the reception desk.

Before the embarrassed girl could reply, a familiar voice shouted, "Doctor Gibson, over here please!"

It was Doctor Campbell, looking drained.

Davy, walked towards Campbell before he turned and gave an apologetic glance at the receptionist.

"I'll look after your coat Doctor Gibson. I didn't know. I'm only a volunteer. I'm sorry!" pleaded the temporary receptionist.

Davy waved a dismissive hand.

"I'm the one that's sorry, girl. It's been one of those nights. I should know better!" apologised Davy.

"What's the problem, young Campbell?" asked Davy.

"Well we have most of the serious cases stabilized but there are a few that, to be honest, we had to deal with in unorthodox methods," sighed Campbell.

"Medical textbooks don't give that much help on repairing damage caused by large explosions in a civilian situation. We have made medical decisions based on a needs must basis but there are no recorded precedents. Some of us are worried about being hauled over the coals for breaking all the standard procedures."

Davy, remained silent for several seconds. Campbell stood equally silent, hoping for an answer he wanted to hear.

"Campbell, son. if I remember correctly, up to last night you were one of my best young apprentices. I told you to do your best and work off your instincts in uncharted waters. So don't you worry yourself. Bottom line is, I have no doubt, you did your best in extreme circumstances and acted under my instruction. If anyone wants to give you stick, refer them to me. It's my problem," assure Davy, as he placed his hand on Campbell's shoulder.

"Right, am I needed in theatre or have you and Doctor Young and the rest got things steadied?" asked Davy.

"There's a few need your knowledge, but we have the life-threatening cases stabilised. The initial surgery needs a bit of time to settle before the next stage," replied Campbell.

"Right, get admin to send the notes of operations into me as soon as possible and I'll run my eye down them. Subject to that, as soon as replacements are available I want you and the rest of the team that's been on all night, out of here, rested, and back at ten this evening."

"Will do Professor," replied a relieved Campbell. He used the term Professor to Davy because he had been a medical student who had attended Davy's lectures at Queens where he had been given the title by the University. Campbell had known him with that title. The habit had become ingrained. Davy never called himself by that title unless he thought it gave him an advantage in a medical debate. The Tom Gibson in him meant he found it a bit boastful and made him feel a bit uncomfortable.

An hour later, Davy walked out of the front entrance of the City Hospital and tried to breathe some fresh air free from the chemicals of the operating rooms and wards. It was almost three o'clock in the afternoon. It had been fourteen hours since the start of the bombardment. His mind concentrated on the most immediate problem. He needed to clear his head for a few hours. If he stayed on until he dropped it would serve no purpose. Home, find Anna, try and get a few hours sleep was the only solution in his head.

Davy crossed the road to Elmwood Avenue, up the Malone Road, past the Eglantine Inn. As he walked as quick as any man who had just done a hard long shift, he heard a motor bike engine, the sound, of which, he thought familiar. The motor bike slowed and stopped beside him.

"Long night, Dad," sighed Roger. "I would offer you a lift! but Bill told me to get my passenger home safe. Don't think this bike would take three."

Davy, looked behind Roger, still leant against the handlebars and recognised a familiar face.

"You seem to be cropping up everywhere, young lady," remarked Davy, as he tried to keep the straight face of a concerned father, while glad to see she had gotten through the ordeal without physical harm. Mental damage, he had no idea.

"Yes Dad, I believed you have already been introduced," smirked Roger, only too glad to compete with his father.

"Agnes lives up the Hillfoot Road, at Knockbreda. Bill told me to avoid going back in the direction of the city, so I went on up to the

116

Royal, over Glenmachan Street, Tate's Avenue. I'm heading up to Annadale Avenue and round to Knockbreda. I'll get Agnes home. Bill should be coming up soon," advised Roger.

Davy, looked at Roger, aware that Agnes, was not to be part of the conversation he wanted to have with his son.

"Where's your mother?" was all he could manage.

"Back home! Bill sent her packing, and she didn't even know it!"

Davy contained his relief. "What about Bill?"

"He should be up this way soon. It's a mess down there. Large hole in the factory roof, and the finishing rooms need rebuilt. Bigger issue is the workers' houses. Quite a few flattened or uninhabitable. Mother has taken it upon herself to deal with that. You'll find we have a few guests this evening!" continued Roger, attempting to copy his father's dry demeaner.

Roger slammed his foot on the pedal and put the bike into gear, letting out a roar from the engine.

"Have to get Agnes home. Let Mum know I am fine. Tell you all when I get home!" he shouted, as the bike, rear wheel slipping from left to right, accelerated away. Agnes managed to keep on the bike by grabbing even tighter to Roger; an act she did not find unpleasant in the slightest.

117

Davy trundled up the Malone as he relaxed knowing that Anna was back home and Roger had, by all accounts, found the evening educational. When he reached Notting Hill and Marlborough Park a car pulled up beside him.

"Get your arse in the motor, big lad!" shouted Bill, as he manfully managed to keep his cigarette in his mouth as he spoke.

"And a fine afternoon it is too, sir, grumpy bollocks that you are!" bantered Davy, to his lifelong friend.

Bill organised two children to get out of the front seat and spread themselves over the three senior citizens huddled in the back before Davy plunked himself and his medical bag into the seat. By the time they had reached Balmoral Avenue, neither had spoken. Davy's, adrenaline finally starting to subside as he tried to gather his thoughts, knowing there were strangers in the back. Bill, knew Davy well enough to know when to say nothing and when to speak.

"Everyone accounted for, Bill?" asked Davy.

"Anna, Roger, Jonty, Adam and Allen, Martha all doing their bit. Got most of the workers sorted for the moment. There's about a dozen we haven't accounted for. Hope they are sitting up Blackmountain. If they aren't," Bill dipped his head, it'll be visits to the Falls Road Baths in the morning. Too many for the morgue. They've drained the pool, and, well you know the rest."

The passengers in the back, looked at each other not knowing the identity of the man in the dishevelled coat covered in dust and stains. Bill sensed the turning of heads in the back, listening to every word of the conversation.

"Sorry folks, This is my mate, Davy Gibson, You'll be staying up at his house for a while, by the look of things," advised Bill, as he kept his eyes on the road.

"Looks like you've been busy, Davy. Bad was it?" asked Bill, still balancing the cigarette between his lips.

"Not good Bill, not as bad as the Somme, but not good. You can only do what you can do. Damage limitations," replied Davy.

"How did Roger end up down there, Bill? That wasn't part of the plan. Thanks for getting him through it."

"He's an Arthur, and a Gibson. Did you expect anything else, mate," laughed Bill, as he gave a brief glance across at Davy.

"We always did wander, if, with him being so protected by Anna, he would have it in him if things got tight. Well we don't need to worry anymore about that, old son.

119

A silence fell again, as Davy's brain continued to relax, then, as they reached the Dub,[16] Davy asked.

"What's with Agnes getting a lift up to Knockbreda?"

Bill let out a contained grunt of laughter.

"Apparently she had been in Belfast doing a St John's Ambulance badge test at the Eye, Ear and Throat place near Shaftesbury Square when the sirens went off and they all went down to the basement and prayed. Must have worked as they weren't in the loop of those bastards. Then, when it stopped, instead of going back home to Knockbreda, she ran up to Millfield with her St John's Ambulance bag over her shoulder. You know the rest after that. I had her and Roger with me all the time. So when it was time to get out of there, Roger volunteered to see the young lady home. That's the Gibson in him," laughed Bill.

---

[16] Area on the Malone Road where the Old Coach Road to Dublin began.

Chapter six

A New Dawn

The Norton motor bike slowed up outside the neat terrace house with a well-kept garden on the edge of Newtownbreda village, Knockbreda. The first of the rose blooms forcing themselves to compete with the daffodils and tulips. Before Agnes could throw her leg from off the vehicle, an ashen faced lady in her mid-forties, rushed out of the front door.

"Agnes, Oh Agnes, thank God you are safe! Your father and brother are away into the town looking for you!" shouted her mother, as she cradled her daughter in her arms. Roger, sat on the bike and took more than a little satisfaction in watching the happy reunion, while keeping his distance. Finally, mother and daughter released their grips from each other and looked towards Roger, who, like any lad of fifteen, was unsure of his position in the circumstances. Meeting with the mother of a young girl he had just deposited from his motor bike was a tricky one, he thought.

"Well that's you home safe and sound Agnes. I'd best get home and face my mother, now," said Roger, as he reached to engage the bike. Agnes's mother was about to ask him in for a cup of tea before he went off, but Roger had already worked that out and had no desire to find himself the subject of an interrogation, no matter how polite and well meant.

"Well Agnes, that's you home. I'll be on my way. I am sure we will meet again," smiled Roger, as the engine roared, and he turned the Norton in the direction of the Milltown Road and Ballydrain. Agnes and her mother barely had the chance to shout a 'thank you,' as Roger sped away from this awkward situation.

When Roger turned the Norton into the tree lined drive up to the courtyard of Ballydrain, he met a different sight to the tranquil surrounding he was used. Gone were the horses strolling the fields either side and the birdsongs of Spring. Instead, children playing hide and seek. Grownups standing in small groups deep in conversation. Tents and tarpaulins being erected by estate staff, neighbours and refugees from streets around the Mill. He slowed up as a few of the men from the bombed-out houses gave him a discreet wave and a nod of approval. He didn't understand what that was about, but he waved back anyway. After he left the bike in the garage and slipped in through the back door of the kitchen he had intended to go to his room and get his head down. He had never felt so tired in his young life. As he crossed the hallway to the staircase a voice stopped him in his tracks.

"Roger, my boy. Would you come in here please?"

The voice, was mellow in tone, but one that was used to being obeyed. Roger pulled a face to himself, as he halted his stride. As he entered the drawing room, the source of the voice, he saw Sir James standing by the decanter of whiskey, as he poured two crystal glasses.

"Have a swig at that Roger and don't bother feigning you don't know what it tastes like. I saw you taking the odd tipple yesterday afternoon courtesy off those two Bamford chancers, Adam and Allen." Roger looked at Sir James, failing to conceal his thoughts.

"Only share my whiskey with men who deserve it," mused Sir James, still keeping the manner of a business introduction.

"You can never know the metal of a man until he is tested. Now I know your metal," continued Sir James. as he handed the Tyrone crystal to his grandson, chinking it with his own as he did. Roger smiled an embarrassed smile, before Sir James continued.

"Count yourself fortunate that it is not the illegal brew I had to share with your Grandpa Tom. Now that will be a pleasure yet to come, but trust me, you are not ready for that stuff yet," said Sir James, as he allowed himself a broad smile.

"All I did was act as Bill's 'go for'," replied Roger.

"I understand you did more than that. Heard a few comments from the 'great unwashed' outside, as I took a stroll amongst them. I got the impression they thought you put in a good shift, young man," continued Sir James.

Roger remained silent as he sipped his whiskey, slowly, just staring at the carpet. Sir James, let out a grunt.

"It would appear you are turning out a fine blend of Arthur and Gibson grit, young man."

"I am what I am Gramps. I try to do what is right. I been taught that by Mum, Dad, Grandmama, Grandpa Tom, and yourself since I was small. It is not difficult when I have been blessed with that," smiled Roger.

Sir James sipped his drink again as Roger's smile reminded him of his own son, Roger, the day in the gardens as they talked before he went to the Somme, never to return.

"When I am old enough, I will have to join up. It is not an option Gramps. We need to stop this evil," sighed Roger.

"Your mother and father might have something to say about that Roger. You know their view on wars. To be honest I have similar views, but this one is different. It's not a question of power struggles or economics. This one is a fight about a way to behave. A fight for decency, against an evil tyranny," mused Sir James.

Roger nodded his head slowly as he looked into Sir James's face before the concerned grandfather continued.

"Well, that is a decision for another day and one I hope it will not be needed," replied Sir James, before he continued.

"Don't go up to your room Roger for a bit yet. I would prefer if you would sit by the fire with me for a while. Life is short my boy, best to remember the special moments."

Roger did as was suggested. The pair sat on the large comfortable fireside chairs opposite each other as their faces started to warm in the glow of the logged fire. Within five minutes they were both asleep, slumped in their chairs.

Chapter Seven

Recovery

Shortly after, Davy and Bill and their passengers arrived at Ballydrain. When they had ushered passengers off to be given safe shelter, Davy started to walk towards the rear door of the mansion house. He paused when he realised Bill was not alongside him. He turned and found Bill getting back into his car.

"Come on in and get something to eat before you go Bill. Like me, you haven't eaten since yesterday."

Bill looked over at Davy. "Thanks Davy, but my own 'wee woman' will be sitting worrying about me, so I'd best put her out of her misery. Besides, I don't want to keep you away from the lovely Anna. She might need you to hold her in your arms, mate. She found last night hard, but she dug deep. Might as well have been back on the Somme. I could see it in her eyes."

Bill said no more, he just gave Davy a feigned salute with his for finger against his head, as he made his way thoughtfully out of the estate and home to Edenderry.

126

Davy, walked wearily through the back entrance, passing the door of the kitchen. Usually by late afternoon it was quiet. Now it was full of bustle like the kitchen of St Patrick's Drumbeg Church Hall in the middle of a social event. He stuck his head through the door and surveyed the scene. Martha was leaning against the sink deep in thought, A few staff were making themselves busy, aided by other women whom he assumed were refugees from the streets of Belfast. He arrived alongside Martha and lent against the kitchen unit beside her. She had not seen him as she was deep in her own thoughts; staring at the floor. Taking a brief physical rest, mind going in all directions.

"How's Jonty, Martha, what's he up to, girl?" asked Davy in almost a whisper.

"He's out there sorting a few things, but I've told him to get his head down for a bit as soon as he can, Davy," was her tired reply.

"Maybe you should do the same Martha, looks like you haven't stopped since last night, advised Davy."

"I'll not be stopping until Anna ends her shift. I've given up telling her to ease off. We have things under control, but you know what she's like more than the rest of us."

Davy shook his head slowly and let out a stifled laugh as he raised himself off the edge of the kitchen unit.

127

"Where is she Martha, any idea?"

"God knows, Davy. Flitting around all over the place. Keeping her mind occupied. Running around with a look in her eyes I haven't seen before. Get her out of it, Davy," urged Martha.

Davy turned to face Martha and placed a hand on her shoulder. "Martha, take yourself away home and take Jonty with you. You look after him. Anna is my problem. Now go!" ordered Davy, as he moved his hand from her shoulder and gave a token gesture of a shove in her back.

As Davy entered the main hall he passed the drawing room where Roger and Sir James were still inside. He could hear the sound of Sir James snoring. As he opened the door he was met with the sight of Sir James and Roger slumped in their seats. Sir James lay with his head back and his jaw open. Roger was lying on his side in the large chair, curled up like a child. In sleep the young 'almost' sixteen-year-old had let go of his pretence of adulthood. Davy saw before him his son, who was really still little more than a child, trying to fit into an adult world. Davy closed the door quietly and smiled at the bond between his father-in-law and his son.

As he turned away, Jack Simpson, a young estate worker was carrying a small tent to put up in the front lawn.

128

"Hey Jack, have you any idea where that woman of mine is, kid?" asked Davy.

"She went upstairs about five minutes ago to see how Lady May was doing!" interrupted Eileen, who was passing by at the same time, and had heard Davy's question.

"Lady May is confused by all the activity about here. She started to have a bit of one her sessions. Mrs Gibson went up to calm her down."

Davy's let out a blow of air from his cheeks as he glanced briefly at the ceiling.

"Jesus, as if she hasn't enough to deal with," he whispered to himself.

"Thanks Eileen," replied Davy, as he turned and took the staircase two steps at time. Eileen and Jack both gave each other a look and pulled their faces. Davy usually strolled around the house in a quiet understated manner. Flying up the stairs two at a time was not his style.

As Davy slowly opened the door of the bedroom he could see Lady May sitting up in her bed with Anna sitting on the bed side, combing her mother's long white hair and talking gently to her. Anna, hearing the door open, turned to see a tired and dishevelled Davy at the doorway. She let the brush fall on the bed sheets and rose to greet Davy as they embraced without speaking. Lady May sat and looked at them with a vacant stare. As Anna and Davy relaxed their embrace, Davy whispered,

"This isn't doing her any good, is it?"

Lady May was in the later stages of dementia complicated by a stroke she had taken a year earlier. She did not recognise Davy, more often than not. Even Anna, on occasions, had to suffer the question, "And who are you my dear?" which almost broke her.

"Right girl, we need a bit of time to ourselves. You can't keep this up. There's plenty running around with enough wit to manage things. Come on Anna, we'll send Eileen up to sit with her until she falls asleep," coaxed Davy.

Anna turned to face her mother who was still staring incoherently in their direction. She rubbed her hands against Davy's back, as she whispered.

"Doctor's orders. Is that what you are saying," she sighed, with a small hint of that look in her eyes the evening at Shaws Bridge when Davy made his first declaration of love for her. Anna turned to look at her mother.

"Mama, I am going to rest for a while. I will have your warm milk brought up," assured Anna.

The pair retired to their bedroom that looked over the lake and the fields, alive with activity, drew the curtains to exclude the late afternoon sun. climbed into bed rapped in each-others' arms and did not speak. Physical and mental exhaustion overcame them in seconds. Even the notion of a bit of romance didn't enter Davy's mind. Now that was the real test of tiredness, he thought to himself.

Later that evening, sitting at the dinner table, Davy could not miss pointing that out to Anna whose response was to lean across the table, give him one of her special slow kisses, followed by a playful slap on his cheek and said,

"That'll have to do you, Big Lad. Now get yourself back to your work. I've plenty to do up here. We'll have a nice afternoon together, away from all this, as soon as it blows over. It's still you and me Davy. The Kaiser didn't separate us and neither with Adolf."

Chapter Eight

The Trust

When Davy walked into the City Hospital at 22.00 hrs on the evening after the Blitz, the lines of casualties had reduced to a manageable number, and a degree of stability seemed apparent. As he met with doctors and senior nurses he was given a list of patients that needed to have his second opinion. He spent several hours attending operations, mostly observing, sometimes stepping in and taking over, when young inexperienced surgeons had taken their skills as far as their competence. As he left one operating theatre a voice caught his ear.

"David, old chap, there's a messenger just arrived from the Royal that they could do with you over there, if possible, urgent!"

It was the unmistakable voice of John Clarke another senior surgeon of similar status to himself. John was a very different character to Davy.

"Phone lines are still out but they've been sending runners between the hospitals. There're a few difficult ones needing help at the Royal. I could do some, but I'm about to start on a nasty one here in a few minutes. Looks like it's your problem, old chap!"

John was an excellent surgeon, but his confident posh accent did not endear him with all of the staff. They saw him as arrogant and aloof, the opposite to Davy, who regularly sat in the canteen bantering with the porters and cleaning staff.

Both were good men, but Davy had more rounded personal skills. Davy got on fine with John as they had both trained together as students at Queens University and they were both members of Malone Golf club, playing regularly, as they unwound from the pressures of precision surgery. Davy knew the real John Clarke that others seemed to misunderstand. He had the advantage of knowing him over twenty years and understood his manner was down to his upbringing in the higher levels of Belfast society. Davy had lived with the upper echelons of Ulster society for half of his life and had learnt to understand their ways. The other half he had grown up living the harsher lives of the rest. Davy had long established that the good and the bad existed across society and it was best to take everyone as he found them. 'Class' had nothing to do with where you lived, how you spoke, how much you had in the bank, but how you went about things, was Davy's view.

"What's the nature of the problem, John?" asked Davy.

"There are quite a few with bone damage at the Royal that need your knowledge. That's your domain more than mine, David. I am more of an organs man." advised John, as he moved his head side to side with a sense of doubt that Davy knew was not the normal John Clarke, before he continued.

"They never trained us for this mess, David. Unchartered waters, my friend. You have the advantage of your earlier life experience, horrible though it must have been," sighed John, as he gripped Davy's arm at the elbow before he started to move towards surgery.

"The notes from the Royal are on my desk!" advised John, as he disappeared.

Davy gathered the other notes from reception and asked a porter to find him some transport urgently. Davy shared a bench in the back of an ambulance that was on its way back to the bombed sites and he was dropped off at the gates of the Royal on route. Once in the Royal he quickly gave advice to junior surgeons on how to deal with some cases, and in others, took the pressure off them by confirming amputation was the only option. One case caught his attention more than others. He decided advice was not enough.

The junior doctor explained the case of a child in intensive care who had lost an arm and her leg was in an extremely critical condition. It wasn't a straightforward broken leg. There was crush damage to sinew, muscle, veins and arteries. If it had been an adult the leg would have been amputated and the next patient would have been wheeled into the operating room. It was down to Davy whether the damage could be repaired, or the leg would have to be removed. The potential of a child being left with no arm and leg down one side was a harrowing thought for even the most-hard bitten of surgical staff. The knowledge that it was the same child he and Muldoon had extricated from the bombed house the evening before, added to the dilemma. It had gotten personal, something that Davy always tried to avoid. It clouded judgement.

"How long would it take for this one to be prepped and ready?" asked Davy, trying to disguise his concern.

"There's a few repair jobs that could be put back. Ten minutes probably," his junior doctor replied.

"Right get that sorted," snapped Davy, before he continued after a brief second of thought.

"Sorry Dr Flynn, I'll need the best you have of the surgical nurses and, if possible, another surgeon to watch what I do so they can do it themselves next time, if it works," advised Davy, as he raised his voice.

"I'll make myself available if that's all right with you," replied Flynn, only too glad to get the opportunity to learn from the legend that was Gibson and improve his CV.

"You'll do me. Just get me a good theatre nurse that's up to a tricky one, Flynn," stressed Davy.

Davy scrubbed up, mind racing as he tried to put together a plan of action to potentially deal with the injury. He had great concerns if he could save the leg, but he had to try. By the time he entered the operating theatre, the child was lying already anaesthetised. He scanned the room and counted heads to make sure there was a full team, walked over to the sedated child, and confirmed it was what he had feared. It was the same child that Gerri Muldoon had dragged from under the rubble, the night before.

"Well, little one, let's see what we can do for you," sighed Davy, as he gave a closer search of the damage, and finally spoke.

"Right Flynn, If I make a 'bollocks' of this, it's up to you to help me out, so concentrate. Don't get in a flap, and don't let anything distract you. Are you with me, Flynn?"

He barked an order to the surgical nurse, without turning to face her.

"Nurse, clamp that artery above the temporary clamp and don't take your eyes off it unless I tell you. Scalpel please," instructed Davy, eyes still looking at the problem in hand.

The nurse opposite leaned over the child, completed the clamp at the first attempt and immediately handed the scalpel, having already worked out the size he would require. Davy caught sight of the face of the nurse that was not covered by her surgical mask, as he received the instrument and smiled to himself from behind his mask.

"Glad to see you did what you were told, Flynn," said Davy, with a deadpan expression.

"I asked you to get the best you could get for this one. Glad to see you did just that," continued Davy, still not taking his eyes off the wounds, as he began attempting a repair to the mess he saw before him. The surgical nurse opposite him made no reaction as she was too intent on watching the effects of the clamp.

"This 'wee' soul wouldn't even be here if it wasn't for Gerri Muldoon. Isn't that right, Muldoon?"

Gerri Muldoon still concentrated on her tasks, but the change of colour of her face, left uncovered, by surgical protection, from a pale Celtic white, to flushed crimson, told a tale.

The full procedure took a painstaking two hours to complete. It was not without difficulty. On several occasion, blood flew in all directions, as each sinew and blood vessel were either, repaired, reconnected or removed.

At the end of the operation, Davy turned to the young Dr Flynn, who was still trying to take in what he had witnessed.

"Well Flynn, I hope that has done the trick. We won't know for a few days yet if it will work or she will lose it, but we have given her a fighting chance," mused Davy, as he gave Flynn an approving nod.

Flynn walked out of the theatre still trying to process and remember the techniques and dexterity he had witnessed. Davy followed behind him and just as he was about to leave turned and scanned the theatre until he picked out Muldoon, who, like the rest of the operating team was busy clearing up the mess, sorting scalpels, clamps and swabs to do the set up for the next operation.

"Muldoon, what time's your next session?" asked Davy.

"That's me done until tomorrow morning, after I get sorted in here, Dr Gibson. Be glad to get my feet up for a few hours, only got a few ours rest this morning.

"See me up in the canteen before you go. Need a chat with you. Don't be long. There's probably some other poor soul that we'll have to 'wing it' with, before the night's out," he sighed, as he disappeared out the door.

Ten minutes later, Davy was sitting with a cup of hot black tea. Even with no sugar or milk, the weak tea of the hospital did nothing for his taste buds. He had been brough up on Tom Gibson's tar like substance. A 'real man's tea' as his father told him. The sort of tea that if you put your finger in, it would be turned into a leather product.

Oh, how he wished his father was sitting in front of him, smiling as he opened a bottle of Armagh's finest and pouring it into his cup. As he looked up from the table he saw Gerri Muldoon walk towards him, looking both exhausted and concerned. Davy stood up and pointed to the chair across the table; Gerri hesitated. She had been preparing herself for a lecture for something she had done wrong during the operation. It didn't make sense to her that the big fish in the pond was standing up for her.

Davy watched as Muldoon settled herself.

"Is it tea, or is it tea, Muldoon?" smiled Davy, as he turned to the canteen queue to get the unappealing liquid.

Gerri Muldoon sat, glad of the chance to settle herself, while Davy returned with a steaming cup. The sight of a senior consultant getting her tea, didn't reduce her level of uncertainty.

"Showed your metal in the last twenty-four hours, Muldoon. How long have you been in this nursing game, now?" asked Davy, keeping his face straight,

"Started at sixteen, five years ago. It has its bad days, but my other option was in the mill, and I wasn't having that, Doctor Gibson. Too many reasons I wasn't going down that route. Had an awful time getting my mother not to send me down there at fourteen. I went to St Dominic's Grammar. The only one in our street that got into there. The nuns from the school came down to the house and more or less told her I was going nowhere until I did my certificates at sixteen. They must have seen I had more in me than my Ma did. Strange the nuns showed so much interest, because they were a hard bunch, always threatening us with hell fire or a beating. Must have been tough love," she shrugged her shoulders.

Davy sat opposite her and tried to keep a smile off his face. There was too much of himself sitting opposite. He sipped some tea, hesitating, as he tried to think of the best way to begin the conversation he intended. As his brain creaked into gear, the memory of his meeting with Sir James, the night he agreed 'The Deal' in the drawing room of Ballydrain in 1919, occupied his thoughts.

"You are in the wrong job, Muldoon," advised Davy, his voice without any emotion. Gerri Muldoon's face dropped, she felt a sinking feeling, the like of which she had never felt before. She held back tears that began to appear from the corners of her eyes.

"But I love being a nurse. There's nothing I wanted to do more, Doctor Gibson. What did I do wrong? I did my best. What did I do wrong?" pleaded Muldoon.

Davy, felt an instantaneous surge of regret. He had forgotten that women can take a different view on things. Like when two women wear the same dress there is potential for friction, but if two men wear the same jacket, it's a bonding expression of kindred spirits.

"Did I say you have done anything wrong; quite the opposite in fact," assured Davy, as he pulled his handkerchief from his breast pocket.

"Here Gerri, wipe those tears. You've no need for them, girl," reassured an embarrassed Davy.

"But if you think I'm in the wrong job how can that be nothing to worry about," sobbed Muldoon, as she tried to discreetly dab the tears.

"Now there, Muldoon, is, your problem. How the hell do you think you can be criticised for what you have done in the last twenty-four hours. Between keeping that child alive last night, being my back up this last few hours; you can hold your head up to anyone," replied Davy, with an expression of disbelief, before he continued.

"Why did you settle for nursing? You have the ability to be a doctor in your own right," questioned Davy, as Gerri settled herself and dabbed the corner of her eyes.

"God, getting into Nursing was a big enough stretch for my Ma and Da. It was never an option. Probably was capable of it. Eimear McGuigan was in my class in St Dominic's. I used to get better marks than her. She is in her fourth year in medicine now, but her family are loaded. Live up in Cadogan Park," explained Muldoon.

"If you had the chance to do it now, would you take it, Gerri? You wouldn't be the first to come into it by the side door," suggested Davy. "It's a nice idea, Doctor Gibson, but that chance doesn't come to girls like me. Nursing is the nearest I'll get in this game." sighed Muldoon.

Gerri Muldoon had heard enough and was content she had not been told off. Even more content that she had been given praise from a legend of Belfast hospitals.

"I'm away home to put my feet up. At least our house is still standing. Have to be thankful for that, Doctor Gibson. Thanks for the tea."

Muldoon, stood to put her coat on, as Davy made his last comment.

"Don't sell yourself short, Gerri. I'll ask you once again. Taking everything else out of the equation. What would you rather be, a nurse or a doctor, girl?" inquired Davy, again.

Gerri stood, thinking, as she buttoned her coat and in a burst of exasperation, raised her voice in frustration.

"Doctor Gibson, I appreciate the compliment. I would love to be a doctor, but I live in the real world. It's easy for your lot in the leafy suburbs but it doesn't happen to girls from the Cullintree. You wouldn't understand. Doctor."

Davy could not contain a smile as he listened to Muldoon's words of wisdom.

"So your answer is 'Yes' then, Muldoon," grinned Davy. Gerri Muldoon gave him another exasperated look and turned to walk away.

143

"Surprised no one ever told you how I got into this game," remarked Davy, irony mixed with surprise.

Gerri turned her face once again in confusion as he waved her away with the back of his hand.

"Gerri Muldoon, will you go home and rest. There's nothing more to be said for the moment." instructed Davy.

Before Muldoon could acknowledge him, a medic came alongside Davy.

"Professor Gibson, John Clarke needs you back over at the City urgently, sir."

Davy got up from his chair and exchanged glances with Muldoon as they both went their ways. Muldoon to her home to sleep, Davy to get back over to the City Hospital and arrive in John Clarke's office.

John was seated in his chair studying the latest reports on patients. Trying to priorities the order of his attention.

"What's up Clarkey?" asked Davy, dropping the formalities that were expected in the public domain.

"The damned men in suits are on their way, attempting to make it look as if they are doing something useful. Didn't anyone tell them the best thing is for them to keep out of our way and let us clean this mess up first," raged John Clarke.

"Get word back to them that all medical staff are too busy dealing with the consequences of the raid to be distracted from their duties. That should do the trick, Clarkey," suggested Davy.

"Too late for that, old chap. They'll probably be half-way up Bradbury Place by now," sighed Clarke.

"Ahh, for frig sake, that's all we need, Clarkey," winched Davy.

My thoughts exactly David, but as head of the Select Vestry at Windsor Presbyterian Church I could not possibly repeat it in those terms," agreed John, with more than a degree of angst.

"Well I don't have the same limitations, even though I do show my face at St Patrick's Drumbeg, to keep myself right. Leave those clowns with me, John," advised Davy.

As Davy attempted to go to his own office to do exactly the same as his colleague, he could see that the great and the not so good of Belfast's bureaucrats were posing in front of reporters and photographers in reception. As he tried to disappear into his office the Chief Administrative Officer spotted him.

"Professor Gibson, would you have a moment, please? asked the administrator, who deliberately gave Davy his academic title to enhance his authority in speaking to the Government's elite.

Davy stopped for a second as he decided that to hide from them was not the best option. He stepped forward towards the group and exchanged greetings and handshakes.

"Well Professor Gibson, it would appear you are coping well with the horrendous casualties the Hun have brought upon us," sympathised one of the men of importance.

Davy recognised him as a man who had called on occasions over the years at Ballydrain and had been entertained by Sir James. He had always seemed an amicable enough character, so Davy did not feel uneasy with the conversation.

"Well, that has been down to the efforts of everyone here and it is the same at the Royal and the Mater," replied Davy. "Now if you would excuse me, I, like the rest of the staff here, have patients to deal with, gentlemen. I will gladly take the opportunity to explain the way of things in this hospital, but now is not the time."

Davy turned to walk away, intent on finding refuge in his office. The Chief Administrator tugged at his arm.

"Professor Gibson, the press would like a photo of us discussing matters with the Members of Parliament and the City Council's concerned representatives."

Davy turned to the Chief Administrator and spoke to him between gritted teeth and in little more than a whisper, not wanting the words to reach the men of importance.

"Desmond, I know you have a job to do, and you mean no harm, but if some of those bastards that's standing around posing to keep their seats in Stormont and the Council had paid a bit more thought into defending this City, we would not have to be clearing this mess. Now I've better things to do. Speak to you later. You are welcome to that lot, Desmond," sympathised Davy.

Unfortunately for Davy, one of the reporters who had been hovering unnoticed, notebook and pencil in hand, had very good hearing, and was close enough to Desmond and Davy to hear every word.

The next morning the headline of the News Letter, Whig, and the Irish News were,

'Top Consultant criticises Belfast defence strategy.'

It took up most of the front page.

Chapter nine

The Inquisition

By the time Davy drove back up into the courtyard of Ballydrain it was early afternoon the next day. He had managed a few short naps in the armchair in his office since his handshakes with officialdom and a steady flow of surgical work. His head was full of plotting and planning surgery that he would attempt when he returned to the next shift. As he entered the hall and passed the reading room, Sir James gave a shout that was more like an instruction.

"David, got a minute please? came an intimidatingly quiet but stern request from Sir James.

Davy stopped in his tracks and ambled into the room. Sir James was sitting relaxed with a copy of the News Letter[17] on his knee.

"Read the newspapers this morning, David?" asked Sir James, as he closed the paper, folded it over and offered it to him. Davy unfolded

---

the journal and scanned the front-page headline. He stood in silence, wanting to curse and swear at the headlines but as he had built up too much of a good relationship with his father-in-law he did not wish to annoy him with an outburst of profanities; it would not be the Arthur way. It had taken him over twenty years to adapt to the Arthur way of doing things. He did not want to blow it all in five seconds of rage. Davy settled for a long sigh from expanded cheeks as he handed the News Letter back to Sir James.

"That's not the way it was, James. Some reporter eves dropping on a private conversation between me and the Chief Administrator; making a name for himself," replied Davy, as he shook his head wearily from side to side. He put his hands deep in his pockets, walked over to the French windows and stared out over the fields and garden. Silent, saying nothing, calming his rage.

Sir James broke the silence. "If you take my advice this is a damage limitation job. Nip it in the bud, before it grows into a monster."

"Aye James, that's your expertise. I am not in your league when it comes to dealing with that lot," sighed Davy.

"Exactly David, so I suggest you go and find that daughter of mine, see if you can get her to slow up a bit, and leave me to do to the strategizing. We'll have a short chat about it over breakfast before you have to face their response. You know as well as I do there will be one. In the meantime, think no more of it," reassured Sir James.

"What was Anna's reaction to it?" asked Davy.

"Ahh!" laughed Sir James, as he raised his head to the ceiling.

"I had to persuade her not to get into that flying machine of hers, head to the News Letter office in Donegall Street, and rip the doors off the place. She backed off when I reminded her that protecting the Arthur family, is still my domain. You David, are a much loved member of this family, come hell or high water. Leave it until the morning and we'll agree the best approach," advised Sir James, as he waved Davy to leave.

Next morning, Davy shared breakfast with Sir James. Anna sat listening, nodding her head at times, containing a laugh now and again. Afterwards, Anna followed Davy out to his car. She gave him a hug, rubbed his back with her hands and whispered.

"Don't let the bastards grind you down, Davy, and don't miss and hit the wall if it comes to it," was her last words, as she gave him a kiss and waved him off.

It was full a week before Davy received a formal letter from Stormont Castle. It contained a request to appear before the Health

Committee with regards to 'matters of irregularity' at The Royal Victoria Hospital.

It was also the same day Gerri Muldoon received an extra envelope with her pay packet from the wages department.

Two days later, Davy walked up the steps of Stormont, the overly extravagant building covered in black pitch in an attempt to make it less of a target of the Luftwaffe. He passed through the main doors and up the imposing staircase with the stone effigy of Lord Craigavon, James Craig, on the landing halfway up the staircase.

He was tempted to make a gesture of disrespect, in the memory of Tom, his father, and his deceased friend, Joe. He bit his lip and kept his hands at his side. Sir James, had primed him in every detail and option depending on the line of questioning. There was no point in messing matters up by a cheap gesture at the founder of the State.

"Remember David, treat this as a visit to the enemy trench. Keep silent, as far as possible, have your exit plan, do not waste your bullets. Make the kill quick. Do not let them see it coming. Leave them a trap so they can not follow after you," was the advice given by Sir James as he summarised the answers he suggested. As he finished his final comment, he added.

"Please David, do not allow them to turn it into a scrap. Eight against one is not the odds for a fight. Stick to my formula, keep your natural instincts under control. I take your advice on matters of health. You take my advice on how to handle this lynch mob. Trust me, if you do what I say, it will work out fine." pressed Sir James.

As he was ushered into the intimidating committee room his eyes scanned the eight faces. He laughed to himself when he realised that only one face would be likely to give him any protection. Harry Midgley, a rare breed of Unionist with a socialist agenda, did his best to give him a supportive glance without being noticed by the other seven. Amongst the other seven, three shuffled their papers and did not make eye contact. The other four glared at him as if they would have happily put his head in one of Jack Graham's mincing machines.

Harry Midgley, like himself and Bill, had been a lifetime Linfield supporter and they had many a pint over the years after a game. Midgley's politics of the working man, had always been Davy's view on life, despite his own personal good fortune.

Davy, settled himself in the chair that had been reserve for his potential professional execution.

The Minister of Health was the first to speak.

"Good morning Professor Gibson. It has been found necessary to call you to this committee this morning concerning the serious matter of your professional conduct during the night and morning of the Blitz. Information has been received by the Department that claims that you broke numerous professional practices and amongst other things instructed hospital staff to carry out medical procedures of which they were not qualified. The Department of Health finds it necessary in the circumstances to investigate this matter and establish whether it needs to absolve itself from failing to protect the health of its citizens by reporting the facts to the British Medical Council. Furthermore, if it is deemed appropriate, the involvement of legal process, criminal or civil," advised the Minister, as he glared over his spectacles at Davy.

Davy, looked directly at the Minister of Health with an expression of complete indifference as Sir James had advised, and sat silent. The Minister continued to look directly at Davy as he settled back in his chair waiting for Davy to reply. No reply was forthcoming. An unsettling silence took over the room. As the Minister's patience wore out, he asked.

"Well Gibson, what have you to say for yourself?"

Davy, sniffed. "I was waiting for you to finish. Was that it, Minister? You have brought me up here to tell me this. I have patients in urgent need of my help, and you order me up here wasting valuable time." He rose from his chair and sighed.

"And the band played on as the ship sank below the waves," he mused in irony, stifling a laugh as he turned to leave. His reference to the Titanic hit hard, as it was intended to. The Prime Minister Andrews, one of those that had given him an intimidating glare, dropped his pen. His family connections to the construction of the doomed ship caused him to flinch. Exactly what Davy and Sir James had wanted.

"Please sit down, Gibson. We have to protect the citizens of Northern Ireland. It is our duty as their custodians. In so doing we are obliged to ensure that proper procedures are in place at all times," demanded The Minister for Health.

Davy kept his face expressionless as he slowly eased himself back into the chair as he adjusted his waistcoat and jacket.

"You will need to be more specific about these incidents, Minister, if you wish me to give this my full attention," instructed Davy.

The Minister gave him at look of exasperation.

"It has been brought to our attention that you authorised non medically trained staff to perform medical procedures. That, if it is confirmed, causes this government great concerns, the potential consequences of which I have already mentioned."

"Well then, I will make it simple and quick, Minister. I can confirm that I authorised experience porters, who had witnessed many small injury treatments, far longer than any newly trained nurse, and asked them to help with non-life-threatening stitches and bandaging. This in turn freed up trained staff to work on more serious cases. I would do it again if those bombers came back again tonight, to, as I understand it, a still underdefended city. As far as the British Medical Council is concerned, perhaps this letter might relieve your concerns for my professional and legal position."

Davy pulled the envelope from his breast pocket and handed it respectfully to the Minister. He felt like throwing it at him or better still ramming it down his throat, but he heeded Sir James's advice to remain calm and professional throughout, no matter how much provocation.

The Minister finished reading the contents. He passed it round the table for the other members. Davy sat silently, and in the process pulled out his watch chain to check how much this meeting was eating into his valuable time.

When the eight interrogators had read it, all eyes reverted to the Minister. He leant forward in his chair and handed the letter back to Davy.

"That letter only confirms that the BMC approved your actions on the night of the Blitz. It does not specifically refer to the concerns of the particular incidents we are here to discuss, Gibson," sighed the Minister with an excessive zeal.

Davy, smiled at him. "Oh, I do apologise. I should have given you this letter as well; quite remiss of me. It is a copy of the original letter that prompted the letter from the BMC that you have just read. It was written by Professor Clarke. He is a stickler for protocol and wrote to the BMC for clarification. It goes into depth about the level of injuries due to an underprepared city, hospital understaffing, both prior to, and at the time of the bombardment. He also explains that there were precedents of a similar nature used at the Front in the last War."

The Minister nodded his head. Davy was not sure if it was a sense of frustration or a sense of understanding. He didn't really care.

"Hope that removes your concern for my welfare, Minister," assured Davy, trying his best to keep any sense of sarcasm from his tone. He cast his eyes round the rest of the table particularly the four who had given him glares as he had entered the meeting.

156

Harry Midgely gave him a look similar to the one he gave Davy when Linfield scored against Belfast Celtic. Davy looked blanky at him. Too early yet to show any sign of victory. There were still a few of Sir James's plans to implement.

The Minister's head spun as he considered his next attack. He was not the instigator of this inquisition, but he had been under pressure from his Unionist Party colleagues to whom Davy's criticisms had been levelled. As the comments came from an employee of the Health Department, it was for the Health Minister to be their front man of the retribution.

The Minister looked around the room again for support from his colleagues. Harry Midgley broke the silence.

"Well, is that the matter settled then, gentlemen?" he asked. There was the briefest of pauses, before a voice rasped from the far end of the table.

"No it bloody well is not, Midgely! I demand an apology from Gibson here, writ large across the front page of the Belfast Telegraph, News Letter, Irish News and the Whig. You cannot get away with making us look like fools. It was always a close call between spending money on defences or increasing production for the war effort. It was most ungentlemanly for you to make those accusations."

Davy, had his response ready. Sir James had already advised him of how to play it if the scenario reached this point.

"No point in gaining a victory if you leave the enemy intact. Remove their motivation and ability to counterattack. End it, so it is done, finished!" was his father-in-law's advice.

Davy looked down at the end of the table to the voice that had reacted badly.

"Sir, may I remind you. I did not make a statement to anyone. It was a private comment between me and the Chief Administrator. It was not for public consumption. It was a knee jerk reaction, under stressful circumstances. If I had the chance to turn back time I would not have let the press within earshot. I certainly deeply regret allowing the press an opportunity to increase its sales. 'Never let the truth get in the way of a good story' is their mantra. I do apologise for that without reservation. Having said that, it has been the thoughts on the lips of most of the population. If you feel the need for a public apology from me, then you'll have to get the rest of the population to do the same. Good luck with that gentlemen," advised Davy.

"You are not getting away that easy, Professor Gibson!" grunted another interrogator. Davy gave him a stare as he began to rise again from his seat.

"I think gentlemen we had best put the last few weeks down to a learning experience for us all and leave it at that. Now if you will excuse me, we all have work to do," added Davy.

"This is an outrage. I demand an apology!" shouted the Member who was receiving the harshest of the public criticism. He came to the meeting wanting the pressure taken off him and transfer it to Davy. Davy kept his face serious and thoughtful as he raised a look, filled with sarcasm, at the ceiling.

"I tell you what, then. I'll arrange for a full front-page apology in the Belfast Telegraph and then on pages two, three, four, five and six; probably have to serialise it for several nights, we'll have a bit of investigative journalism done," suggested Davy, with a sense of keenness in his voice.

"We can start with," Davy pointed to one of the protagonists, "The amount your business has profited from the 'black market' since the War started."

Before the subject of his glance had time to speak he moved on to another sitting next to him.

"There'll be one on how you got your contracts for supplies, and, as for you," Davy pointed to a third, as he shook his head. "I don't think we should even go there."

The third embarrassed interrogator, knew well what Davy was referring too. He was more than grateful that David could not refer to his discreet visits to the sexually transmitted disease clinic at the Royal, curtesy of his all too frequent visits to a house of ill repute in Customs House Square opposite the Liverpool boat dock. It would not have gone down too well with the congregation of his Church who saw him sit in the front row every Sunday praising the Lord at the top of his voice. Davy stood looming over the table as the silence filled the four walls. Sensing the right moment, he continued.

"If you want to have a bit of time to think over it, you know where to find me. In the meantime I'll get myself back to my work. Good day to you gentlemen!"

After he closed the door behind him, the committee members sat in silence. They all knew that Sir James Arthur was a significant shareholder in the Belfast Telegraph and that the investigative journalism suggested by Davy would take place at the drop of a hat.

Midgely was the first to leave the room. He descended the staircase two steps at a time and out to the car park. He could see Davy's Ford car disappear out of the gates at the Netherleigh entrance. Midgely caught up with Davy as he reached the junction of the Templemore Avenue on the Albertbridge Road. Through the junction he pulled out ahead of Davy's car and turned in at the Mount near the Woodstock Road and got out of his vehicle. He leant against the side of his car, lit a cigarette, and looked at the sky. Davy pulled up alongside him, leaned across to the passenger side and put the window down. Harry spoke across to him through the open window.

"Nice one David, old son. Twenty-five yards strike. Straight into the top corner. Near bust the net!" laughed Harry.

"Just glad it worked out, Harry. Could have ended up over the bar and out of the ground," laughed Davy, nervously.

"Remind me never to play poker with you, mate," laughed Harry.

"Can't take the credit for that session. I was schooled on that by the best. Sir James Arthur himself." laughed Davy again.

"Time for a quick one before you head on?" asked Harry.

"No thanks, Harry. Have to give it a miss. I wasn't joking when I said I had better things to do than sit in that meeting. It's all hands to the pumps at the moment and I need my hands steady at any minute. Just hope there's not another raid. Although it's highly likely there will be one," Davy mused.

"Aye and if there is, it'll more than likely be this side of the city. It'll be the Shipyard, Aircraft factory, Sirocco Works and Ropeworks," sighed Harry, as he inhaled his butt before he threw it on the ground and twisted his foot on it.

"See you when I see you, 'Auld Hand' then," sighed Midgely, as he got back into his car. Davy gave him a wave as he drove off.

The letter Staff Nurse Muldoon received with her pay packet was different to that received by Doctor David Gibson. When Gerri collected her wages packet, the wages clerk called back.

"Hold on Gerri, there's another envelop here for you," advised the hospital clerk.

Gerri pulled a face, as she took the white embossed envelop. She stuffed both in her bag and raced out of the door intent on getting prepared for a scheduled operation. She didn't open it until she got home. As usual, she opened her pay packet, kept what she needed, and handed the rest to her mother for the house keeping. That weekly ritual done, she pulled the white quality envelop with a fancy logo on the front, from her bag. She turned it over and read 'the return to sender' address on the back.

Queens University, Belfast.

Gerri opened the envelope. It was a request that she attend at the University to 'discuss matters relating to Nursing.'

She stuffed the letter back in her bag before her mother or any of the family asked what she was reading.

A few days later, she walked through the imposing entrance to the University with the chess board flooring. She was well out of her comfort zone. A rabbit in the headlights. "This was worse than going to confession," she laughed to herself."

As she looked around the walls and the statue of the studious looking gentleman in the toga, hand under his chin, in deep contemplation, a voice with the tone of a Regimental Sergeant Major rasped, "Can I help you Miss. Look a bit lost there!"

Muldoon pulled the letter from her bag and handed it to the Head Porter, Sam Murray. "I've an appointment to see this man here. No idea where his office is. Can you help me please?"

Murray, read the letter. "Well you are in luck, you haven't far to go. See those double doors to your left. Straight up those stairs, turn right and his office is the one with the big door at the end of the corridor."

Muldoon, smiled at the Head Porter, "Thanks sir, that's great."

"My pleasure, Miss. Good luck with him. He can be a grumpy bugger when he wants to be. Don't let him intimidate you," advised Sam.

The well intended advice did not help Muldoon's apprehensions about the whole event. It crossed her mind to turn and run out of the front entrance, through the sacred lawns, and not stop running until she got to Shaftesbury Square. As she knocked the solid oak door with Dean of the Faculty of Medicine, Sir William Glenn on a brass plate, she took a deep breath, knocked the door, and walked in as confidently as she could manage.

"Ahh, Miss Muldoon, please take a seat," instructed Sir William, as he gave her a quick glance above his reading spectacles, before he returned to dealing with forms scattered about his large desk. Muldoon had seen smaller communion tables. She sat quietly as he signed a document.

"Well dear, so you are Geraldine Saiorse Maria Muldoon, born 13th May 1920. Address 126 Cullintree Road, Belfast. Is that correct?" inquired Sir William, whose manner reminded her of Winston Churchill. All that was missing was the cigar and the whiskey glass.

"Yes Sir, that is correct."

Muldoon was in surgical operation mode, keeping everything formal, short and precise.

"Well, I am sure you wonder why I have asked to see you, and, as we are both busy people, I will get to the point, without delay."

Sir William sniffed as he opened a file that had been sitting beside his right hand.

"Here is a Letter of Offer which you should sign in triplicate and hand back to me. You will be commencing your studies for a Doctorate in Medicine in September," advised Sir William, as he looked directly into Muldoon's face, watching to see her reaction, which was predictable.

"I cannot sign this Sir William, it just won't happen," sighed the exasperated Staff Nurse.

"I have to put my pay into the house. There's seven of us and my mother and father. I cannot do this. It just isn't on, Sir," continued Gerri, as she held back her frustration. She began to rise as she fumbled for her handkerchief in her pocket.

"Perhaps you should read this document first, which also requires your signature; only once this time," urged Sir William, still containing his stern persona, while enjoying the whole situation.

Muldoon, still standing, reached across the desk and took the second document. As she began to read the document she unconsciously sat back down in the seat. Half-way through reading it she looked over at Sir William, who stared back at her. This time there was the sign of the slightest hint of a smile.

"Keep reading, my dear. If your answer is still, No, then you are not cut out for the job, and you will have wasted the time of several people who have put themselves out to help you. Please read on," advised the ageing academic.

As Gerri finished the last words of the document, Her eyes were full of tears that dripped down her cheeks as she looked up at the ceiling. Sir William, smiled to himself, as he proceeded to scan a few other papers on his desk. He decided it was best to let her sort herself out in her own time. It took a few minutes for her to dry her eyes and return to some form of normality.

"What is this Roger Arthur Memorial Education Trust? I don't understand this. I have never heard of it?" asked Muldoon.

"It is a fund that was set up by the Arthur family. Roger Arthur died on the first day of the Somme Offensive 1916. His father and sister set up a trust to help fund education for exceptional cases whose social status makes it difficult for them to do so. You, my dear, fit that category. Take the benefit of it, Miss Muldoon. The world is hard enough without turning down such an opportunity. As you will have read, the Trust will cover your Medical School fees and provides a bursary. I am reliably informed by Professor Gibson that you will be offered part time duties in the City Hospital only a few hundred yards from here. The combined amounts of your wages, together with the bursary, should mean your gross income will not be effected," explained Sir William, as he handed her back the pen to sign the forms. Geri Muldoon, blew out her cheeks, shook her head, and signed the forms, three times on the Letter of Offer and once on the Grant funding document. As she handed the papers back across the desk to Sir William, she asked,

"Sir William do you mind if I ask how this Trust got to know about me?"

Sir William, looked at her over his spectacles.

"Roger Arthur's sister Anna Arthur, has been married over twenty years. Now goes by the name of Anna Gibson," smiled Sir William, unable to contain his sober persona.

"Oh Fu…" sighed Geri, stopping her expletive in mid-sentence. The old academic gave her a few seconds to gather her thoughts before he continued.

"It would seem Professor Gibson sees at little of himself in your circumstances. If you get the opportunity to speak with John Clarke he will fill in the gaps for you."

Sir William raised himself from his desk and extended his stumpy hand to Muldoon, giving her the slightest hint of the best he could manage of a smile. " I look forward to seeing you in September, young lady."

By the time Gerri Muldoon reached the top of the staircase to walk down to the Head Porter's office her head was full of a thousand thoughts. She walked down the steps, taking a few seconds to each step, lost in her thoughts. Sam Murray, noted her thoughtful demeaner as she passed his small window at the entrance. He pulled back the sliding window frame.

"What's up, Miss. Did your meeting not go too well? He can be an awkward character when he wants to be. Don't take it to heart. He's the same with the rest of us," sympathised the Head Porter.

Muldoon turned, to face the voice from the window.

"No, I'm fine thanks, just confused. Seems you'll be sick of the site of me for a few years. Didn't see it coming. Trying to work out how my Ma and Da will take this," explained Muldoon, pulling her face in concern.

Sam stuck his head through the small window in an effort to strengthen his advice. "It's your life, girl. If you've been given a chance in life, it's not for anyone to get in the way. Stand your ground and don't turn back, is my advice. See you in September!"

By the time Muldoon reached her front door she had settled her thoughts. As she walked into the tight single room downstairs, kitchen house, her mother was at the sink. Her father was sitting in the only good chair, sleeves rolled up, still dusty after a hard day lifting sacks off a ship at the Belfast Docks. It wasn't a bad week. He had got work four days in a row unloading cargo as a Deep Sea docker. That category of docker only got work on the days vessels from beyond Britain arrived in port. The work was not as regular as the seven day a week local ships from the mainland ports. Even then, the number of dockers waiting on the quayside for work may not all find employment. Four days in a row was not a bad week. How he wished he could get working for Kelly's coal boats. Steady work every day. It would be like he'd won the football pools, he often thought to himself. Two younger brothers wrestled with each other in the corner. They looked at her, wondering why she was all dressed up and not in the usual dishevelled garb coming of a shift in the Royal.

"I've something to tell you and there's nothing you can say will change it." announced Gerri. Her mother's shoulders dropped as her hands rammed to the bottom of the sink..

"Oh no, Gerri, you're not pregnant, are you?" gasped her mother, face still looking at the soap suds. "Wondered why you went out all dressed up this morning. Away to the doctor, were you?"

Gerri Muldoon raised her eyes to the smoke-stained ceiling and let out a short laugh to herself.

"Well thank you very much for your faith in me, Ma. No I am not 'up the duff', although you're heading in the right direction when you mentioned the Doctor."

Gerri took another deep breath, as her mother turned to face her, hands on her hips.

"I am going to be one, and, before you start gurning, I'll still be bringing in my wages. It's all been sorted," snapped Gerri, her expression full of defiance. Her mother was about to open her mouth as she turned her back to negotiate the narrow staircase in the corner of the room.

"I'm away to get the 'glad rags' off!"

Chapter Ten

Bad Judgement

Back at Ballydrain, Roger, in between doing his bit around the estate, mostly trying to organise the children living in the scout tents and outhouses, occasionally thought of Agnes. He began to roll it through his mind how to make contact without the risk of looking silly or suffering rejection. Roger had always been comfortable in the company of teenage girls in his social circle, but they were just friends, good company. He didn't go to sleep at night thinking about them. Agnes filled his brain until sleep took over.

Almost three weeks after he had dropped her off at the front of her home on the Norton and left as quickly as he could, unprepared for any conversation with her mother, he hatched a plan.

She had said she went to Knockbreda Parish Church. He assumed she would be there on Sunday morning. He didn't think arriving up on the Norton outside the Church was a good idea, so he settled for his Elswick Hopper bicycle. He would wait outside and wait for his chance to speak to her and arrange a date. What could be simpler he thought to himself.

It took longer than he anticipated to cycle over Shaws Bridge, Milltown Road and over to Newtownbreda village. By the time he got there, the church service was over. He could see groups of the congregation dispersing in all directions, some towards the Ormeau Road, some up the Saintfield Road, others up to Newtownbreda village, others in the direction of the Hillfoot. His eyes concentrated on the line of walkers returning to Newtownbreda village.

He peddled his bicycle slowly until he got fifty yards behind the walkers as he scanned for the shape of a diminutive teenage girl. His eyes finally picked out Agnes as she walked with her back to him. Then, without warning, the privileged young man suffered his first real set back in a life, that, up to now, had always opened out in front of him.

Agnes laughed at the boy beside her, gave him a playful slap, and then linked her arm under his. The boy, who seemed a bit older than her, gave her a reassuring pat on her waist, as they continued their seemly intimate conversation. Roger stopped the Elswick Hopper beside a tree so that if she looked back he would be hidden from view. Roger stared at the sight of Agnes on such good terms with the youth

172

beside her. He stared at the couple, consumed with disappointment and jealousy. Agnes looked back over her shoulder as if she was looking for something. Roger kept himself hidden from view. He stayed motionless, deep in his thoughts until Agnes and her friend disappeared over the horizon into a dip in the undulating road ahead. This was his chance to get himself out of this nightmare.

He peddled back home to Ballydrain as he cursed his misfortune. How could he be so stupid to think she was being anything other than polite when she gave him a smile confirming she would see him again. If she did mean it, how fickle was she to not wait for him. First chance she got, she was off with someone else. To think he had dodged the advances of several of the pretty girls evacuated from the Shankill to keep himself loyal to Agnes. That was the last time he would fall for that idea.

"When it comes to the young ladies, Love them and leave them. Don't let them get into your head," was the advice his honorary uncles Allen and Adam had given him. They were right, thought Roger, to himself, as he got on his bicycle and peddled home.

Chapter Eleven

Coming of age

By the time the second raid came in May to heap destruction on the East Side of the City many had been evacuated and makeshift shelters hastily constructed. The damage to the shipyard aircraft factory and engineering companies was severe, but the death toll was thankfully not as bad as the first. Again, the medical teams, general practitioners, nurses and volunteers did their best at coping. Working long exhausting shifts until the pressure eased. shifts, and a sense of control emerged. Thankfully, as the Germans became bogged down in besieging Stalingrad, Leningrad and pushed back at El Alamein, no further raids took place in Northern Ireland.

On a Spring morning of 1942, Anna, dressed in formal black, shook hands with more than she could count as the mourners paid their respects to her after the burial of Lady May in the family vault at St Patrick's Church of Ireland, Drumbeg. Roger, at Davy's suggestion, followed on her shoulder wherever she went, receiving each handshake after his mother. Davy, hovered a few feet away watching how his son dealt with the formality of the situation. Roger had done the same at the funeral of Sir James a few months earlier and, understandably, had been a bit out of his depth, but on this occasion Davy was glad to see that Roger was a good learner and was bearing up well in his new role as the future of the Arthur dynasty.

Even twenty-three years of marriage to Anna and being part of the Arthur family, Davy could never presume to replace Sir James, nor his deceased brother-in-law Roger, who had just been reunited with his mother and father in the family plot. The honour had to fall to young Roger. The only thing that Davy wanted from the Arthurs was Anna. That was more than enough.

"Let them all get on with their empire. Not my shift," thought Davy.

He had never, despite his success in the medical profession, felt it was his place to ever move into Sir James's shoes.

The crowd outside the Church yard was large enough that it spilled out through the gates and extended to groups leaning over the Drumbeg bridge just waiting to pay their respects. The numbers had swollen by some who had been the workers and families who had been given temporary shelter the previous Easter.

They did not need to slowly filter up into the church yard to pay their respects. Anna had decided that it would be best to walk back up to Ballydrain. Sir James and Lady May had always taken great pleasure in their Sunday morning walk to and from the Church. She felt it would be a gesture they would appreciate. That bridge also dug deep into Anna's heart. It was the same bridge where she had made her decision that she would be with Davy for the rest of her life, no matter where it took her. The morning Sir James, broke the wild rose from its stem tossing it angrily into the flowing Lagan River.

As she walked up over the Bridge, Roger and Davy linked arms with her, one on each side. Davy looked down at Anna and across at Roger. He smiled to himself as he noticed his son was the same height as him. Roger had grown up always wanting to be tall like his father. Davy used to tease him.

"Aye, you may be bigger, son, but you'll never be as good looking," was Davy's only way to maintain the upper hand and not let Roger get too big for his boots. Tom Gibson, still lived.

As they ambled up the footpath to the gate house, Martha came out of the door with Joseph and Kathleen in each hand.

"Hope those two behaved themselves, Martha," smiled Anna.

"Ah, my lips are sealed, Anna," assured Martha. "That right, kids?" laughed Martha, as she gave them a wink.

"Bye, Auntie Martha," shouted the two remaining offspring as they ran off up the drive ahead of the three mourners.

Anna and Davy had left them in the care of Martha as they felt they were both too young for the occasion. "Everything is set for them all calling in up to the house, Anna. I'll be up in a few minutes," assured Martha.

As Davy, Anna and Roger walked, thoughtfully up the elm tree lined drive, Roger broke the silence.

"Grandpa James didn't have long to wait for Grandma May. He'll be holding his arms out for her this very moment," as he walked, head looking at the sky. Davy looked at Anna as they shared looks of surprise mixed with pride.

"You did well this morning, Roger. Funerals are difficult at the best of times. I wouldn't have done as well when I was your age, son," praised Davy.

Anna, close beside her son, linked her arms under his, briefly resting her head against his shoulder. Davy smiled at the pair and kept walking along side.

As they reached the bottom of the mansion steps, Roger broke the thoughtful silence that had overcome all three.

"There is another duty I am going to have to perform, but I know it is not one you will agree with Mum, Dad."

The word 'duty' immediately hit the back of Anna and Davy's brains. That could only mean one thing. They both said nothing, hoping Roger would not pursue the topic any further. It was a vain hope.

"It is my duty to do my bit against Hitler and his monsters. It is not an option; it has to be done," Roger continued, with an assured confidence that might have been Sir James himself.

Davy continued to walk alongside Roger and Anna before he made his final remark.

"You are upsetting your mother and I'm not going to allow that to happen. Drop it until you have finished school. You have to be over eighteen to enlist as an officer. Join the Officer Training Corp at school, get a bit of training done, if you must. In the meantime, until June '44 don't dare raise the conversation again. That is not a request, it is an order. Now no more talk about it son," growled David, as the thought crossed his mind that he was sounding a bit too much like Sir James for his own comfort.

Anna remained silent, only giving Davy a glance of approval. She knew this was a conversation between too men. All three looked across the lake, Roger working out his reply, David and Anna, giving him the chance to gather his thoughts. Roger turned and looked at them both in acceptance and made what was more a statement than a reply.

"End of June 44, it is then," with a sense of inevitability that haunted David and Anna

Chapter Twelve

Preparation

The rest of the year, the German war machine was fully occupied on the two fronts of North Africa and the Russian defence of Stalingrad to place the Belfast on their main hit list. Ulster was predominantly involved in supplying the war effort and being a residence for United States and Canadian troops and Polish airmen. The only member of the Arthur - Gibson greater family that was directly involved in the war was Alexander (Alec) Price.

Alec, Jonty and Martha's eldest, had the physical genes of his mother and the quick brain of his father. He was a few inches over six foot and as quick witted as any. He had joined the Inniskillings after Dunkirk. On completing initial training, he had been picked out as ideal material to be placed in a Commando Unit and by 1942 he held the rank of Sergeant. Sabotage and advance scouting, was right up his street. Allen and Adam had taught him all they knew about appearing invisible, His father, Jonty kept him informed in the art of reading a situation and making the best of it. Working with a tight group, with a specific mission, not being used as cannon fodder in an infantry unit with no control of events, suited him. Specific targets, well planned, with a group of fellow lads he knew he could rely on. Not unlike the lads of Edenderry at the Somme.

David and Anna had managed to delay the prospect of Roger having to face the German's, the same could not be said for Martha and Jonty. Alec had been involved in North Africa most of the time since 1940 and had been in the thick of action at Tobruk and El Alamein On his occasional trips home he would say little, but enough to give them the impression he would be fine and nothing to worry about. Jonty played along with the façade in an attempt to ease Martha's worries.

On one of his brief leaves, from a base in Hereford, Jonty got him alone, making the excuse that a large broken tree branch needed a bit of lifting.

"Right son, it's me you're talking too, not your mother. What are you getting up to out there? was Jonty's blunt question as he passed a cigarette to his son, who towered over him.

Alec looked out across the lake, pulled a grimace on his face, sighed and explained.

"Well you know the way I joined up in the Inniskillings because you said they were the best of our regiments. Well you were right about that Dad, but then problem is your skills get noticed. I got transferred to a Commando Unit. It was fine at first, few months back in training camp. Taught how to do raids behind lines, sabotage to prepare for a main attack, but a lot of the times it was learning how to get close to the Germans and watch what they get up to. Funny enough a lot like what you did. It's not any riskier than being in an infantry unit, in fact I have better chances of getting through it. We have plans drawn up, practiced, know what we are up against, specific targets. In and out, back to base. The infantry, don't have that luxury. I'll be fine, Da," reassured Alec.

Jonty, shrugged his shoulders as he replied.

"I know what you mean son, but you'll need to come up with something better to curb your mother's concerns."

Alec, drew in his breath, as he looked to the sky.

"Well she's going to have to run with it, Da. I don't have any other answers," replied Alec, as he looked into his father's eyes. He paused before he continued.

"Tell her I have every intention of surviving so she can be a grandmother someday. That's the best I can do. Now where is this log you want shifted!"

Until the Spring of 1944 Alec had kept his word and was still, like all of the Special Ops men, been a constant elusive pain in the German backsides, doing reconnaissance, disruption, sabotage on a regular basis. Only once had Martha and Jonty found themselves unable to sleep with the fear of the unthinkable.

St Nazaire, was the venue of that concern. Word had come through of a daring raid; some called it a suicide raid, on the German U boat harbour on the West Coast of France.

The raid by the British consisted of a large number of commando units intent on destroying the harbour and putting it out of action to make a large dent in the German naval threat in the North Atlantic.

Word filtered through on the radio that one third had been captured and made prisoner, on third had got back out and one third had perished. The odds of Alec being in one of the units were high. They waited for three weeks hearing nothing from Alec. Jonty made a few inquiries at the Inniskillings through a Staff Officer he knew from the Somme. His body froze when he saw in the list of dead the names of three commando's, originally Inniskillings, like Alec. What made him freeze was they were the three Alec had named as his mates that made up his unit of four; the normal break down of a team. Jonty's biggest fear had come to life. His mind turned to thoughts of Joe Shannon. 'Nothing to retrieve'.

As he returned home to Ballydrain he was so confused that the horse on the trap, had made its own way home without any instruction from the reins hanging limply in Jonty's hands. As he turned through the gates and stopped at the gate house that had been his and Martha's home for most of the last twenty years, he stopped the cart and sat rigid in fear at the prospect of telling Martha.

Martha, meanwhile, had seen him sitting in the cart, silent and motionless.

"Jonty, will you get in here. I can't keep your dinner warm all evening!" she instructed.

Jonty took a deep breath dropped his good leg on the gravel path and limped towards the door. He opened it to see Martha ahead of him bent over to take his dinner out of the iron cooking range. She had her back to him as he spoke.

"Martha," he sighed, "Leave the dinner in the range. I'm not in any mood for it."

Jonty stayed at the door, slumped against the door frame; the door still opened back to his left side,

A silence broke out in the room. Martha set the plate back in the cooker before she put her hands on her hips and gave a look of scorn.

" Well make your mind up or I'll give it to someone else!" replied Martha.

Jonty stood, speechless. He did not want to break Martha's heart.

Martha's eyes glanced in the direction of the far side of the door that lay open, opposite Jonty.

"If you aren't hungry I'll eat it!" shouted a voice from the far side of the door.

Jonty felt a surge of disbelief. He staggered almost falling as he swing himself around the far side of the door. Alec sat casually at ease in the rocking chair his mother had sung to him as a small child.

"Are you not dead?" were the only words that Jonty could get out of his mouth.

"No Da, but there's a few German's would like to do the job if they got the chance!" laughed Alec, as he rose and gathered his stunned father in a bear like hug something similar to Martha's.

"I'm just back from seeing my old boss down at the Barracks and he had a list saying your mates were dead and he had no details of your whereabouts, Jeez, son, what's going on?" pleaded Jonty.

"Got pulled out of my unit to go and freeze my balls off in Norway watching the goings on at a factory making something. We were told they were making something called 'Heavy Water'. Hid in the forest. watched, gathered information, then back over the mountains, rowed out to a submarine and home. Dander up the Mournes wont quite feel the same again," smiled Alec.

As Alec returned to the rocking chair, he looked over at his mother.

"Think you can pull his dinner out of the oven now, mother," he continued.

"Get your arse out of that rocking chair. You're far too big for it and you'll bust it!" shouted Jonty, at Alec, as he gave him a prod with his stick and smiled across to Martha.

"Rab Tate's prayers must have worked, for a change, Martha," sighed Jonty, with a grin.

Don't you laugh at the Lord, or you'll get this plate round you!" laughed Martha, not wanting Jonty to have the last word.

Alec returned to England, back to his unit and for the next year and more managed to survive the invasion of Sicily, Salerno landing and Monte Casino. It would not be until he reached the Po Valley in the Spring of 1945 that Alec would find himself knocking on the Devil's door.

Chapter thirteen

The Siege of Ballydrain

During 1943 and early 1944 the Ballydrain household was very much involved in keeping life manageable. The fields that had housed the temporary refugee from Belfast had been cleared and ploughed to produce vegetables to add to the 'Dig for Victory' push. Davy continued his surgical duties. Anna and Bill got the mills repaired and back to working order. Life however was never devoid of new challenges.

The arrival of the US forces caused not only social tensions in the cities and towns but specifically Ballydrain.

One morning, two Army staff Jeeps, one British and one American arrived at the front entrance of Ballydrain. Out got two officers of the rank of Captain, one American, one British.

They asked to speak with Mrs Gibson. By the time they were ushered into the drawing room and offered tea, Anna greeted them, wearing her riding boots, corduroy trousers, thick shirt, sleeves rolled up, hair tied back and hidden behind a scarf. Looking everything like the pretty 'land girl' adverts on the bill posters.

"Well gentlemen, to what do I owe the pleasure?" asked Anna, dryly. Her father was already entering her brain to adjust for an awkward business dispute. She knew full well the reason they were sitting in her drawing room. She had anticipated it for weeks. She wondered actually why it had taken them so long.

The British Officer stood up and introduced himself and his fellow American officer before he began.

"As you know Mrs Gibson, there are quite a number of Military forces from all around the world who are at the present time stationed temporarily in this small patch of this island. The government is therefore obliged to find accommodation for troops and also Headquarters for numerous garrisons. Ballydrain has been listed as being very suitable to fill such a role in many different aspects. I am instructed to formally advise you that it is the Government's intention to turn the Estate into a military camp for the duration of the war. You will of course be appropriately financially compensated for your temporary departure which I trust you will understand is necessary in times of war," advised the Captain, before he continued.

"I have brought Captain Donegan, Adjutant for the Battalion of the United States Army that has been allocated Ballydrain, to familiarise himself with the facility."

The British captain, stopped talking and waited respectfully for Anna's reply.

Anna remained silent as she struggled to pull the heavy working gloves from her small hands. As she successfully pulled the first from her hand, she cast it like a jousting gauntlet on the surface of the coffee table in front of the two young officers. Neither of them failed to get the message and significance of the gesture.

"Please be seated gentlemen and enjoy your tea and biscuits before you go on your way," suggested Anna, making it clear by her tone that this was not a suggestion but a simple statement of fact.

"Thank you, for the refreshment, Mrs Gibson, but we cannot leave before we have completed our inspection of the premises and our report for Joint Command," explained the American officer.

"Oh, but you most certainly will be leaving, gentlemen. But please take your time, and if you need any more biscuits please do not hesitate to ask. Now if you would excuse me, I have to organise a lorry load of potatoes to pack for collection shortly. Good day gentlemen."

Anna began to turn to leave the room as the British Officer spoke again.

"But Mrs Gibson, you do not understand the government has decided the property is to be requisitioned. It is not a matter of choice," said the officer as he tried to maintain a respectful tone towards Anna.

Anna turned back to face the two officers as she replied.

"Gentlemen, I am afraid it is you, who do not understand. This is my home. I own it lock stock and barrel. My family traces back to Moses Hill and Arthur Hill, Wellesleys and the Trevors. This family has given enough to this country, and it will continue to do so. but this house, these grounds, are the soul and heart of this family; have been for three hundred years. I have no intention of letting it be usurped by officialdom and let it be used as a doss house for the military who will graciously hand it back to me wrecked and ruined. So please, take your time with your refreshments and then be on your way," instructed Anna.

"But Ma'am" exclaimed the American officer. "I can assure you the United States Army would not destroy the property and will return it to you in the same condition they find it."

Anna gave herself the indulgence of a laugh filled with sarcasm.

"Oh really, do you think so" mused Anna.

"Listen to me young man; both of you for that matter! Unlike yourselves, whom I presume, have never been the far side of a desk so far in this war, I am too well aware of what happens to property used in a war. They are either bulldozed or returned in a condition not fit for human habitation. There are plenty of other mansion houses that are scattered around the country lying empty because their owners went back to the shires in England. I suggest you requisition some of them. They would probably be glad to take your money." ordered Anna.

The two officers smirked at each other.

"Mrs Gibson," sighed the British captain, "we are under orders to carry out a report on the premises for the purpose of requisition," said the British officer. "If you do not take my advice, we will have to play it a different way, then."

Anna lifted a serving bell that sat on the coffee table. Eileen walked into the room. After fifteen years working at Ballydrain, in between, marriage, two children and a husband, she had by now nothing to learn from the ways of life at Ballydrain.

"Eileen would you be so kind as to ask Allen and Adam to come into here and ask them to bring Bill and Ben with them, please," sighed Anna, in an apparent tone of resignation.

As the officers sat defiantly taking their tea, preparing to inspect Ballydrain, Adam and Allen sauntered into the room and stood either side of Anna's shoulders. The two young officers both stopped sipping their tea as their jaws stopped chewing the fresh oatmeal biscuits.

Adam and Allen stood with their shot guns cradled in their arms, both weapons broken open with the barrels facing the ground.

"Adam, Allen, These gentlemen are trespassers intent on malicious acts on my property," advised Anna, to the twins as she began to exit the room.

"Allow them to finish their refreshment and then please ensure they are removed from this property with as minimum force as you see fit."

At the same time Adam and Allen, with military precision, cocked the barrels to firing position and cradled them in their arms like they had done with their rifles at the Somme. They grinned from ear to ear at the officers.

The officers drained their cups of tea, stuffed a few oatmeal biscuits into their pockets, stood up, adjusted their uniforms, and began to walk out of the door past the twins, whose gaze never left them.

The US captain spoke quietly into Allen's ear, with more than a hint of intimidation.

"I would advise you to explain to your boss, sir, that we will be back, and the requisition will take place."

Adam and Allen exchanged glances.

"Take it you'll be coming back with a few big guns and reinforcements," asked Adam.

"You can bet your life on that sir." promised the American.

"Will you be bringing a few tanks?" asked Allen.

"You'll need them!" laughed Adam, as the officers left.

That evening Anna recounted the whole episode of the visit by the requisition team with Davy. Both agreed that Anna had won the battle but not the war. They had only a few days to get the defences in place to make the castle impregnable.

Bill, Anna, Davy, Canon Rab Tate, Jonty, Adam and Allen, all met around the boardroom table at Ballydrain, late afternoon the next day. A plan of action was agreed. It had to be carried out by Friday evening.

As anticipated, on the following Monday morning, two military cars drove up to the steps of Ballydrain House, accompanied by a black Bentley. A fourth vehicle followed but kept its distance at the end of the driveway. It was a vehicle of the Royal Ulster Constabulary.

Eileen was the first to see their arrival. She scampered into the kitchen and told Martha,

"Eileen you go out, invite then into the drawing room. Get them some tea and tell them Mrs Gibson will be with them shortly. You know the plan, just play your part girl," advised Martha, between gritted teeth. "Our jobs could depend on it, girl!"

Eileen, straightened her maids dress, adjusted her cap, took a deep breath, and walked steadily, but confidently, out to meet the visitors who had already rung the bell at the front door.

Martha disappeared out the back to find Jonty, washing down a pony, Adam and Allen were working in the greenhouses.

"They're here gentlemen. Get your backsides in here and remember what we agreed," Martha instructed. The lads gave her a nod, smiled to themselves and proceeded to play their parts.

Eileen had invited the entourage in with a smile. By the time she got them into the drawing room and offered them tea, a few minutes had passed. As they sat sipping the tea and assessing where office furniture might fit in the drawing room, they could see through to the hallway. Eileen had deliberately left the door to the hallway wide open, as instructed. First they could hear the sound of laughter mixed with the sound of wood hitting the parquet floor in the hall.

They lowered their cups to see two heavily bandaged soldiers of the Royal Ulster Rifles hobble past. Seemingly oblivious of the visitors in the drawing room.

As they returned to their tea, they could hear the sound of feet walking around in the rooms above their heads. Their ears strained to what sounded like,

"Ok son, we'll get you turned over. One, two, three. That's it now!" Martha always did enjoy a bit of amateur dramatics.

The officers and one official looking gentleman sat in their seats, waiting for Anna to enter, while they took in the sense of activity in the house. Eileen, in the meantime, offered them more tea and biscuits apologising again for Anna's delay.

A full five minutes later, Anna arrived through the door, her hair tied back in a bun, a working skirt and blouse covered by a nurses apron, recently stained. All of the visitors set their cups and saucers down and stood up in respect for the Lady of the House.

"Good morning gentlemen. If you had given me some advanced warning I would have arranged for a full breakfast for you all," she sighed in disappointment, before she continued.

"I assume your failure to give me some advanced warning suggests there is a matter of urgency in your visit. Please enlighten me as I have

196

matters to attend," as she glanced down at her soiled apron, half raising her arms, opening her palms.

The gentleman in the dark business suit was the first to speak. "Mrs Gibson, we are here to serve you Notice of Requisition of Ballydrain for the benefit of the War Effort. It will be most suitable as a brigade headquarters for the United States Army and the grounds for billeting of servicemen. I understand that there was a bit of difficulty in conveying this to you last week. I, as Minister of War for the Northern Irish Government have come in person to ensure that the process is carried out, Mrs Gibson.

Anna, dropped her head and stared at the ground. Face devoid of any emotion. The room took on a deathly silence. No one spoke as they waited for her to respond. In the silence Adam and Allen appeared through the door on either side of Anna, double barrels cradled in their arms.

"Everything ok, Ma'am. Saw those uniforms coming back. Just checking if you needed a hand, Ma'am," asked a concerned Allen.

"No it's fine, lads," replied Anna. "These gentlemen have had a wasted journey. They have come all this way for a cup of tea and a few biscuits. I am sure they have better things to be doing for the War Effort," sighed Anna, before she continued.

"Were you out shooting some game to fill Martha's soup supplies? Our guests enjoyed yesterday's. Big improvement on the gruel they got before they came here?" laughed Anna, as the boys gave a respectful, nod to Anna and the visiting entourage, adding cheeky winks at the British and American officers that they had sent packing the previous week.

The military officers and government official looked at each other with blank faces. The man from Stormont decided he was the one to take control of the situation.

"Mrs Gibson," he sighed, "Whilst this is an official visit of some importance I have felt obliged to address you formally. I would much prefer to address you as Anna, as we have been on first name terms for many years at all sorts of events. I may be the Minister of War for Northern Ireland, which is the capacity in which I am here today, but, you know me as Wesley. I would much prefer to solve this difficulty on good terms, my dear." as he shook his head from side to side a little too condescendingly for Anna's liking. She just managed to bite her lip. Everything was going to plan, so far.

Anna looked at The Minister of War and returned the same condescending shake of the head back at him.

"My husband has for a long time always had a dim view of 'the powers to be', Up to recently, I have not paid much attention to his foibles but now I wonder he may be right after all. He often makes comments such as 'they couldn't organise a piss up in a brewery.' A rather uncouth turn of phrase, but I think you get my drift."

"Now Anna," replied the Minister." Stormont has not come to this decision lightly. It is most inappropriate to regard the government as incompetent," he retaliated.

Anna, paused as she waited for the next part of the plan to unfold before she walked past the still standing visitors and looked thoughtfully out of the window over the grounds.

"Wesley, would up come over to the window and share the view with me, if you please?"

Wesley, did as he was asked, strolled across to the window and survey the view. He saw before him a group of wounded soldiers, some sitting in chairs, others in beds rolled out onto the patio, some leaning on crutches. As he processed his thoughts, Anna spoke again.

"It would appear Wesley, that the 'dots are not being joined up' at Stormont, Wesley. Ballydrain, is a Nursing Home for badly injured military personnel, which as I understand, means it's out of bounds for the gentlemen with you here today. Imagine the fuss if the people of

199

Belfast thought brave invalided fighting men were kicked out of their oasis of healing by a bunch of Brigadiers," mused Anna, in mock concern.

Wesley stood back and turned away from Anna, raging that he had been outwitted by her. He looked at the officers who looked blankly back at him. He turned again in anger to Anna.

"Look here Mrs Gibson, I don't know what little scheme you have going on here, but it will not wash, my dear. I have a document here that officially serves notice to you of the government's intention to requisite the premises.

Now that I have served this writ, I will be taking it directly to the Law Courts in Belfast where it will be signed and sealed by a High Court Judge. That is the end of the matter. I wish we could have completed this transaction on more favourable terms. I regret it has not been possible. Good day to you Mrs Gibson!" he raged, as he picked up his hat from the chair, beside him.

As he and the officers turned to face the door, Anna intervened.

"Piss up and brewery, Wesley; David was right," sighed Anna, with a contained grin, as she held her gaze into Wesley's eyes.

"Now there's no need to get nasty. It doesn't become a lady of such class as yourself. I would have expected better," he snarled.

"When the left hand doesn't know what the right hand is doing, that is surely a piss up in any brewery," laughed Anna, still staring at Wesley.

"What are you rambling about, Mrs Gibson, enough is enough!" snarled Wesley, once more.

Anna turned to the locked writing bureau in the corner of the drawing room, pulled a key from her apron pocket, unlocked the drawer and pulled out a crisp new legal document still in its embossed wallet.

"Surprised you were not informed of this transaction, Wesley. It contains a contract stamped and signed by a High Court Judge, Sir William Boyd QC. Willie, lives just down the road.

"If you take a seat and read it, you will see that Ballydrain has completed an agreement with the Department of Health to make itself available as a convalescence retreat for wounded servicemen for the duration of the War. It is also signed by Mr Midgley, the now Minister of Health. It was signed and sealed last Friday morning," explained Anna, in a tone of complete indifference.

The Minister stared at the document which was still in her hand. He knew there was no point in sitting down to read a document with the only result being that she would only gain further superiority.

"It is not necessary, Mrs Gibson, I will refer this back to the Military people. I will save my angst for Mr Midgley. He should have discussed this with me.

Good day to you, Mrs Gibson," mumbled Wesley as he left the room along with his entourage.

As they drove out of the gates of Ballydrain, the wounded soldiers waved them off, rather too enthusiastically for the departing visitors' liking.

Back inside the house Anna stood at the bottom of the staircase below the balcony to the first floor.

"It's ok, you can stop bounding around up there. They've gone!" shouted Anna.

Martha, Eileen and Jonty appeared on the balcony smiling from ear to ear. Jonty tapped his stick on the floor several times, identical to the sound of a wounded soldier walking with the aid of crutches.

"That was more fun than the church hall pantomime last Christmas, girls!" he chuckled.

"Get those gentlemen outside a few beers while I phone Harry Midgely to warn him of imminent contact from Mr McClure," advised Anna.

That evening Jonty, Martha, Bill, Davy, Anna, Eileen, Adam and Allen all sat around the dining room table recounting the plan that had operated better than any night raid to the enemy trenches. Only Canon Tate was missing, as he had a sermon to write.

He decided 'The Story of Esther' would be fitting in the circumstances.

Around the table, as they shared bowls of Martha's best stew and a little liquid refreshment they smiled, laughed, shook their heads in approval of the sequence of events.

During the seven days since the previous call from the Military attack they had managed to build their own defence.

Anna, had used her position as head of the Nursing Veterans to have offered Ballydrain House to be made available as a convalescence home for wounded servicemen. It was immediately accepted by the Ministry of Defence in Westminster, bypassing the local government. As a second assurance, so they could not be overridden locally, Bill and Davy had contacted their good friend Harry Midgely who had no hesitation in scuppering McClure's plans. Midgley, did not like the man. Chalk and cheese was an understatement. Harry Midgely was Minister of Health at the time and because of the war, he, like other Ministers had considerable powers of decision making that did not require parliamentary debate. It was well within his remit to sign an agreement to set up any hospital facility. The only other matter was it needed to be signed and sealed by a High Court judge at very short notice without it coming to the attention of any one at Stormont other than Harry Midgely. Bill solved that problem by taking the papers with him to his Masonic Lodge meeting, and after a quick chat with a fellow member, Sir William Boyd QC, he returned to Ballydrain with the legal documents all correctly completed, feeling quite full of himself. Whilst the paperwork was all in place, Anna decided that the invaders, as she called them, needed wiped out so they could not return. A bit of humiliation would achieve that, she thought.

How better than to complete the rout than to have the establishment appear to be up and running. 'Fait a compli'

In the normal course of events it would take a few months to get part of the house turned into a working convalescence facility. The immediate answer to that problem was solved by rounding up a dozen injured servicemen scattered around the Royal and City Hospitals who were about to be released, to continue their recuperation at home. Offers to spend a few weeks, treated like the gentry at Ballydrain was eagerly accepted.

A lack of facilities in place upstairs in the mansion house was covered by Martha, Jonty, Eileen and the Bamford boys clattering about upstairs reminiscent of a busy ward.

During the middle of the celebrations, the doorbell rang. The diners held a silence, wondering whom it could be at this time of the evening. Jonty shuffled his way out to the door. After a few long minutes that seem like an eternity, he hobbled back through the door into the dining room, his face pensive.

"There's a man from Stormont. Says he is here on urgent business. A matter of national importance."

"Oh bollocks, I knew this had gone too well!" grimaced Bill, as he looked across at Anna who closed her eyes and put her hands in her head.

"Where is he now, Jonty? Is he still at the door?" whispered Davy.

Jonty nodded without speaking.

Davy dropped his spoon into the bowl of stew as he rose wearily from his chair and walked out to the hallway to the front door. As he crossed the reception area and got near the half opened front door, he could see the shape of a man with his back to him, wearing a homburg coat and large hat tilted slightly to one side, like the detectives in the movies.

"Good evening sir. What do we owe the pleasure of your calling without notice at this time of the evening," asked Davy.

The man in the homburg and hat, turned.

"Jeez Davy, that's not a very nice reception for a man that's brought a bottle to join the party!"

Harry Midgley opened his coat and produced a bottle of Bushmills which he handed to Davy, as he brushed past him, eager to join the crowd in the dining room.

Midgely walked through the door smiling at the worried faces.

"Somebody told me there was a 'wee' celebration going on in here. Looks more like a wake to me!" he laughed.

Anna rushed towards him and gave him a hug that was a bit too appreciative for Davy's liking.

"She's taken, Harry! Sit yourself down before I knock you down," joked Davy, as he slapped Harry on the back.

"Well, have you seen your mate Wesley yet, Harry?" asked Bill.

"Indeed I have Bill. Most enjoyable meeting it was too, old son!" laughed Harry.

"Came bursting into my office. Near took the hinges off. Took plaster of the wall when the door handle slammed back against the wall," continued Harry.

"Who do you think you are Midgely, he shouts, leaning across the desk, close enough I could smell his bad breath."

"Minister for Health, last I knew. At least that's what it says on the door you've just near taken off its hinges, Wesley, says I" continued Harry.

"I have just been made a complete fool of, Midgely, because you did not have the decency to advise me of your arrangement with Ballydrain, he shouts at me, still bent over my desk!"

"Wind your neck in Wesley, says I." added Harry.

"I deal with Health. You deal with the War. Now let me get on with my work, and while you're at it, try not to take anymore plaster off my walls on the way out," says I."

"What did he say to that, Harry?" asked Bill.

Midgely looked round the table at the ladies present and grinned again.

"Definitely not repeatable in the present of these young ladies here!" advised Midgely. "Now is there any chance of a bowl?"

Chapter Fourteen

May Ball

By the Spring of 1944, Anna had managed to keep a degree of normality at Ballydrain, albeit they had to share it with a steady stream of convalescing military wounded, residing at the House. It was not a difficulty, it was the least they could do. Ballydrain was a lot better place to be than for many in Europe.

On a personal level, Anna and Davy had the pending sense of fear of an issue that they had managed to push down the road.

Roger was now only a few months off leaving Campbell College completing his exams for entry to Law School at Queens, as he had agreed with them two years earlier. They had also agreed not to discuss the matter of him enlisting as an Officer in the Inniskillings. Their hope that the war might have ended, and the discussion might not be necessary, had not worked out. The war was still in full swing. The Russians had turned back the Germans and were progressing steadily from the East towards Germany, intent on revenge and humiliation at every mile. Allied forces, had control of North Africa and were making advances in Sicily and Southern Italy. An Allied invasion of Europe was imminent, but when and where, was unknown.

In April of 1944, Roger, was cycling home from Campbell College on a wet afternoon. He was cursing to himself that the school would not allow him to make the journey on his Norton. School policy frowned on the idea of pupils racing up the hallowed grounds of Campbell College like a bunch of ruffians, on noisy, smelly, symbols of rebellion. Hardly what was intended to nurture the future pillars of Belfast Society.

As he cycled past Knocklofty Park, past Shandon Park, across the Castlereagh Road towards Knockbreda and Newtownbreda village, intent on going down the Milltown Road, Shaws Bridge, up the towpath and through the back entrance his mother and father had used a lifetime earlier, he spotted a girl in a nurses uniform walking quickly, almost running, holding her cape over her head. She must have got off the tram at the end of the lines at the top of the Ormeau Road and was going in the direction of Newtownbreda.

She arrived at the crossroad of the Saintfield Road and the Hillfoot Road just as he was about to pass her. Being a young man who had been brought up with good manners, nothing to do with not missing the chance to pass judgement on her appearance, he slowed up and waved her across. The girl lifted her head from under the cape, raised her hand and smiled. Roger lifted his right hand from the handlebars and gave her a casual acknowledgement. The young nurse continued to trot across the junction.

Roger's mind rushed. "She looks a lot like Agnes, but she's grown up a bit!" he thought to himself.

Before he could allow his mind to work out what to do next, he instinctively shouted.

"Agnes, is that you, Agnes?"

The young nurse reached the kerb of the road and turned to look in the direction of the voice. She screwed her eyes to try and focus on who it was.

"Oh," she laughed in irony. "It's you. What happened to your motor bike!" as she feigned a total lack of respect by making fun of him.

"How are you, Agnes? Glad to see you have gotten into nursing. It's what you wanted. That's great!" replied Roger, as he guided himself and his bicycle to the roadside next to her.

"I started just last Autumn; still get all the rotten jobs. They said I'd have to start at the bottom and that's just how it has been," explained Agnes, as she instinctively pulled her handbag further up her shoulder; folded her arms in a defensive pose.

"I am tempted to imagine you have seen quite a few bottoms then, Agnes," teased Roger, not wanting to miss the opportunity of a risky joke. His Uncles Allen and Adam had told him the girls like a man with a bit of humour. What they didn't explain to him there was a time and a place for it.

Agnes, tugged at her bag strap on her shoulder again and turned without speaking. She was not in the mood for an overconfident, Campbell schoolboy, whom she had sobbed herself to sleep about on a few occasions, wondering why the boy who had left her safely home on his motor bike almost three years earlier, had never called to see her. He had seemed so genuine. Had he taken cold feet, or was he just another rich boy with the attention span of a gnat? Had he just been polite when he said he would see her again?

Roger's mind raced, as he realised Agnes had finished speaking to him and was going on her way. He bent his head and looked down at the handlebars of his bicycle. Drastic measures were necessary. No time for his uncles' advice to maintain the upper hand.

"Agnes, are you still going out with that boyfriend?"

Agnes walked on a few paces, as his question filtered through her brain, still reeling with the memory of holding his waist, as she hung on to the back of his motor bike, three years earlier.

She stopped, turned, with an expression suggesting he was not making any sense.

"Boyfriend! What boyfriend?

"The one you were having such a good time with walking home from church. Seemed very close. Realised I would be getting in the way. Left it at that," explained Roger, as he shook his head ruefully.

Agnes was about to continue on her way, but Roger's drop of his head made her wait for more information.

"When was this? she asked.

"A week or two after the Blitz. I was trying to meet up with you outside church one Sunday. Didn't feel ready to go to your door, and you might not have been at home. I was a bit late, but I saw you walking with a boy, and you seemed quite close. I'd seen enough. Kept out of sight and went back home," continued Roger, as he stared sincerely into Agnes's face, while she stared back at him.

Neither spoke for several seconds.

Agnes turned full circle and looked back again at Roger and laughed in disbelief.

She gave him a flash of her eyes.

"You are one idiot!" laughed Agnes, "That was my big brother, Willie!"

The mutual sense of relief overcame them both as they stood smiling at each other. The rain was falling, but neither of them noticed it, as it soaked their faces, like tears of joy.

"Maybe we could turn the clock back and start it all again, Agnes. We could start with me giving you a lift home out this rain. Sorry it will have to be on the handlebars of this bicycle and not the Norton," suggested Roger.

Agnes shook her head to refuse his offer.

"Thanks Roger, but I only live a hundred yards from here. I'll be home just as easy," smiled Agnes. Roger thought quickly.

"Well then, I'll walk with you to your door, if you don't mind," smiled Roger, glad that he had given himself a few more minutes to gather up the courage to ask her out.

As Agnes reached the latch of the small garden gate at her house. Roger drew in his breath.

"Agnes, The Campbell May Ball is on Saturday week. It's the last one I will be at, before I go for Officer Training with the Inniskillings, in the summer. I would really like to take you to it. Please say you will?"

"I couldn't go to that sort of fancy do!" gasped Agnes, as she recoiled in horror. "1'm on a shift that night, anyway," she added with a hint in her tone that told Roger she was disappointed, and not just making an excuse.

Roger, gave a look that mirrored her disappointment, which turned into a smile.

"Don't you worry about any of that," reassured Roger, as his Arthur organising skills overwhelmed his thought processes.

"Are you in the City Hospital?" asked Roger."

Agnes, nodded her head.

"Do you know a senior surgical nurse by the name of Gerri Muldoon?" Agnes nodded again.

"Speak to her, she'll sort out your work shift for that night," said Roger.

"But I haven't anything to wear for a do like that!" sighed Agnes.

"Agnes, I don't care if you come in a sack, as long as you are there, Please Agnes, speak to Muldoon. She'll get something sorted with the dress. I'll call here this Sunday after lunch time. We'll go on a picnic. Leave it with me," assured Roger, as he began to move his face towards Agnes's, who began to close her eyes and open her lips in advance of a kiss. Just as he was about to seal the deal, Roger noticed the curtain move in the window behind Agnes's head.

"Oh, better not; best leave it for another time," sighed Roger.

Agnes pulled back, stunned and confused, assuming he had been teasing her, all along.

"Your mother is looking through the curtains, Agnes. My bad timing again," whispered Roger, trying not to move his mouth.

Agnes, smiled in relief, as she gave Roger a casual wave for the benefit of her mother.

Roger threw his leg over his Elswick Hopper and cycled home, never noticing he was soaked to the skin by the persistent deluge. Apart from the euphoria of meeting up with Agnes and the prospect of the Campbell formal. his mind was filled with how to cope with Jean Cunningham, the daughter of a wealthy Belfast family who would have been under the assumption she would be his partner at the School Formal. He had been on good terms with Jean and other young ladies of Belfast's elite; they had always got on well, and neither were thinking of anything more than enjoying the moment. Still he knew it wouldn't go down too well.

"Need to get a bit of advice from my Uncles Adam and Allen. They'll tell me how to sort it." he reassured himself.

The following Sunday afternoon, Roger arrived at the end of the road to Agnes's house. He got out of the Alpha roadster he had begged his mother to lend him, under strict instructions he was not to think he was Fangio[18]. He left the car out of sight of Agnes's house, not wanting to appear to be showing off at her front door.

As he approached the house he was relieved to see Agnes come out of the front door, down the path, and meet him in the road outside her gate.

"Just keep walking, my Dad is looking out the window," she whispered.

Roger linked her arm as he guided her back down the road.

"You didn't bring the Norton today. You didn't walk all the way over?" asked Agnes."

"No, thought you deserved a bit more than that, Agnes," he replied apologetically.

As they reached the Alpha, Agnes was still walking at full speed, keen to get out of sight of her discerning father, assuming they were walking to Shaws Bridge. Roger pulled her back.

"Hey, where do you think you are going, those nice shoes of yours aren't fit for walking," advised Roger, as he opened the passenger door, waving his hand for her to get in.

---

[18] Famous Italian Racing driver.

"You are kidding me," laughed Agnes. She gave Roger a long look until she saw in his expression he was not joking.

Roger joined her in the car and before he could put his hands on the steering wheel, Agnes, in a panic demanded,

"Quick, let's get out of here before any one see's us!"

Roger laughed "I'm bad for your image, am I?" teased Roger.

"No, but some of my neighbours will tell my Mummy before the day is out. Just drive please," she gasped, before talking to herself.

"Blooming sports car arriving to pick me up. I'll get an inquisition and a lecture when I get home if they find out."

Roger laughed as he drove off, wheels spinning, engine growling, which was the last thing Agnes wanted because if the car had not been noticed before it certainly would be now. Roger drove up the Saintfield Road, rather than across in the direction of Shaws Bridge before he let the car grind to a stop at the roadside and pulled up the handbrake.

"Just sit there a second, Agnes, I've a bit of unfinished business to attend to. Wanted to do it for quite a while now. Nearly got it done the other day, but circumstances got in the way," explained Roger as he looked into Agnes's confused face.

She looked across at him, wondering what it was.

Roger leant over to her and gave a slow kiss on her cheek, before he pulled back, and caressed her hair with his hand he had placed casually across the back of her seat.

Agnes gave him a look of approval out of the side of her eye, grabbed him by the lapel of his jacket and put her lips hard against his before she pulled back, and giggled.

"That's what I call making up for lost time!"

Roger smiled approvingly, started up the Alpha, and drove in the direction of Carryduff.

"Thought you might like a picnic down at Strangford Lough near Killinchy. Martha made a hamper up, it's in the back," said Roger.

" I normally get taken a walk up to Lisnabreeny[19] and a fish supper on the Ormeau Road!" Agnes laughed.

"Nothing less, than you deserve, Agnes," replied Roger, as he continued his journey, driving the car sedately, as his mother had instructed him.

The afternoon passed off successfully for both of them. They stopped at Whiterock Bay, walked across the causeway to Sketrick Island and sat at the viewpoint looking over Strangford Lough, across

---

[19] Neolithic hill fort at the top of Hillfoot Road near Newtownbreda.

to Greyabbey, Kircubbin and back up to Scrabo Tower and Newtownards.

As they sat taking in the view, Roger opened the hamper, before Agnes, instinctively took over the catering as she set everything out and poured the tea from the flask.

"China cups on a picnic!" she laughed to herself.

As they tucked into the food, Roger, taking care his mouth was not full; good manners had been instilled in him since birth, asked.

"Did you get next Saturday sorted out with Gerri Muldoon?" he asked.

"Oh yes, she has said she will do my shift on Saturday. Really surprised about that. She's a senior nurse whose studying to be a doctor. Thought doing my work would be beneath her," replied Agnes.

"That's great. Did you find yourself a decent sack to wear yet?" teased Roger.

"I think so, I was going to get the lend of a bride's maid's dress and camouflage it a bit, but Gerri says she will sort something. She did a few measurements and said leave it with her. Said she knew someone could make me up something that would do the job. She just said to leave it with her, and something about the Arthurs have been good to her. I'll not let them or you down. Don't understand what that's all about. Who are the Arthurs?" asked Agnes, screwing up her face.

Roger smiled, Agnes obviously did not know the connection. All she knew was his father was a Doctor Gibson in the City Hospital who had treated her like a child on the night of the Blitz, who lived somewhere up the Malone Road. In her few months at the City Hospital she had heard Doctor Gibson's mentioned but she was nowhere near surgical at her early stage of nursing. Bed baths, making beds and wiping fluids had been her limited experience of hospital life. It reassured him that Agnes was not going out with him because he was part of Belfast's aristocracy. It was still too early for him to show his hand. He had a plan in mind for that. Too much of the 'Arthur' in him, not to maintain the upper hand.

"Arthurs, name does ring a bell, Agnes. I'll have a think about that. It'll come to me, I'm sure," assured Roger, as he feigned an attempt to test his brain.

At the end of the evening, Roger stopped the Alpha at the end of the road where he had collected her earlier in the day. Agnes had still refused to let him drive to her door, in fear of her parents' concerns.

Roger walked her to the gate, gave her a short hug and as he turned to walk back up the road, he said,

220

"Saturday night. Seven o'clock. I will have to bring your chariot to the door. Can't have you walking down the street like a May Day Parade.

On Saturday night, at ten minutes to seven, Agnes was pacing up and down her front room looking out the window, turning to the mirror to adjust her gown and check her lipstick for the tenth time. As she faced the mirror again, she saw before her a face full of fear, excitement and insecurity. Thank God that Gerri had done her proud with the gown. She reckoned it would have cost a week of her father's wages at the Sirocco Works to pay for it in one of the high fashion shops in Belfast. How a neighbour of Gerri's, who made Confirmation and Irish Dancing dresses in her kitchen house had managed to combine the two with spare material, she would never know. She felt like a film star. None of this made the instinctive fear that she was well out of her depth, subside.

She heard the sound of a car door close, but it was not the normal metallic sound of a Ford Standard. It had a strange muffled, full-bodied tone. Strange it had sounded very quiet, none of the usual rattling engine sound.

She stretched out over the chair in front of the window to get a better look out, and froze. Roger was bounding up the garden path but behind him on the road side was the largest car she had ever seen and there was someone driving it who had a chauffeur's cap on their head.

Agnes stood motionless. "Oh God, I can't do this, I can't cope with this, I'll make a fool of myself and let Roger down!" she gasped.

Roger rapped the door. She stood, motionless, head spinning.

The door knocked again with a greater sense of urgency.

"There's your date at the door. Are you not going to answer it, girl!" shouted her father from the kitchen.

Agnes, turned to the mirror again and began thinking of what to say to call it all off.

Finally, as the door began to rap for the third time, she opened the parlour room door to go up the narrow hall to the front door. Her father was already taking large steps past her. As he reached the door handle he told her off.

"Agnes, what is up with you?" as he opened the door.

His eyes caught Roger, holding a bunch of flowers, and the Silver Shadow Rolls Royce and driver, idling at the kerb side.

"Agnes, there is a young man here waiting for you!"

Agnes emerged cautiously from the front room and walked slowly towards Roger who was standing, smiling nervously, dressed in formal evening wear, complete with white silk scarf.

Her father stood back to let her past him as she put her arm out to take the flowers. The adrenalin of the moment pulled her through the fear and doubt in her head.

"No Agnes, I have flowers for you out in the car. These are for your mother. It is part of the tradition of the May Ball," before he continued, as he looked at her father who was retracing his steps up the hall.

"Good evening Mr Miller. My name is Roger. Perhaps you would give these to Mrs Miller."

Agnes's father stopped and opened the kitchen door.

"Maggie, there is a young man here has something for you!"

"Come on in son and give them to her yourself," advised Bertie.

Roger hesitated, he was well versed in the manners and etiquette of the upper tiers of Belfast society but meeting mothers and fathers in a normal terrace house, at close quarters; he was as nervous as Agnes.

Margaret, got up from her chair, wiped her hands on her pinafore and advance into the hall.

"My mother picked them herself and hopes you will enjoy them," explained Roger.

Margaret, looked at Roger, as she shook her head from left to right. and turned to Bertie.

"Now, do you see that, Bertie. Here's a man who knows how to treat a woman," scolded Margaret.

"Twenty-five years we have been married. Never brought me home flowers once, as she gave him a playful slap on his arm."

Roger sighed and looked at Agnes." I hope I haven't caused a row," he joked.

"There'll be no rows in this house as long as this young lady is back by midnight. One minute later and you'd be best keeping that engine running," laughed Bertie, with only the slightest hint of a threat.

"Now away and enjoy yourselves!"

"And thank your mother for the roses. I'm away to put them in water, if I can find a vase big enough," smiled Margaret.

Roger led Agnes out to the Rolls Royce. As he opened the door to let her in, he could see curtains twitch in the houses either side and across the street. They settled into the back seat with the soft leather in a space that Agnes thought was bigger than her front room,

Roger announced, "Drive on driver!"

The driver, cap well down, and high 'choker collar' uniform, nodded to acknowledge the instruction and calmly cruised off in the direction of Campbell College.

"Roger I know your father is a doctor, but this is mad. You didn't need to go to this expense. It must have cost a fortune to hire this," scolded Agnes, as she sat in embarrassment.

Roger, in an attempt to settle Agnes's nerves explained.

"Agnes, this is the Campbell May Ball. The last one I will attend. I want to make it a great night for you. Now relax, stop worrying."

"That's ok for you, but I fear letting you down with your friends," stressed Agnes.

"Agnes, you are better than any of them. Now, where is the girl that crawled round rubble one night and was in great form last Sunday. I'm with you. Just be yourself. I'll look after you," assured Roger, as he pushed his hand against her knee.

At the front entrance to the dining room of the College, the Rolls Royce pulled in line behind other expensive automobiles, but none quite up to its standard.

Roger and Agnes got out of the car and Roger leant into the driver's window.

"Pick us up for eleven thirty please. Don't want to incur Mr Miller's wrath," said Roger.

The driver nodded in approval and drove out of the grounds.

The rest of the evening was the best they had both enjoyed in their young lives. Agnes had only ever been to local Church Hall dances and had just started to attend a few nurses dances, The evening's grandeur and atmosphere was like something out of the movies. Roger was her Clarke Gable. It never occurred to her that she was Roger's Vivienne Leigh. He could not believe how beautiful she looked as she walked down the hall of her house, as he led her to the Rolls.

Roger revelled in his friends asking him out of the side of their mouths,

"Where did you find her, Roger old chap. Great things come in small packages" was mentioned on several occasions, referring to her small petite stature of five foot one, with the heels."

The girls present, all from the top grammar and public schools for young ladies were divided on their opinions of Agnes, who was the centre conversations. Some, were intrigued by her, not in the least jealous and wished her well, as they had their own targets of attention amongst Belfast's elite. They did have a giggle to themselves at the sour faces on the ones who resented her because the pretty little nurse,

226

had achieve what they had not. Those ones bitched about her at every opportunity. Agnes was aware of all of this, but she did her best to remain at Roger's shoulder, smile and be polite to everyone she was introduced, determined not to let Roger down.

At eleven thirty, Roger grabbed Agnes by the arm as she finished a dance with one of his best friends. A good enough friend that he knew would not try to move in on her.

"Grab your coat, you've pulled young lady," laughed Roger. Don't want your father chasing me down the Hillfoot, do we!"

Outside in the dark, the Rolls sat in the driveway behind a few other cars.

Agnes got into the back of the car as Roger held open the door.

"Great night, driver. Best ever!"

Agnes smiled to herself as the sense of relief overcame her.

As the car cruised slowly along the Hillfoot Road a silence had fallen over the couple in the back seat.

Roger began to be concerned, Agnes seemed pensive, in a world of her own. A silent girl, was, and still is, not a good sign to any youth just turning nineteen.

Roger attempted to probe for information.

"Well Agnes, that, was the best night ever. Couldn't have wished for better. I am really glad you came," thanked Roger.

Agnes did not reply, Roger looked into her face, and could see her eyes were wet.

"Agnes, what's wrong. Did I offend you?" asked Roger, as he glanced forward at the back of the driver's head. The driver slid the glass partition over so as to avoid hearing the couple speak.

"No Roger, you did nothing wrong. I'm happy, that's why I'm like this," sighed Agnes, as she took out her handkerchief, dabbed her eyes and wiped her nose.

"But that doesn't make sense, crying when you are happy," sighed Roger.

"You wouldn't understand, Boys don't understand," sighed Agnes. "This has been a wonderful evening, it was just the best, but Ahhh!" sobbed Agnes, as she shook her head from side to side, and stared silently out of the side window, not wanting to look at Roger.

By the time the Rolls pulled up outside the kerb at Agnes's house, she had regained her composure. Roger's mind had raced to adjust to her outburst. He had to do something to end the night on a good note. "Well its eleven fifty-five so your father won't be chasing me down the road; that's something," he laughed, nervously.

228

"Can I see you tomorrow afternoon. I'll call about two o'clock. Sorry it won't be the Rolls. I believe it is booked for tomorrow anyway," Roger joked.

Agnes paused as she got out of the car.

"Yes I'll see you tomorrow, but we'll have to talk. No picnic, and definitely no Rolls Royce, please, lovely thought that it was, Roger." She turned and gave him a quick kiss on his lips.

As they walked to the door, Roger spoke again,

"Agnes, if you want to have a talk about something tomorrow, we can walk to Minnowburn and sort out what is bothering you?" asked Roger, in a clumsy attempt to understand the source of the change of mood.

Agnes, nodded and waved him off before she disappeared through the door.

Roger walked pensively back to the Rolls Royce, opened the door of the front seat passenger side and slumped into the seat, as he spoke to the driver.

"I really don't understand women. We had a great night, she seemed to really enjoy it. Then she ends up crying and telling me we have to talk about something. Women!"

The driver unbuttoned the choker collar, threw off the chauffeur cap onto the dashboard, and shook their hair.

"Your Dad still doesn't understand me sometimes, so don't beat yourself up about it," advised Anna, as she laughed in irony.

"Deal with it as it comes, Roger. She seems a lovely girl. Listen to what she has to say tomorrow and work off your instinct."

You are still eighteen. Don't complicate your life, unless you really need to, is my advice. Now, it's home, young man," instructed Anna.

At the same time, Agnes quietly opened the door to the living room where her mother and father had waited up, while they listened to the late news, which had just finished. The final pips rang out to signal, midnight before the station closed. She was about to speak but the strains of "God save the King" filled the airwaves.

Her father stopped drawing on his cigarette, her mother stopped knitting. Agnes stood in the living room doorway, looking at the carpet until the final strains of the anthem ended.

"Back home, I'm away to bed," was her only comment, as she turned and closed the door before they could start an interrogation of the night's events.

Margaret raised her eyebrows and frowned at Bertie.

230

"Don't think that went to plan, Bertie," quipped Margaret.

"As soon as I saw the Roller I though it didn't fit. Our 'wee girl' is too down to earth for that lot. Seems like she had a bit of a hard education in life this evening," sighed Bertie. "Maybe you should go up and check how see's doing, Maggie," he added in reflection.

"Best leave her to it. Take it from me the last she wants is motherly advice. I'd only make it harder for her," instructed Margaret. It was not a suggestion.

At the Sunday service of St Patrick's Drumbeg, Roger sat, head still full of self-doubt and fear of pending gloom. He didn't listen to a word of the sermon and even the hymns he liked, seemed dirges.

His head was full of thoughts he processed and filtered down to one question.

"Why was he more concerned about Agnes and not himself. He had successes and failures with enough of the young ladies of his social circle. Never lost a night's sleep over any of them. Why was he feeling different about Agnes?

Allen and Adam had warned him enough times not to let a girl get into his head. Agnes had got into his head.

As soon as he finished his lunch, he mounted the Elswick Hopper and cycled, thoughtfully, in the direction of Newtownbreda. Anna had refused to let him use the roadster. Her response to his request.

"Roger after last night's little 'blip' I fear you swanning over in a sports car, is the last thing Agnes wants to see. She feels intimidated, is my guess. Take you bicycle, leave it at her gate and do whatever you have to do. Now get a move on!"

When Roger got within distance of Agnes's house, his chest began to tighten, as he became more fearful of what might be ahead of him. The fear subsided a little when he saw Agnes already at her front gate out on the footpath, her arms folded, pacing slowly up and down a few yards back and forward, her head staring at the footpath.

"At least she was there, that was a relief," he reassured himself.

He dropped off the Elswick as he reached her side and searched into her face for a reaction.

At first she kept her face to the pavement, swinging her foot back and forward across the pavement, seemingly in deep concentration.

"Hello Agnes, I worried about you all night and this morning. Please tell me you are ok!" asked Roger. "I wanted to make last night a great night for you. I never intended to ruin your evening. That was

232

the last thing I wanted to do, Agnes I am so sorry if I caused you any grief," pleaded Roger, as he continued to search her face for a reaction.

Agnes half raised her head and gave him a strained look out of the corner of her eye.

"Let's walk, Roger, I need to explain," with a sigh of regret.

"Fine" replied Roger, as he held out his hand to clasp it in hers.

By the time they had reached Belvoir, almost at the Milltown Road they had walked in silence. Roger waiting for some dreadful announcement. Agnes, the words she wanted to say sticking in her throat. Finally Agnes stopped and tugged his arm.

"This has to be the last time we go out, Roger, Best we stop now. I can't cope with it. I'm afraid, Roger," she announced as the tears welled up in her eyes.

Roger stared at her and spoke instinctively, without forming a clever thought-out reply and shook his head in angst.

"What has happened to the bundle of fun. The little lady with the heart of a lioness," he sighed, before he continued.

"If you are trying to dump me, you aren't doing a very good job of it," said Roger, with a grin.

" I don't want to, but I have to, Roger," replied Agnes, as she turned back in the direction of Newtownbreda.

Roger replied in panic.

"But that doesn't make sense Agnes. "If you don't want to, you don't need to. I don't want you to!"

Agnes looked at him, her expression a mixture of sadness and embarrassment.

"Come on Agnes, at least walk with me to Minnowburn and finish the day out. It's calm up there. We can talk this through," coaxed Roger.

"If you don't, I'll walk you back home and I'll know it's over and I'll not embarrass you any further."

Agnes stood and looked at Roger, mind in even more confusion.

"You don't embarrass me Roger, you idiot. It's me, I'm afraid. I'm afraid, that I will not be able to cope in your world and it will all fall apart. I can't face that. It's better for both of us."

"Agnes, I'm not asking you to marry me. I'm just asking you to be my girlfriend. You are seventeen. I am nineteen in a few weeks. I, will be away to Officer Training in a month's time. Let's not complicate things. Let's enjoy a bit of time together. Who knows what the future holds for any of us." Roger held out his hand.

"Now walk with me up to Shaws Bridge, at least, and see how you feel."

Agnes gave him a weak smile, wiped her face, and reached out to hold his hand.

Roger felt a sense of achievement as he walked silently with Agnes up to Shaw's Bridge. He smiled to himself, remembering his Grandpa James's advice when trying to reel in a big fish.

"Don't reel it in fast or you will snap the line and it'll be gone. Let it run a bit, reel it in gently."

At Shaws Bridge they lent their backs against the wall of the bridge, the same wall his mother, father, Joe and Kitty had leant against on their first dates back in the Spring of 1915. As they looked downstream in the direction of Belfast. Roger, broke the silence first.

"Do you remember that night of the Blitz. The night we met. It wasn't exactly the most romantic of first dates, was it?" joke Roger, trying to encourage some level of closeness to the atmosphere.

"I remember your father treating me like a six-year-old," growled Agnes.

"He was concerned about you, that was all. He was also very impressed by you, but he isn't the sort of man to show much emotion. He saves that all for my mother.

He wasn't born with the 'silver spoon in his mouth' like me.

I, on the other hand have been handed the baton of responsibility to keep the family name in the manner it has done for several generations. You aren't the only one faced with daunting circumstances," sighed Roger.

"Listen to him!" laughed Agnes in irony. "The poor 'wee' soul, has to live in a house on the Malone Road, and cycle all the way to Campbell College, just so he can feel like a real person," mocked Agnes, making sure to give him a smile out of the corner of her eye so the ridicule would not be taken too seriously.

Roger laughed, grabbed hold of her. lifted her up like a sack of potatoes and pretended to throw her over the bridge into the fast-flowing Lagan, swollen by the previous night's heavy rain.

"Put me down!" screamed Agnes. "People will think you are mad. Everyone's watching!" she scolded, almost whispering.

"Well, are we going up to Minnowburn, or do you fancy a swim in the Lagan. Your choice?" laughed Roger.

"Why not go to Minnowburn and swim down the Lagan from there!" laughed Agnes, unable to keep her frosty image any longer."

That's more like the Agnes I know!" replied Roger.

By the time it took the ten minutes to walk up the Ballylesson Road to reach Minnowburn, the feeling of doom and gloom had vanished. Their mood had changed to the day they had spent at Sketrick Island. As they sat on the grass beside the river they watched some lads who had waded out from the low gravel bank to commence a water fight as they stood knee deep in the river, their trousers rolled up to their thighs. Roger and Agnes smiled at the antics of the boys that was reminiscent of a slap stick Chaplin comedy.

Roger and Agnes lay back on the grass and turned to face each other and kissed. Just as the kiss was becoming serious, a shout rang out from the river.

"Help, I can't swim!" The two young lovers sat bolt upright.

One of the boys had lost his balance and fallen into the water headfirst. By the time he surfaced he was being dragged down the river in the fast following current.

Roger threw off his shoes and removed his jacket as he waded into the stream, swam a few strokes, before he grabbed the boy by the collar and pulled him ashore. The lad lay on the gravel riverbank, motionless. His two friends went to lift him up, still laughing at his stupidity for falling into the water.

237

Their laughter changed to panic when they realised he was not breathing.

"He's not breathing!" yelled the bigger of the boys.

Agnes was the first of the riverbank spectators to reach the boy. She turned him on his side, and within a few seconds water spouted from his lungs. He coughed and spluttered as he dragged himself from his knees.

His two mates pulled him up to his feet and they all ran from the riverbank, still holding their shoes, trousers still rolled up to their shins. Roger and Agnes looked at each other.

" Not even a thank you!" laughed Agnes, in irony. Roger shook his head in disbelief.

"Well that sort of puts our plans in a bit of a pickle, Nancy Miller," replied Roger, maintaining the mood, using the name only her close friends called her, as he took off his shirt, and put his shoes and jacket back on.

"We'll have to go to my house and get a change of clothes; better go quick. That water is a tad cold, Agnes," instructed Roger.

Agnes nodded in agreement as she turned to walk back down to Shaws Bridge and the leafy avenues that ran between the Malone and Lisburn Road where half of the doctors of Belfast lived.

Roger took a few steps the other direction towards Edenderry. "This way is shorter Agnes, come on!" urged Roger.

"No Roger it's shorter this way to Malone Road," advised Agnes.

"Trust me, Agnes, up to Edenderry, across the bridge up there and there's a short cut to my house. Come on I'm bloody freezing!" coaxed Roger.

As they reached Edenderry and crossed the footbridge, Agnes noticed a few villagers point at Roger and speak to each other out of the sides of their mouths. Some gave him a friendly nod of their heads. "Roger, do they know you around here?" panted Agnes, as they ran over the bridge that took them to the Drumbeg side of the Lagan canal.

Roger again began to walk southwards up the towpath, ignoring her question about the villagers.

"Roger you are still going the wrong way. The Malone Road is down the way!" urged Agnes.

Most of it may well be, but I do know my way home!" shouted Roger, making sure he had a smile on his face, ensuring Agnes would not be offended,

"The Malone Road is down the way, Roger!" she insisted again, as she became more infuriated.

"The Malone Road goes all the way from Queens University to Drumbeg, Agnes, now come on!" Roger insisted, as he offered her his hand.

They trotted up the towpath for one hundred yards when Roger stopped and turned to go through a gap in the hedge.

Agnes tugged against his arm.

"Roger you can't go in there. That's some bigwig's estate. We'll get arrested if we are caught in there." advised a panic-struck Agnes.

"Don't worry Agnes, my father knows the owner quite well. We will be fine," assured Roger, still hiding the truth, hoping Agnes would not have another of her panic attacks when she would soon find out.

As they climbed the steep slope from the bottom meadow Agnes could see the corner of the lake and a tall man fishing with two children in the distance. Then the formidable Ballydrain House loomed over the hilltop as they climbed higher up the field.

"Is that the House? I've been past the walls on the road to Drumbeg but I never actually saw the House. Some shack, Roger, isn't it?" announced Agnes in awe.

As they reached the edge of the forecourt, Jonty was washing down the Rolls Royce, as he looked up and saw the dishevelled pair.

"What happened? Did you forget your swimming trunks, kid!" grinned Jonty.

"Ah. so this is where you got the lend of the Rolls, Roger," announced Agnes, feeling quite pleased with her deductive powers.

Unknown to Roger and Agnes, their entrance up the field had been noticed by Davy, who was now walking back up to the house with Joseph and Kathleen either side of him.

Jonty noticed Davy advance behind the intrepid couple.

"What were you up to Roger?" asked Davy. Agnes turned to see where the slightly familiar voice came from.

"Doctor Gibson, Roger said you knew the owners. I thought he was joking!" she acknowledged, in surprise,

Davy looked at Jonty and then to Roger who was behind Agnes as he progressed towards the front steps. Roger pulled a face asking his father not to let any cats out of any bags just yet.

Agnes, sensing that Davy had looked over her shoulder, turned to see Roger disappear into the house. Before she could get the chance to speak, Roger gestured to her that he would be out in a few minutes.

"Well then Agnes, it would seem we are destined to always meet in situations of chaos," teased Davy.

Agnes hesitated. Part of her wanted to flee back down the meadow and not stop running until she got to her front door. The other part decided to take Roger's advice and take things in her stride. She was determined not to let him down again.

"Roger pulled a drowning boy from Minnowburn, Doctor Gibson," announced Agnes, in pride. Davy just nodded, smiling like any proud father, but not wanting to show it. Almost at the same time, Agnes could hear the sound of footsteps coming down the steps of the front entrance. She turned to see a lady with an almost regal manner.

Joseph and Kathleen, ran excitedly towards her.

"Mummy, Mummy, we caught two fish today and Daddy only caught one!" exclaimed Kathleen.

"Well, run in and give them to Martha and she will cook them for your dinner. Would you like that?" offered Anna, as she touched them both on the cheek and chased them inside.

Agnes's brain jumped again, "Martha, that was the name of the lady who had made up the picnic hamper for Strangford Lough."

Anna, stepped towards Agnes, and offered her hand.

"Hello Agnes, I am so glad you are here. Roger would have been so disappointed otherwise," smiled Anna.

Agnes, froze in confusion, her face showed it.

"Please call me Anna, I am Roger's Mum. He assures me he will be out in a minute," doing her best to make Agnes feel at ease.

"We were about to have afternoon tea on the veranda with Martha and Jonty. Please join us. Roger will be down when he has changed. By the look on your face he has a bit of explaining to do," teased Anna.

Roger came out of the front door with a fresh change of clothes, to see Agnes and his mother talking together. Davy caught his son's eye and pulled a face suggesting he might be in a bit of bother, and he could do nothing to help.

As Anna and Agnes continued to talk, Roger quietly drifted alongside Davy.

"You'll have to get yourself out of this one. The game I fear is up. This should be fun, kiddo!" before he stepped forward to break up the girls' conversation.

"Well folks, let's go round to the veranda, for a bite of grub!" advised Davy, deliberately being as informal as possible to reduce the level of intimidation in Agnes's head.

He knew better than anyone what it was like being introduced to the Arthur dynasty for the first time. Agnes was doing fine, probably better than he had many years ago, he told himself.

As they sat on the veranda, around the garden table, Roger was silent, as his brain tried to weave an explanation for Agnes, He feared a relapse of Agnes's insecurity.

Anna broke the silence. "Well Agnes, it sounds like you had an exciting afternoon."

"Yes Mrs Gibson it's not every day you see someone being fished out of the Lagan," replied Agnes, containing a nervous laugh.

Roger interrupted. "Agnes was the real star of the show. She got him breathing again. He brought his guts up, but it did the trick!" laughed Roger in typically bad taste boys' humour.

"Roger, behave yourself!" scolded Anna.

A silence returned. Davy, decided his son needed a bit of help in this tricky situation.

"Well then Nurse Miller, it would seem you are a good learner. Well done. Anyone can learn the theory if they put their minds to it. The real test is when you are faced with the situation. You can give yourself a pat on the back, young lady," smiled Davy, as he offered a plate of blackberry tarts to Agnes. Agnes lifted a tart, her throat, so tight in fear, she doubted she could swallow it.

Davy laughed quietly again.

"Roger, it is time you put Agnes out of her misery," advised Anna, as she gave her son a look of despair, followed by a reassuring smile.

As Roger opened his mouth to speak, Agnes saved him the embarrassment.

"I think I have got the picture, Roger," interrupted Agnes, as she stared across the garden table, expressionless, holding her gaze.

Roger did not know what might happen next. His life was passing before him. Agnes slowly moved her blank stare into a broad affectionate smile. Roger, relaxed, as Agnes continued.

"Roger, didn't want to be a show off and I made it more difficult with behaving badly last night. That's all there is to it, Mrs Gibson," said Agnes.

"You didn't behave badly last night, Agnes, I did. It was rather silly of me to offer to take you both to the formal in the Rolls. I thought you might enjoy the experience. Please forgive me, I meant well," apologised Anna.

Before Agnes or Roger could contribute to the conversation, Martha interrupted.

"Roger, take Agnes down to the Italian gardens and show her around. There are some lovely blooms that started early. What sort of a gentleman are you?" she scolded him, laughing at the same time.

Roger and Agnes rose from the table and made a hasty retreat down the path.

"Thanks Martha, always my guardian angel," smiled Anna.

"Sure, God put me on this earth for that very purpose, Anna!" replied the big girl, with an even bigger heart.

Jonty placed a reassuring arm round Martha's shoulder and looked, smiling contentedly, across at Davy. She was more than just Anna's guardian angel, she was his as well," he thought to himself, "and he knew it."

Chapter fifteen

D Day

On the morning of the 5^h June 1944, Davy and Anna were having breakfast as the morning news reporter began to introduce the News on the BBC radio station. Even before he began to hear the announcement they looked at each other across the table in anticipation. They were well aware the mock landings on the beaches around Northern Ireland had stopped, and the army camps were on the move. Any morning now there would be some announcement. It was not a matter of if, but when and where.

The newsreader's polite, stiff upper lipped, clipped accent, could not conceal the magnitude of the report he was about to read. Davy dropped his spoon still full of his next mouthful of porridge back into the bowl. Anna, extended her hand to grab his forearm tightly.

"The Prime Minister, Winston Churchill has announced that Allied forces have landed on the shores of Normandy. There have been heavy losses on all fronts. Firm footholds have been established along the

Normandy Coast, supported by the largest land, sea and air invasion in the history of mankind."

Anna and Davy leant back in their chairs, Anna, put her hands on her cheeks, Davy, his hands round the back of his neck as he looked at the cracks in the cornice on the ceiling.

"Casualties will be worse than the Somme. No frontline hospitals, more powerful weapons, Jeez!" sighed Davy, still looking at the cornice, as his medical training took over his brain.

"Thank God, Roger has missed that!" added Anna, the instincts of a mother, filling her brain.

"Maybe it'll be all over by the time he goes through training. It should be a few months before he could be over there," replied Davy, not really believing a word of it. He just felt the instinctive need to protect Anna.

"He will not be going, Davy, I will not allow it," insisted Anna, as she dropped her hands from her face and slammed the sides of her fists on the table, making the teapot lift as the lid bounced on the table, rolled off and crash on the floor. Anna cursed to herself for her lack of self-control,

"You had better have a serious conversation with him this evening. We've swept this issue under carpet for nearly three years. He needs to be told," sighed Anna.

"I am going out to tack the horses. Need a bit of air. Speak to him tonight, Davy. It's a man-to-man conversation. He'll not take to being protected by his mother. He is too much like me. It would just make him more determined" announced Anna, pausing and breathing out before she continued.

"It would seem it is retribution time, twenty-nine years in the making," sighed Anna, referring to her rebellion against her father in 1915, as she disappeared out of the door to the kitchen on her way to the stables.

David sat for a moment, thinking. He was relieved Roger had already left for school. At least it gave him a chance to work out a way to speak to Roger that evening.

On the second Day of the Normandy landings, A Company, 2nd Royal Ulster Rifles landed on Sword Beach. They had the good fortune of arriving on a beach where the German defences guns had been either blasted by Allied Naval power or systematically wiped out, at heavy loss, by the first wave on the first day.

249

Corporal Willie Miller, from Newtownbreda, Belfast, waded out of the water, looked up at the sand dunes and rocks of Sword Beach and surveyed the destruction of the German defences. His eyes moved down from the shoreline to the beach in front of him. His mood changed as he froze at the sight of the bodies of soldiers floating in the waves. Young men like himself, who would never have the opportunity to walk with a pretty girl on a summer day, laugh with their mates over a beer. Make decisions in life, good and not so good. Hold their children in their arms. All gone because of an evil corporal of the Reich.

Miller himself, was a corporal, twenty years of age. He was brought out of his thoughts as he felt a nudge on his calf that he ignored. A few seconds later it nudged him again. He turned, looked down and saw in horror the remains of a body in a torn uniform, floating in the tide as it ebbed and flowed. Miller felt his stomach retch as he spewed his last meal into the English Channel. "Poor sod!" he said to himself as he breathed out, wiped his mouth, and looked around hoping no one had seen his reaction.

"Keep moving, Miller!" shouted his Sergeant. "Find cover at the base of the rocks. There'll be snipers around, just to slow us up!

"Are the German's not running all the way back to Berlin. Is the worst not over, Sarg?" asked Willie, as he strode forward eager to find a place of refuge as his sergeant had advised.

"Not a chance Miller, those bastards will fight every inch of the way. Every, road, village, town and city. This is just the start!" growled the sergeant.

That evening, when Roger had returned home from school he was full of the news of D Day. His friends at school had nothing else on their minds. The house was unusually quiet. His mother was not in the house, Martha and Jonty were both nowhere to be seen. He was not aware that everyone close to him, were told to make themselves scarce until Davy had spoken to him.

By almost six o'clock, Davy parked his Ford car at the back of the house in the rear courtyard and walked thoughtfully through the kitchen and into the drawing room. He put his medical bag in the corner, slumped into his armchair and looked at the cornice once more. He had spent all day running over the way to get Roger to listen, understand, and accept.

Roger, who had been cleaning the Norton out on the front drive, had seen his father turn into the back of the House. He knew his nightly ritual was to sit in the drawing room when he got home and cleared his head from the daily pressure of the hospital.

His father always made a point of not bringing his work home with him. His family was too important to him. He had never had a normal family; just him and his own father. He wanted more for his own.

Roger burst into the door of the drawing room, excited to tell Davy all he had heard about the events in Normandy.

"Dad, they've landed. They've given Gerry a bloody nose!" shouted Roger, in triumph.

Davy dropped his gaze from the ceiling to the carpet pattern below him and shook his head.

"Glad I am not having to deal with the casualties this time, Roger." sighed his father, as he shook his head.

Roger looked at him in confusion at his lack of enthusiasm.

"But Dad, we have landed in Europe. We have the Germans on the run. I can't wait to be part of it. School term ends this month and I'll be able to enlist. You said the Inniskillings are the best Irish Regiment. That's who I'll be joining," announced Roger, with the same defiance his mother had shown in 1915.

"Roger, son, sit down. Let's have a talk, man to man about this," sighed Davy.

"There's nothing to talk about. I'm going!" replied Roger, as he remained standing.

Davy gave him a look of frustration and sighed again.

"Sit down, son. You are wearing out the thread of the carpet. Please sit down," advised Davy, in a tone that meant it was an order.

"The last time this subject was raised was after Grandma May's funeral. I asked you never to raise it again until you had finished school and got your entry to Queens. Being the good lad that you are, you kept your promise and never spoke a word of it until a few weeks ago. For that you deserve credit," remarked Davy.

Roger sat down and leant forward in his chair as he thought of the best thing to say. He sensed that this was about to be the first time in his life that he would defy his father and stand on his own two feet.

"I did father, I have never mentioned it. Grandpa James always told me to honour my word in life and in business."

Roger took in a deep breath and let the air flow heavily back out of his mouth.

"He also told me to stand my ground. Not to give in to something I cannot agree with," replied Roger, as he looked apologetically across at his father.

Davy forced himself to remained relaxed in his chair, knowing that to sit forward would send a signal that it was not a conversation but confrontation.

"Well then, it looks as if I am going to have to make it clear to you that you are making the wrong decision and you should stop the whole idea," groaned his father, before he got up and took a few steps towards the drinks cabinet and continued.

"I don't want this to be an argument, Roger. I would rather we talk this through and agree that the most important person in the dilemma is not you, me, Winston Churchill or Jesus Christ; it is your mother. If you do not agree with me on that point then this conversation is a waste of time."

Roger did not speak, just nodded in approval.

He was taken aback by the heavy nature of what his father was saying to him. His father was not one for heavy conversations, just words of wisdom and often humour. He did not normally take his conversations to this level. Roger needed to hear more.

He sat silently watching his father reach to the back of the top shelf of the drinks cabinet and retrieve a brown bottle with no label and pour a small amount into each crystal glasses.

Davy handed one to Roger and took a sip of the other, himself.

"Don't take a big gulp of that. Sip it slowly, son. Too good to waste!" advised Davy, as he stifled a laugh."

"What is it, Dad?" A Bushmills Twenty-year malt?" asked Roger.

"God knows, son," grunted Davy. "A barn in North Armagh somewhere. Apples and barley; most likely eighty percent proof. Doubt if anyone bothered to work it out, though," as he took another sip.

Roger, not heeding his father's advice, took a swig.

Two seconds later, the sensation of heat began to rise from his stomach to his chest and finally his airwaves. He adjusted himself in his chair, attempting to camouflage his uncomfortable feeling.

Davy smiled to himself, knowing full well the effect on his son of not taking the poteen slowly as he had advised. It was starting already to have the effect he expected and wanted to achieve. By the time Roger would have finished the glass, his mouth would feel like rubber, and he would not be in the mood for an argument. The world, would be a place of tranquillity.

"Right Roger, you seem determined to go and do your bit in this war. I understand that. Did it myself, as did your mother, and the rest of the crew around here, but the circumstances are different this time round. There are more reasons for you to stay here than go off to fight the Hun," advised Davy.

Roger looked across at his father in despair.

"Father," sighed Roger. "I have to go. Some of the sons of our workers are off to the war. How would I ever gain their respect when the day comes the Arthur businesses are my responsibility?" Agnes's brother, Willie, is with the Rifles[20]. Alec has been with a Special Operations Commando unit since the early days. I can't be seen to be sitting in cotton wool, at home."

Davy, looked across at him.

"I understand all that, Roger. It still doesn't sort the bottom line. I will protect your mother, should it mean destroying the whole Arthur empire. I'll open up the Lockkeeper's cottage and we'll spend our days down there, if I have to, without a second though, son," stressed Davy.

The illicit brew, thankfully, was beginning to make Roger's brain less confrontational, as he replied.

"So there it is father, we have an unsolved problem," mused Roger.

Royal Ulster Rifles

Davy did not expect such a mature comment that meant his son was standing his ground.

As he rolled round in his head, the next reply, something Roger had said seeped into his immediate thought processes.

'Cotton wool', Davy sat in silence as he contemplated the remark before he leant forward to look Roger in the face. Roger did not move in his chair, as he braced himself for a harsh reaction from his father.

"The May fly look a bit active out on the lake; the trout even more so. I'll see you down at the lake in an hour. We'll continue this conversation soon enough. In the meantime, let's, just enjoy the present," suggested Davy.

Roger looked across in confusion, before his father continued,

"Leave it until the end of the month when you've left school. Sunday afternoon, that weekend. I might have answer to this that might do the job," sighed Davy, as he emptied his glass, and got up from his chair. Roger began to do the same, before his father, let out a grunt.

"Best you don't take the rest of that stuff until later if you want to cast your line straight!"

One week into the invasion of Normandy, Willie Miller walked into a village the Germans had withdrawn from under the cover of darkness the previous night to join their comrades in making a stand several miles further up the road.

Willie, and three other fellow Royal Ulster Rifles, walked carefully down the main street, taking regular stops in doorways and corners. Basic training had been drummed into them. "Don't stay in one stop too long. Find cover as much as possible. Snipers could always be about."

By the time they assured themselves there were no errant Germans remaining, their sense of caution eased.

Micky McCann from the Woodstock Road was the first to see it at the next corner. The only inn of the village. Micky's eyes lit up.

"Now there's a lovely sight for a thirsty soldier. It's a week or more since I had a beer!" he shouted to Willie and the other two thirsty comrades.

"Don't even think about it Micky, if the Sergeant catches you, you're a dead man!" reasoned Willie.

"Frig that, Willie. Might never get another chance!" shouted Micky, as he put his foot to the door of the inn. He looked inside as the smell of stale alcohol met his nostrils.

"Think I'm back in the Oakley on the Ravenhill!" he laughed, as he disappeared inside the building. The other three looked at each other, and over their shoulders, to check the Sergeant was not around. They shrugged and disappeared inside the inn.

Micky McCann was already behind the bar, scanning the names on the beer pumps.

"That's the one for me!" he laughed, as the other three ambled to the bar counter. Micky pulled the pump. The bar exploded.

Chapter sixteen

The Deal

The morning after Davy and Roger's conversation and evening fishing, Davy walked into John Clarke's office. As usual, John, was perusing the reports on the surgery he would have to perform and check the procedures his juniors had performed the previous day.

"Morning, Clarkey," grinned Davy. "I would appreciate it if you could cover for me some day in the next week if it's not too much bother. We could swap a few if it makes it easier. I'll even do a Saturday morning and miss the golf at Malone," offered Davy.

John looked over his reading glasses in pretend concern.

"It must be serious, David!" mocked John.

"It could be a matter of life and death," replied Davy, without any sense of humour.

John paused, realising that whatever it was Davy had in mind it was not a laughing matter, reprimanding himself for his lack of sensitivity.

He set down a report he was perusing and lifted his large leather, bound diary and flicked the pages, while he considered. Next Tuesday would be the best day for me, David," assured John.

"Tuesday it is then, John. Gentleman and a scholar!" announced Davy in appreciation, as he walked out of Clarkey's office.

"Also a better golfer, David, Don't forget that!"

"Aha! Don't push it, Clarkey!" replied Davy, as he closed the door and breathed a sigh of relief.

"Let's hope the rest of the plan goes as straight forwardly," he thought to himself.

The following Tuesday morning, Davy drove the long and uneven roads through Lisburn, Portadown, Dungannon, Ballygawley and on to Enniskillen. As he reached the top of Enniskillen town he turned left down to the River Erne where he could see his destination ahead of him. The Inniskillings Barracks, stood proudly at the far end of the town at the shore of the Erne River, the link between the weave of islands and waterways that make up the Upper and Lower Lough Erne. At the entrance to the barracks he was stopped by a soldier and asked for identification. The lance corporal, studied his papers and ID.

"Oh right, Dr Gibson, the Major is waiting for you, Sir!" as he stood back and saluted him with enough enthusiasm befitting a General.

261

Davy, chuckled to himself at the soldier's reverence.

"What's that all about?" he thought. Davy walked into the reception area and another young soldier with a gloved artificial hand stepped towards him.

"Hello Corporal, I have an appointment to see the Major," advised Davy as he offered his papers.

"Don't worry about that Dr Gibson, the Major is waiting for you. Please follow me."

The soldier tapped on the Major's door and opened it with his remaining right hand. Davy's thanked the corporal as he closed the door behind him. The Major looked up at Davy.

"Good morning Corporal Gibson, forgive me if I do not stand," he smiled, as he put his drop shaped pipe on the ash tray at his hand.

Davy stood rigid and saluted the Major.

"Corporal Gibson reporting for duty Captain Montgomery, Sir. Sorry I'm a bit late; about twenty-eight years to be exact!"

Davy gave an embarrassed laugh as he leant forward to shake the Major's hand.

"Well David, I assume you have a matter of importance to bring you down here. I am forever in your debt, so if there is anything I can do to help, just ask." reassure the Major.

Davy slowly sank himself into the chair opposite the Major at his desk, as he unbuttoned his jacket.

"The problem is my wife and my son, Roger Jnr," sighed Davy.

Montgomery looked in surprise at him.

"I am sorry to hear they aren't getting on. Last time I called to your house a few years ago, when I was up in Belfast to get a new bit of metal to this contraption, you all seemed in good spirits."

"No, they are on the best of terms. It's the war that isn't on the best of terms with either of them," said Davy, as he breathed out heavily. He wants to join up. She doesn't want him to go, haunted by her brother Roger. I'm in the middle trying to keep them both content. I'm losing this sortie. You might be my last chance," explained Davy, with a sense of hopelessness.

The Major gave him a lingering look. "What has happened to the youth he knew to be such an assured character," was the thought that passed through his mind.

The Major remained silent as he allowed Davy to continue.

"You had been a career soldier before our war started and you didn't let your leg change any of that. A lot of men would have thrown it all in. You took up desk duties and have been in the logistics end of things ever since. As I understand it you have a say in deployment of all ranks. You decide which jobs the members of the regiment are to be attached."

Davy paused, embarrassed by what he was suggesting, but if his embarrassment resulted in Anna being content, and the affections of his son intact, so be it. The embarrassment would be a cheap price to pay.

Montgomery sensed his mood and broke in to speak before Davy could continue.

"It's fine Davy, I think I get your drift, my friend," sympathised Montgomery.

He leaned back in his chair, as he lifted his pipe, stuffed in some tobacco, lit it, sucked in a few times, and watched the smoke rise to the ceiling. Davy sat silent, knowing his routine all too well.

"I assume he has had his offer to Queens for next September. What subject does he intend to study?" asked Montgomery.

"Law, same as Roger," replied Davy, with only the slightest hint of irony.

"Perfect" whispered Montgomery, almost talking to himself.

"Has he been in the Office Training Corps at Campbell?"

"Yes, since the Blitz in 'Forty-One'." replied Davy, keeping his answers short and sweet. That was the way the military did things.

"Good, good," reflected the old soldier, as a silence settled over the room again before Montgomery set his pipe down on the ash tray and continued.

"You do realise that all the newspaper nonsense about smashing Hitler in a few months is a lot of bollocks. The word amongst senior command is it will take until this time next year. If we don't come off with something special by the Autumn the Germans will grind it out until next Spring and beyond. We will win, they know it, but they will not roll over. I understand they are pinning their hopes on a few scientific breakthroughs or belief that we will settle for a ceasefire and they all go home. You and I both know that is not an option. Their heads have got to roll, and their whole structure brought to heel."

A silence invaded the room, again. Davy continued to bite his lip. He was not in charge in this situation. He had to wait for whatever, morsels, scraps of hope, would be thrown over the table.

"Brigade Staff, how would that suit, Corporal Gibson?" announced Montgomery.

"The 'five miles back brigade' as we used to call them," grunted Davy, with uncontained irony.

Montgomery let out a restrained laugh, before he finished his explanation.

"There's always a few 2nd Lieutenants get posted to Brigade Staff out of each batch. Young Roger having a legal bent, covers him as, potentially, a good analyst. His time in the OTC covers him as understanding the mode of operation of the military and more experience of training than some of the poor sods we are churning through Sandhurst.

"If he joins end of July, it'll be near Christmas by the time he is posted. Officers appointed to Brigade, normally only get six months in it before they get designated out to Active Service. That would take it to this time next year. It might be all over bar the shouting. We'll cross that bridge when we come to it, David. That's the best I can do," offered Montgomery, before he continued again.

"Although do not forget he does not have to go at all. There's no conscription here. There are thousands who have no intentions of joining anything more than the Boy Scouts, so don't feel any embarrassment about having to ask me this favour. I see a concerned parent trying to keep a good son in one piece." consoled Montgomery, as he looked over at Davy, who, by this , was bent forward in his chair, elbows on his knees, his face buried in his open palms. He stood up took a deep breath, waved his head from side to side.

"That'll do me, my friend," as he shook the Major's hand.

"Nothing to thank me for, David. I have had three sons, a daughter, and my wonderful wife; none of which would have existed had it not been for you!" smiled Montgomery, as he finally lifted himself awkwardly from behind the desk as he dragged his artificial limb around the desk, grabbing his stick propped beside him.

"The Officers Mess is where we are going. You must be hungry after the long run down here, David."

As they made it slowly across the parade ground, Davy spoke.

"Well how are your four and the good lady?" asked Davy, making polite conversation as much as anything else.

Montgomery did not change his stiff walking pattern as he crossed the parade ground.

"It's three and the good lady now, David," replied Montgomery quietly, still not changing his pace.

Davy, felt that feeling you get when you could dig yourself a hole and want to crawl into it.

"Oldest, Freddie, was posted with the 9th to Burma. Captured, died in a labour camp. Forced at gun point to dig a railway, until he could dig no more. I refused to let the other two join up!" he explained, without any emotion, or change his slow but steady pace.

"I'll do my best to look after Roger, and you, stop beating yourself up about it. David," reassured Montgomery, before he changed the subject.

"Ah, I can smell the grub, already. A tad better than that crap they used to feed us!" he announced, as they reached the canteen door.

As Davy drove home a lot less stressed than he was on the journey down, he rolled around in his mind what was the next part of this campaign. He decided to explain it to Anna first, leaving the discussion with Roger for the end of the month as they had agreed.

Chapter seventeen

At the going down of the Sun

On a bright summer evening, the day after Davy had returned from his successful mission in Enniskillen, Roger parked his Norton at the front of Agnes's house, intent on taking a walk to the top of the Manse Road, up to Lisnabreeny Fort, one of several Neolithic sites scattered around the hills of Belfast.

The sun was setting behind Divis and Blackmountain, which caused it to shine directly into the houses of Newtownbreda, Knockbreda and Glencregagh. It was nothing unusual for the blinds of the houses to be pulled down to cut out the glare and stop the wall paper and carpets from fading in the front rooms always kept immaculate for visitors. He strode up the pathway in good humour. He had thought all day about this evening. His knock on the door reflected his mood. Normally Agnes would come bouncing out, give him a kiss, and they would begin their walk.

The door did not open and there was no sound of Agnes's feet skipping up the hall when he knocked the door. He knocked again with an impatient wrap.

He could hear the sound of the living room door open slowly followed by a ponderous sound of heavier feet on the linoleum hallway floor.

The door opened slowly to find Bertie leaning against the door frame. His face was void of its usual gait. It was a face of devastation. Empty of any sense of anything.

He looked at Roger, without speaking. His eyes were looking at Roger but there was no focus, just a distant haze. He forced himself to speak.

"Agnes won't be going out tonight Roger, son," said Bertie.

"Is she alright, Mr Miller?" asked Roger.

Mr Miller, had to force the words from his mouth.

"Willie has gone, son. 'Killed in action, is what they've told us. son," announced the strong Sirocco Works foreman.

"Best you leave it a few days. She's in her room and she hasn't come out since we told her when she got home from her shift."

Roger's mind spun, shocked.

"Oh no, Mr Miller that is awful. Agnes talked about him all the time. They were very close. She must be in an awful state," continued Roger.

"We are all in a state, Roger. There's nothing but sadness in here. You'd be best leaving things for a while," urged Mr Miller.

Roger paused as he thought for the right thing to say.

"Would you mind if I sit here at the step for a while, Mr Miller?"

Bertie Miller, up to that point had regarded Roger with more than a degree of doubt. The Belfast working man was in his soul. He had been worried that Roger was just another spoilt rich boy who was just enjoying himself with Agnes before he would let her down and leave her in tears. The look on Roger's face, lessened that fear.

"Roger, lad. You can sit there any time you want. I'll bring you a mug of tea out. Don't think I'm being rude not asking you in, but there's nothing but sorrow in this house. There's no need for you to be in the middle of it."

Mr Miller returned a few minutes later, handed him the tea.

"There is a memorial service at Knockbreda Parish, Monday, at 10.00 am. There's no burial service. He won't be coming home," winced the mourning father as he turned and shut the door.

271

Roger sat until the evening chill of a cloudless night started to get to his bones, as the sun set over Divis Mountain. His head was full of the fate of Agnes's brother, the effect it was having on her mother, father and younger brother.

He sat for nearly three hours. Thinking, hoping Agnes would come out. He just wanted to hold her in his arms and protect her.

As he rose stiffly from the step, he heard the sound of a window frame above, open slowly.

"Roger," came the voice in almost a whisper. "I love you!" before Agnes closed the window without another word.

Roger looked up at the window, but Agnes had already slumped back on her bed. He walked out of the front gate and pushed the Norton a hundred yards or more, not wanting the growl of the engine to intrude on the solemnity of the row of terrace houses with the small, neat gardens.

"She loves me. That's the first time a girl has said that to me. This is different, but a nice different," he thought to himself, as he slammed back the throttle of the Norton and rode over Shaws Bridge faster than ever before.

At breakfast he broke the news to his mother and father, telling them he intended going to the service on Monday morning. Anna looked across at Davy, who read her mind.

"We'll go with you Roger. Young Agnes is one of my nurses, Gerri Muldoon might want to be there too," sighed Davy.

The mourners filed into the pews at Knockbreda Parish. The church was almost full by ten minutes before ten on the Monday morning. Bertie Miller had turned his head from the alter and surveyed the faces behind him. He gave a nod to his workmates from the Sirocco Works He was about to turn and face the front again when he saw a group entering and slide into the back row; trying unsuccessfully, to draw as little attention as possible.

Roger, led the group, followed by Anna, Davy, Bill, Jonty, Allen, Adam, Martha and Gerri Muldoon.

Mr Miller turned to face the alter as he bent his head to whisper to Margaret. Agnes looked round at the same time as her mother to see a back row of men, all wearing their Medals of an earlier conflict and Anna, in the uniform she wore at the Cenotaph each year, complete with her medals. Agnes caught Roger's eyes, full of compassion for

273

her, and pride at being able to give her brother the best respects he could muster.

The chief mourners turned back to the alter as the vicar proceeded to the front. Martha gave Gerri a nudge with her elbow.

"Looks like you and me aren't half dressed without our medals. Lord knows I deserve a few, with Jonty," she whispered.

Never wanting to miss the opportunity to make light of a difficult situation. Gerri nudged her back.

"Don't thing a medal with the King's mug[21] on it would go down too well in our house. I'll give them a miss, Martha." she whispered back.

At the end of the service the mourners passed the Miller family at the vestibule exit. Each in turn, shook hands with them. All with the exception of Rogers group, knew the family and needed no introduction.

As the line came to near the end, Roger led the group, to pay their respects. They shook their hands and explained who they were. Davy and Anna were the last two in the line. Davy, introduced himself,

---

[21] Belfast slang for a face.

"David Gibson, I'm Roger's father, and Agnes here, is one of my best 'wee' nurses. "Isn't that right, Agnes?" as he placed a reassuring hand on her shaking shoulder.

Agnes gave him a tearful attempt to smile. Bertie Miller looked on down the line at the woman about his own age in her nurses jacket and medals.

"Hello Mr Miller, I am Roger's mother, Anna Gibson. I do hope he has not been making a nuisance of himself.

"He hasn't, Mrs Gibson," sobbed Agnes, from beyond her father.

Mr Miller gave Anna a knowing smile, before Anna gave Margaret Miller a hug and moved on to Agnes.

Agnes offered her hand, as Anna cradled her in her arms, like her own Kathleen.

"Just think of the good memories, Agnes, Trust me, I know," consoled Anna.

As the group broke away, Bertie, stepped forward and grabbed Roger by the arm.

"Thank you, son. I didn't know what to make of you. Sorry I doubted you. Tell your ones' to head over to our house, for a cup of tea. I'll get you a proper cup, not an 'aul mug!" sighed Bertie, before he turned to speak to some of his work mates from Sirocco.

Roger walked slowly behind his group, content that the show of strength of the Arthur clan had worked. Grandpa James would be proud of him, he thought to himself.

Chapter eighteen

The Long Winter

On the last Sunday in June, Davy, Anna and Roger, sat in the drawing room with the evening sun of summer glinting through the French windows.

Roger sat, bracing himself for the mental torment he was about to suffer as his parents would not accept his insistance that he was going to war, with or without their approval. It would be painful, but war is painful, he thought to himself. Davy, started the conversation.

"Well Roger this is your D Day. What is happening about this 'joining up caper?" asked Davy, face straight, as he sipped his glass of Bushmills. Anna sat silent, glass of her favourite Chablis at the small table beside her chair.

Roger shifted nervously in his chair, before he sat forward and forced the words out of his mouth.

"Neither of you want me to go. Agnes is begging me not to go. Even Mr Miller is saying to leave it, that Agnes has suffered enough."

Roger, hesitated, as he shook his head ruefully.

"I have to go. I don't want to go, not when I see what it is doing to Agnes and you, Mum, but I have an obligation, a duty; a need, to play some part in defeating this evil. If I don't I would be betraying myself and I would not be the person you think I am. I am sorry but you will both, as will Agnes, have to accept me and my decisions, my responsibilities."

Roger paused and squinted as he tried to look out of the French windows. He was expecting a sudden response of disapproval from his parents. There was no reaction, just a silence. He began to speak again, confused by the lack of a response.

"I have to gain the credibility of the Arthur name, or I will not hold any respect. Grandpa James would understand if he was here!" he announced in frustration as he directed the comment to his father.

A silence returned briefly. He had said all he could say. He had made his case to his father. He did not look his mother in the face.

"That's fine, it's decided. When will you be leaving, Roger?" asked Anna, as she reached for her glass of Chablis to take a small sip.

Her manner was as serious as if she was deciding what to have for dinner. Roger turned his gaze from his father to his mother; surprised at her reaction. He had run through his brain all the possible questions and demands his mother and father would throw at him. This situation was not in his thinking.

Anna, let the silence hang, before she gave Davy a discreet dip of her head in approval that Davy put Roger out of his misery.

"Roger, you are a good lad, we are both proud of you. Proud of your efforts back at the Blitz. Proud of the way you have kept your word, not to rhyme on about joining up.. Proud of the way you have been a gentleman in your dealings with young Agnes. Proud of the way you stand up to us, without getting silly about it."

Davy looked at his son, right into his eyes.

"However, you are only eighteen, almost nineteen, and a lot to learn before you will be one step ahead of either of us. Here is the situation. It is not a deal. It is not negotiable.

I, have made an arrangement with Major Montgomery, my Captain at the Somme, He has organised it that you will be appointed to Brigade Staff on completion of your officer training. You understand what that means without me going into the details. In essence, it means that you will be doing your bit in the war, but your mother, and Agnes, will have less to worry about than they already do, when you hammer that Norton over Shaws Bridge. To the world back here, when the war is over, you will have been seen to have done your bit. No one will be any the wiser," explained Davy.

Roger sat gathering his thoughts.

"But that means I would be getting special treatment. That is not fair!" exclaimed Roger, full of indignation.

Davy was about to respond, before Anna interrupted.

"Enough Roger, Enough!" raising her voice in frustration, unable to maintain her calm façade, before she continued.

"The world is not fair, otherwise, your Uncle Roger would be down at the lake painting or strolling through the rose beds. Jonty, would be getting ready to race at Down Royal.[22] Bill would be able to hear with both ears and not suffer from blinding headaches, without warning. Poor Kitty wouldn't be waiting for a lifetime to be with Joe," she scolded.

"And me, I wouldn't have become so overly fond of this bloody Chablis!" Anna sank the rest of the glass and poured herself another, her hand shaking so that some of it splashed on the small table and dripped onto the carpet below.

Davy lent forward into his son's face.

---

[22] Horse racing course in Northern Ireland

"Welcome to the world of the grownups, Roger. When you play Monopoly with Kathleen and Joseph, do you turn down a 'get out of jail free' card. There'll be plenty of times in life things won't go your way. Don't through away good fortune.

"Only you, the Major, your Mum and me, need to know. Army rules, son!" assured Davy.

"I think, dinner is ready, gentlemen," announced Anna, as she regained her poise.

Roger went in ahead of them. He had just got his appetite back.

Davy and Anna followed behind, holding each other, relieved that their plans seemed to be working out.

They were not to know the twist of fate that would awaited their son.

Roger said goodbye to his mother and father in early July. Like Davy and his uncle Roger before him, he bid his 'fair wells' from Ballydrain. The only face at the Donegall Quay in Belfast that he said goodbye to was, Agnes. Roger was leaning against his kit bag on the quayside, taking in what he hoped would not be his last sight of Belfast. He felt a sharp tug on his arm. As he turned ,Agnes had already begun to embrace him.

"Agnes, I thought you were on shift this morning. Thought last night was the best we could manage."

"I'll be here when you get back, Roger. That's a date. Don't stand me up, Rodge," whispered Agnes, using her pet name for him.

"Fully intend to; get back I mean. No chance I'd stand you up, 'Nancy' Miller, assured Roger.

"Willie, will be watching over you. Told him to, last night," replied Agnes, as she planted a loving kiss deep into his mouth. The beautiful moment was abruptly interrupted by a taunting shout from behind them.

"Roger, get a move on. The war can't wait for your love life!" shouted a fellow cadet he knew from school.

Roger gave her a last hug as they parted. He grabbed his kit bag and joined the queue walking up the gangway. He looked back several times to see Agnes waving discreetly to him. She didn't want it to be a wave for all to see, just Roger.

As he disappeared inside the boat, she turned and walked as fast as she could, eyes full of tears. She had done her best to give him a last show of her love. To watch the boat disappear over the horizon was more than she could cope with

Chapter nineteen

The Po Valley

While Roger went off for Officer training until December, before taking up his post with Brigade Staff in Europe, Alec Price, attached to the Eighth Army, Desert Rats had travelled the length of Italy from Sicily, the crossing at Messina to mainland Italy and on to Monte Cassino, Rome and finally to the North of Italy and the German last stand in the Po region in the Spring of 1945. It was a strategic place of vital importance to the Germans rear guard action. It blocked the way of advancing Tito's Yugoslavs force from the Balkans, covered the French borders of the Cote D'Azur, but most importantly the escape route and supply routes through Switzerland and Austria. The Swiss government may well have been neutral, but if German troops and supplies wanted to pass through unopposed, there was nothing they could or would do about it.

Alec and his fellow Special Forces were involved in what they were trained. Reconnaissance and sabotage behind the lines was their bread and butter. The further they got northwards they had an additional task;

one they found the most difficult. Going in advanced parties locating mine fields and booby traps in villages and towns. Alec and his unit had survived it all because they had always done their homework on the raids and incursions behind the lines they would the take part in. By early April 1945 the German army, packed in the Po Valley, had their backs to the Alps and could only hold their ground as they gave the remains of their beleaguered force time to beat a steady retreat through the Alps to regroup and fight to the end in the fatherland.

Alec and his comrades would not say it, but they began to think to themselves, that the odds had improved that they might just get back home to their farms, favourite hostelries, sports clubs, old flames, wives and girlfriends. The only negative thought was that knowing their special skills, they could probably be packed off to the Far East to grind out a campaign with Japan.

The less they dwelt on that prospect the better, was the general thinking. Alec began to think he might actually get back home and take the job he had wanted that had been side lined by Adolf and his cronies, as he described the Nazis.

He had grown up wanting to be a policeman. He liked the idea of stopping the 'Bad Boys'. The odd scrap, especially after what he had been through for four years, did not cause him any apprehension. The odd street riot would, to him, have a degree of entertainment. His quick brain, gave him the confidence that he could progress through the ranks. The sooner this was all over the better. Back home, find a girl to enjoy his company, and sign up for the Royal Ulster Constabulary was his next mission.

Plans don't always work out exactly in the manner expected.

In what would be the last months of the war in Europe, Staff Sergeant Alexander Price sat in a corner of a makeshift room a few miles behind the front lines listening to instructions and asking questions. Their mission was heavy duty, not a case of slipping behind the lines, assessing the opposition defences, minefields and get out.

This mission was riskier than most, but it had the potential to help finish the war in Italy once and for all. It would also cut off the remaining Germans attempting to slip back to their homeland and drag the war out longer.

"So that is it, gentlemen!" rasped the Major. "Nip in behind their lines, sabotage their exit routes, stop any supplies coming through," he continued in a tone of complete indifference.

The group of commandos sat silent, most looking at the ground, smoking their cigarettes.

"Ehh, Major, Sir? asked Alec, "While we are over there making life difficult for the bastards, what will the rest of the boys be doing?"

"The 'rest of the boys' as you describe them, will be hitting them with everything we have, and if you lads do your bit they won't be able to escape. They will surrender and we will join up with you all for the biggest piss up in Italy," replied the Major, attempting, but failing, to give the impression the whole plan would be a simple fait accompli.

A silence returned for a few seconds.

"One other question, Major, if you don't mind," continued Alec. "If it doesn't go to plan. What is our exit strategy? Usually we have one. It seems there is no mention of it up to now," sighed Alec, as he put his hands behind his neck and leant back. He waited for the Major's reply. The Major shifted in his chair.

"When you have your bit done, you dig in and wait for us to reach you. Hide out until they surrender. If you try and get back through you'll get in the way of our attack, Staff Sergeant," rasped the Major, who was getting a bit annoyed at the questions. Alec, being his father's son, was not bothered if the Major was annoyed or not.

"One final thing, Sir. What's the options if it all goes belly up and you don't reach us, Sir?"

"Price, you have served in this regiment for longer than I have. I believe you know the answer to that." The Major spoke without any sense of angst, just resignation.

Alec took a long draw on his cigarette, looked around at some of his comrades that had fought alongside him since Messina.

"Get the drift boys!" growled Alec, before he turned back to look at the Major and continued.

"So we need to do a good job over there and the rest of the battalion better do their bit, or this could turn into another mess like the Somme my Da and my uncles told me about," announced Alec.

"That is it in a nutshell," agreed the Major, as he gave them all a respectful nod.

The room went silent again as Alec and his comrades began to rise from the floor of the makeshift operations room.

As they walked outside, Jim Wilson, a young private who had only been in the unit for a few weeks, moved alongside Alec.

"Sarge, what did he mean when he said, "You know the answer to that?" asked a confused Wilson.

"If we find ourselves outnumbered against Wehrmacht troops we can surrender. If it's SS troops we can't," explained Alec, without moving his eyes from the pavement in front of him.

"If it's SS troops and it goes belly up, we aren't coming home, son. We go down taking as many of them as we can with us. Surrender isn't an option with those bastards," continued Alec.

"Right kid, think it's time I bought you a beer. You can owe me one when we get this over and done with. Is that a deal?" grinned Alec, in a vain attempt to reduce the lad's sense of doom.

A week later after they had practiced the incursion and familiarised themselves with the target arrears enough that they could have got their almost blindfolded, they sat in the dark amongst the bullrushes of the south bank of the PO river near Piacenza, waiting to be rowed across on flat boats, hidden by a dark moonless night sky.

The crossing went smoothly, as the German forces were sufficiently depleted that the night watch was thinly spread.

As they regrouped, Alec led his platoon of men beyond the north bank as they ventured towards their selected target. The other platoons disappeared into the darkness intent on locating their own target zone.

"So far so good," thought Alec to himself, as they approached a track that they had seen on their maps. Alec led the way several yards ahead of the platoon, all in single file behind him. They had been instructed to melt into the bushes if Alec gave a signal.

Still on the track they could see the first of the targets, a fuel dump. It didn't take long to place explosives and a timer detonator on the nearest fuel tank. A small timed explosive charge would set off a chain reaction that would take the whole dump out and distract the Germans from the commando unit who by then had moved off to target number two.

After the unit completed their sabotage of the fuel dump they moved to their main target, a bridge crossing an estuary that flowed into the Po River. More importantly a bridge that allowed access to the Swiss border and Alpine passes beyond. It was hoped that the distraction of the blazing fuel dump would make the task easier for the Special Operations.

Lying in the ditches near the bridge, they smiled to themselves as the sentries rushed to deal with the blaze down the road they had come from.

When the time was right they moved towards the target, crouching and trying to keep below the skyline of the background.

The team got to a small strip of open ground within fifty yards of the bridge. Without warning the sky lit up with explosions from flares in the night sky. At the same, the ground around the unit began to explode as mortar shells landed amongst them. Alec instinctively ran to dive into a deep ditch at the edge of the open ground. His last memory was being in mid-air as his eyes sought out the bottom of the ditch.

Chapter twenty

Nightmare

It was the middle of the night in the gate house of Ballydrain. Jonty was sound asleep after a long day supervising the collection of the first crops of early potatoes from the not now so hallowed slopes of the Estate, reinforced by a few beers with Adam and Allen in the stable yard. Martha sat upright beside him, in silence. She had been woken by a sudden bang, which lifted her from her sleep with a lurch that made her sit up in her bed. Her head hurt and she felt an excruciating cramp build up from the back of her hip. It gripped and tore like a dagger, deep into her muscle and tore at her hip bone. She had sat gritting her teeth and stifled a moan as the sensation eased and disappeared as fast as it came. She continued to sit in silence not wanting to waken Jonty.

It was not the first, nor would it be the last time, she would be woken by the arthritic pain and bad circulation which was one of the downsides of being a woman carrying a large frame around her strong hips. The wear and tear, was beginning to take its toll. The heavy noise of a bang, like the slamming of a door, was the bit she had not experienced before. She sat upright and decided a cup of tea was the best remedy in the circumstances. As she pulled her legs over the side of the bed to shuffle her feet to find her slippers, Jonty emerged from his sleep.

"I'll take one as well, girl," he muttered, his face still buried in the pillow. Jonty had never been a deep sleeper since the Somme. The slightest noise or movement would waken him. On any other occasion Martha would have given him a cheeky rebuff before making him his tea. This time she was not in the mood. Her head was full of anxiety, but she could not work out the source of the feeling.

As she made the brew, Jonty pulled himself upright and hobbled into the kitchen where he saw Martha, hands around the steaming cup sitting at the table. He slumped himself into the kitchen chair as he grabbed the cup of tea that was sitting waiting for him.

"What has you up in the middle of the night, Mattie?" asked Jonty, as he put his arm around her shoulder. "What's annoying you. Have I put my one foot in it again?"

Martha, uncharacteristically did not reply with one of her usual reposts. She sat head buried in her hands. Jonty realised it must be serious and not the time for clever comments. He sat silent as he continued to caress her shoulders and back.

"Something has happened to Alec, Jonty. I just know it," announced Martha, her face still looking at the table and her head still in her hands.

"Ach Mattie, you've had a nightmare, girl," assured Jonty, as he tried to cradle her in his arms.

"It doesn't feel like a nightmare. It feels more than that, Jonty," she explained, still staring at the table.

They both sat in silence arms wrapped around each other. It was one of those rare occasions that Jonty put Martha to bed a full hour later as dawn was almost rising.

When he crossed the Po River the Major of Alec's Special Forces unit was intent on only one mission, to find his men and extricate them, if they had survived the attack. None had returned to report. He hoped they had dug in and waited as ordered. He knew the group had completed their two objectives, blowing the fuel dump and taking the bridge out of action, but he was well aware they would possibly have paid the ultimate price. While he had always maintained an air of detachment from his men, as he had been trained back in 1940, when he was conscripted from his job as a civil engineer, his concern for the welfare of his men consumed his every thought. He knew them all by name, knew where they were from, knew their background and their hopes and aspirations after the war. How cruel it would be if they had got this close to the end of the war and not survived it. Some of them had been there since the early days. Alec Price, his Staff Sergeant, was one of those. Price had often been a source of angst on many an occasion for his cleaver remarks at the worst possible times, his impertinence, and his several attempts to wreck a bar when off the front line. For all this, the Major and the rest of the unit liked the big Ulsterman who hated being called Paddy. Alec was an Ulsterman, being called Paddy was to him, an insult. He was no Irishman. No one ever called him that twice and stayed upright.

As the Major got within site of the bridge he scanned the horizon for any of his men. He could see some sitting on the edge of shell holes sitting sharing a cigarette, others helping wounded comrades amongst the smoke, burning wood and twisted metal. A rough head count said about ten were still available to take on whatever was asked of them. Another fifteen, where injured but didn't seem to be in any danger of dying. That meant that the rest, about another twenty who were still to be accounted for. Staff Sergeant Price, was one he had still not either seen, nor more likely heard. As he got amongst his men, he counted six or seven more that were dead. He tried to identify them by, tags, insignia, faces, if possible. The German mortar attack had reaped serious havoc amongst his elite troop. Still no sign of Price, he walked amongst a group of relieved smokers, who began to rise from their positions.

"Stand easy lads, finish your smoke," ordered the Major, before he continued. "I reckon there are about a dozen missing. What do you reckon?

"That's about right, Sir. Haven't seen the Sarg, or the lad that just joined us a few weeks ago," replied one of the commandos, as he took another drag from his cigarette and let the smoke blow out of his nostrils. The Major looked briefly to the sky before he began to walk beyond the group, towards the riverbank of the bridge. The rest of the smokers took the hint and followed him.

The Major, had the benefit of a sun rise as he surveyed the steep drop between the top of the bank and the river. It had been pitch dark when the surviving commandos had dug in as the main force reached them. He sat on his hunkers and searched the bank and river. His eyes concentrated on the areas that there had been explosions, the most likely source of any casualties.

"There's something over there, Major!" shouted one of the unit. "I can see boots. There's more than one of them. See there, amongst the reeds!"

They scrambled down amongst the boots. They could see four combat boots close together. They were relieved to find that both were attached to bodies. They were both face down. One was a Private laying half across a body lying motionless, face down. They slowly lifted him off the soldier below him. They set him down on the grass bank beside the river. To the relief of the Major he opened his glazed eyes.

His attention turned to the other body lying face down in the mud. Sergeant's stripes visible on one arm. He touched the body to feel for a pulse and looked across the river as he waited, hoping he would find one. He could feel nothing.

"Come on you daft Irish bollocks. Just one more sortie and you can go home," whispered the Major. The three commandos around him looked at each other, unsure of what could be done. The Major continued to look for a pulse.

"Come on Paddy, you can do it. Medic over here now!"

The medic dropped into the steep bottom of the riverbank, as a muffled voice came up from the mud.

"I'll chin the next man that calls me Paddy" before the voice fell back into unconsciousness.

It was five days before Alec woke in a hospital bed with clean sheets and the voice of a Belfast girl drifting into his head. He opened his eyes briefly and could see a concerned, compassionate girl, staring into his face. He was about to attempt to speak as a thermometer was

297

stuffed unceremoniously into his mouth. The nurse waited before she pulled it out. Read it, lifted the chart at the bottom of the bed, and as she walked away said,

"Glad you are back in the land of the living, sleepy head!" as she smiled back at Alec.

"Ah Jeez, I thought I'd died and gone to heaven," replied a groggy Alec before he fell back to sleep again. The Nurse smiled again and shook her head as she walked past a doctor checking a patient further down the ward.

"The patient in bed four has come round. Don't think you have to worry about any brain damage."

Five days earlier, Alec had been given triage at a field hospital. He had a gaping wound in his hip, clean to the bone, The result of a large piece of metal ripping into him as he dived to avoid the mortar attack. That was repairable with the skills of a good surgeon, but the extent of his head injury was the greater concern. He had fallen into a comatose state as he was dragged from the riverbank. The dent in his helmet told that he had taken the impact of some heavy object on the helmet. The result was that there was no outward wound, but the brain would have suffered a degree of movement within the skull. There was no facility for potential brain injury treatment if it was needed. In Alec's case it was best to keep him sedated and see if the trauma in the head would settle itself when he woke. Either way his war was over.

Word of Alec's 'return to the land of the living' got back to Davy as he sat in his office in the City Hospital. Soldiers, with injuries in battle that would render them unfit for combat in the longer term were quickly removed from the frontline hospitals and returned to hospitals near their homes. Alec's injuries left him in that category.

By the evening, as Davy reached the gatehouse of Ballydrain, He stopped his Ford and walked to the door. He was about to knock it but the door opened first. Martha looked apprehensively into his eyes.

"He's awake and talking. I'll be back down in an hour to take you up to the City. He's on the mend, " announced Davy with a smile.

Martha burst out in tears as she hugged Davy.

"Hay, get your hands off my woman, big lad. You've got one of your own. Don't get greedy," shouted Jonty, as he hobbled to the door. Davy smiled and waved as he got back into the car looking forward to telling Anna the good news.

In the days that followed, Alec's knock to the brain recovered. His hip was another matter. He wasn't in danger of losing it, but the damage could mean his hope of joining the Royal Ulster Constabulary was in serious jeopardy. He could be left with a weakness in the hip that would mean he would not pass the Police Medical Board.

John Clarke and Davy sat in Clarke's office one morning studying the X rays of the shattered bone, which should heal but the muscle and ligaments were ripped apart. How to repair this enough for him to even bluff his way through a medical was the dilemma. They decided another close look at the gaping wound was required.

"I'll bring Muldoon to listen and learn on this Clarkey, if you don't mind," suggested Davy.

Later that day, John Clarke, Gerri Muldoon and Davy stood around Alec as he lay on his side, wound side up. Alec was already caught in two minds.

"What was the bad news he was about to hear" and at the same time, "I could take this nurse, with the dark hair and even darker brown eyes for a stroll some evening when I get back on my feet. Very nice indeed."

Davy knew Alec too well and could see that he was not fully focused on the forthcoming discussion.

"Right Alec, kid, this is Dr John Clarke and this is Gerri Muldoon the best surgical nurse in this place. I need you to listen to John here, as it's better coming from him. I'm too close to you for a bit of independent thinking," advised Davy, as he looked over at John and Muldoon.

John Clarke, in his short to the point tone, explained that if they left nature to heal itself, Alec would be able to function with normal everyday mobility except for a degree of pain in cold weather. Enough for anyone in normal circumstances to enjoy life to the full, but The RUC[23] was out of the question, unless he was prepared to take a risk on remedial surgery which would either correct the problem and just about get him through the Medical Board requirements or leave him with a permanent limp for the rest of his life. The choice was his to make.

---

[23] Royal Ulster Constabulary

At the end of the monologue from John Clarke, Alec focused on the bed side cabinet to his left and said nothing for several seconds, before he glanced up at Davy and John Clarke.

"I'll take my chance on getting this fixed on one condition," announced Alec. The three at the bedside all stared at Alec awaiting for his condition. Alec began to smile slowly; his father's glint in his eyes.

"As long as the nurse here takes me a walk round Botanic Gardens. It would be part of my recuperation," announced Alec, as he gave Gerri a look of admiration. Davy and John looked at each other and shook their heads in disbelief and embarrassment for Muldoon.

Muldoon, being well capable of looking after herself, and having been on the receiving end of much worse suggestions in her short life, let out a muffled laugh of irony, as she replied.

"Botanic Gardens it is then, Mr Price. Hope you are up for a bit of rigorous exercise. No shirking or the deal is off," retorted Muldoon, as she backed away from the bedside before she looked at Davy.

"I've a prep for an operation to sort out in twenty minutes. I'm away unless you need me for anything else."

Muldoon turned her back to walk away, as Alec was about to attempt further embarrassment on the nurse, Davy gave him a look that said, "Don't even think about it."

Gerri Muldoon, meanwhile, as she disappeared into the corridor, cursed under her breath. "Me, walking around with an RUC man. My mother would have a fit, and my Da, he'd never be able to show his face in the pub again. What have I agreed to?"

When Gerri disappeared out of sight, Alec looked at Davy and across to John.

"Only having a bit of fun with the 'wee' girl, Uncle Davy, you know me; too much of my Da in me," laughed Alec, in an attempt to pacify Davy, who gave him a look of ridicule.

"Might have bitten off more than you can chew there, Alec, son," laughed Davy, in Alec's face, with the slightest hint of concern.

"Why Uncle Davy? asked Alec, determined to have the final say. Davy spoke quietly enough that no one else could hear.

"St Dominic's finest, that one," whispered Davy.

Alec grinned back at Davy. "You know me. Never do anything the easy way!" he laughed.

One month later by the end of May 1945 Alec sat in the Botanic Gardens just beyond the gatehouse, at the first bench facing Lord Kelvin's statue, with a pair of hospital supplied crutches stacked against the edge. It was a fine lunch time, an early sign of summer attempting to break through.

He hadn't long to sit and reflect on the situation before Gerri appeared walking briskly through the gate past the head gardener's gate lodge. She had just had a lecture at Queens University next door to the Botanic Gardens. As she got to within a few feet of Alec, he began to rise awkwardly. He almost lost his balance, but Muldoon grabbed his arm to help him steady himself.

"Looks like we've a lot of work to do, soldier," joked Gerri.

"The more sessions the better. Might take a while then," replied Alec.

"Doctor Gibson was right, he said you would be a nightmare," sighed Gerri, with a smile.

"Right, Alec, we'll see if you can go as far as the Palm House, over to the Bandstand and back to here, for a first session. After that we'll see how it goes," instructed Gerri, attempting to maintain a professional manner.

"Don't you worry yourself, Gerri. After a few sessions I'll be chasing you round the rose beds," replied Alec, acting out his façade of confidence.

"You'll never catch me. I'm the fastest in the Camogie team!" teased Gerri, as she gripped his arm to begin his therapy session.

Inside, Alec was worried sick the operation would not be enough to get him through the medical, while at the same time saying to himself.

"This one's worth getting to know, never mind the complications. Faced worse in Tobruk and Monte Casino."

Chapter twenty-one

"Something is burning"

Back on the European mainland Roger was analysing information for a Brigadier at the mobile headquarters not far from Hamburg. The allies had driven deep into the North of Germany. It was by no means a place of refuge or safety. Germany was clearly losing, but their resistance was resolute. The advance had reached the stage that there were pockets of resistance and other areas where they had surrendered, scattered across every townland. It was difficult to know where the front lines begun or ended There was always the possibility of overextending and being cut off by German units. On some occasions groups of German Wehrmacht soldiers marched up to Allied units and surrendered. On those occasions Roger's language skills in German were in demand.

As Roger flipped over the next page, a Corporal burst open the door,

"Lieutenant Gibson, the Major needs you urgent. He says drop what you are doing. Says your skills are require up the road," said the Corporal.

Roger let the sheet of paper fall from his fingers, lifted his cap, and followed the corporal. Thirty seconds later he was standing in the Major's temporary room.

"Right Gibson, follow me and I'll explain on the way," instructed the Major as he walked past him. Roger followed on his heels, not having a clue what this was all about.

The Major pointed to a jeep that was waiting for them. Driver and a captain in the front. The Major gestured for Roger to get in the back as the wheels of the jeep spun as it began made its journey in the direction of the ever fluid German front lines.

"Need your language skills again, only this time it's not about sorting German prisoners, it's a bit trickier this time," sighed the Major, as he tried to condense the conversation to a minimum.

"We are going across to have a chat to a few concerned Germans, on their patch, actually," explained the Major, as he spat his words out when the jeep found every pothole on the damaged road.

Roger, did his best to appear calm but his sense of self- preservation began to swell in his brain.

"This should test my German, sir," replied Roger.

"We received a message from the German occupied town of Bergen. Seems they have a problem with which they cannot cope. A problem, they say, that could affect us all, on both sides," explained the Major, as he tried to light and smoke a cigarette as the jeep hit another pothole.

"Their concern is sufficient that they are offering to make the area a neutral zone, in the 'interests of public health' is all we know. The purpose of this meeting is to be informed of the finer detail," continued the Major, as he offered Roger a cigarette.

"No thank you Major, I don't smoke. Heard too many stories from my father about them. I'll give it a miss, sir, if you don't mind," apologised Roger, before he continued.

"Have you any idea what it is, Sir?"

The Major, took a few draws on his cigarette. "Not sure, Gibson, but it might be something to do with what the Soviets are rumoured to be coming across in Poland and Eastern Germany. I sincerely hope it is not," sighed the Major, as he lowered his head.

Roger gazed out of the side of the open top vehicle and said nothing.

The jeep continued along the road, before the Captain, sitting in the front, spoke only five words, all without turning round to the Major or Roger, still fixing his gaze on the road ahead.

"Best not to shake hands."

Roger noticed he was from the Medical Corps. He had failed to pick up on this earlier as he was engrossed in the Majors instructions.

"Had no intentions of it, especially if they are SS," spat the Major with venom in his tone.

"Nothing to do with etiquette, Major. It's a medical reason. Contagion is the concern," the Army medical doctor replied, still keeping his words to a minimum. Most of his brain was occupied with how to deal with what was probably coming.

As they passed beyond the next bend, they could see a German army vehicle sitting in the road ahead with a flag of truce on the roof and a tall German officer stand at ease, with no visible sign of carrying any weapon.

"Stop ten yards ahead of them, let the three of us out and turn this jalopy round, just in case this doesn't work out well, Corporal," instructed the Major.

"Right Gibson, let's see how good your German is, young man."
The Major walked slowly toward the German officer of the same Rank as himself. Roger and the Doctor walked a foot behind him on either side.

"Good morning Major, I understand we have, what has been described to me as a mutual medical issue of some importance," he said, as he turned to Roger and gave him a nod. Roger interpreted the Major's words to the German officer. He in turn spoke to a young German Lieutenant who replied to Roger.

"There is a breakout of typhus in this area which we are unable to control, and we consider it prudent to ask for your cooperation in a difficult situation and in changing times."

The Major looked at Roger sideways. "Ask him how many cases, are we talking about," he instructed.

Roger passed on the request. His counterpart looked at his own Major, who gave him permission to answer. The expression on the German senior officer's face suggested that the information was more than likely to be the truth; the body language gave the impression of complete deflation.

" Nine thousand confirmed, possibly as many again infected, but not yet confirmed. We cannot cope. Either to treat them or more importantly to contain them. Our fear is that if this area becomes a battlefield the group involved will disperse and spread the contagion in all directions," explained the young officer in a tone devoid of any emotion. He could have been a bank clerk refusing a loan.

"How many have died?" asked Roger, without referring to the Major.

"Thirty thousand, at a rough estimate," replied the Lieutenant, a little too 'matter of fact' to Roger's liking.

"Thirty thousand, at a rough estimate. What do you mean, a rough fucking estimate!" shouted Roger in the face of his counterpart.

The German Major glared at the British Major, with an expression which said, "keep your dog under control!"

The Major, looked at Roger. "What kicked that off, Gibson!"

Roger explained what the German translator had said. The British Major looked to the ground for a few seconds, then to the heavens, as if looking for some spiritual guidance. Preferably, he thought, a few lightning bolts slamming into the enemy officers standing before him.

"Tell him I make no apologies for your reaction. Ask them to come to the point. Is there a Death Camp up the road?"

"No it is not a Death Camp!" replied the offended officer interpreter.

"It is a Labour Camp for criminals, enemies of the Reich, and undesirables." The sense of being personally insulted swelled from his neck muscles.

The British Major turned his back on the German officers as he looked back at the driver of his jeep, who had, as instructed earlier already his machine gun resting flat on his knees. He scratched his left breast pocket, a sign for the driver to place his finger in the trigger and be prepared for all hell to let loose. The Major spoke.

"Tell that bastard that we need to be taken to this place to assess the situation for ourselves. Tell him also, that if I consider he has any responsibility for this carnage that he will face retribution went this war ends. There will be nowhere to hide. On the other hand his full cooperation will be noted, if and when, there is an investigation into his part in it," insisted the Major.

"Major, We, as you will have noticed, are Wehrmacht soldiers, loyal to our German nation. We have, and will continue, to fight for the fatherland for as long as we are commanded. The situation at the Camp was under the control of the Waffen SS. We are not the SS. We have only become involved because they have decided that their skills can be put to better use elsewhere. We have been left "carrying the can" I think is an expression of the English," interpreted the German Lieutenant, who had now discarded the tone of superiority in his voice and changed it to one of humility and feigned innocence.

The German senior officer stood back and gestured that the British follow in their Jeep. The cortege of two vehicles travelled up the road and passed through the town of Bergen. As they drove past, Roger could see tired, shocked, resentful and deflated eyes of the local people, staring at him as they sped through. "This must be worse than what my Dad and his friend Joe had to go through in Belfast when they found themselves in the wrong place at the wrong time."

On the far side of the town, they turned off a road that led to the edge of a wood. At the end of the road deep in the wood, Roger could see barbed wire fencing and a sign across a closed entrance gate, with 'Belsen' across the top.

At the fence there was a gathering group of detainees who stared vacantly at the mixed group of British and German soldiers. They looked frightened, drained and dishevelled, but did they did not look particularly unhealthy.

"Are you sure you got the translation right, Gibson?" rasped the Major.

Roger, looked at the Major as if he was a child, an innocent. He took in a deep breath and looked at the sky.

"Well Gibson, did you interpret this correctly or are we being played here!" rasped the Major again.

"Breath in Sir. Take a deep breath. What can you smell, Sir?" asked Roger, in as calm a manner as he could manage.

The Major and the Doctor took in deep breaths. There is a certain 'wiff' of something, Gibson, but I do not have the time for games, young man. Get to the point!"

"Back home on the Lagan, down at Newforge, there is a meat factory. Once a week the carcasses are incinerated. It's the same smell, sir," exclaimed Roger, as he looked to the sky in silence before he spoke.

"I'll take one of those cigarettes now, Sir, if you still are making the offer."

The Major turned to the Medical Officer captain, who felt a little inept not having assessed the stark reality ahead of them. The captain gestured to the Major to walk over to the Jeep.

Roger concentrated on keeping his stomach from emptying as he stared at the German Major and lieutenant. All he could see in their eyes was stoney indifference.

"Major, that smell is one of burning bodies, presumably dead ones. I suggest we state our case and get out of here, as soon as possible, sir." advised the captain.

"But do we not need to inspect this situation further, Captain?" asked the Major as he drew slowly on his cigarette.

"Sir, It is clear that those prisoners at the fence are the few that are still in reasonable condition, deliberately house in an area the public can see. Gives the impression this place is just a labour camp with a food shortage. We don't need to go further to confirm the worst.

Gibson has identified that quicker than I should have done. There is nothing we can do for any of them without the manpower, medicine and a quick course of dealing with deadly diseases before anyone has to go in there. If we don't, it will be a suicide mission for us all, sir," advised the medic.

The Major shook his head up and down a few times and turned to look in the direction of Roger, who was beginning to feel a little out of place, left standing alone in front of German officers.

"Gibson, over here please!" shouted the Major. Roger was only too pleased to retreat from the German soldiers.

"Go back and tell them, that if they want our help it will only be if the area around Bergen Belsen surrenders, and a one-mile stretch either side of the road between her and our lines is also surrendered. Tell them that a truce is out of the question. That's the offer, take it or leave it. Go back and tell them that, and do not wait for a reply if it is not immediate. Get yourself back into the Jeep, and we will get the hell out of here. It will let them see it is not negotiable," ordered the Major, as he lit a cigarette and without thinking gave one to Roger. Roger gestured for a light, inhaled, coughed, and turned in the direction of the Germans. He took another drag on the cigarette

Which achieved what he had hoped. It masked the smell of burning flesh in his nostrils and mouth.

Roger repeated his Major's response and for a few brief seconds looked all three German's in front of him in the eyes before he turned to walk steadily back to the Jeep.

"How do we convey our reply, Lieutenant!" shouted the German interpreter.

"You know where we are. There's nothing to talk about. March your men to the crossing you met us at. Leave your weapons there. Then we will see what can be done!" shouted Roger, without looking round at them.

As the Jeep sped back down the road to Allied lines, the Major asked Roger.

"What was that last bit they said to you, and what did you say, Gibson?"

"They asked how they could get back to us with their response. I told them if they arrived at our lines without their weapons, that would be a start, sir," explained Roger, before he continued.

"Those bastards aren't Wehrmacht, they are SS. They have Munich accents. The one on the left, that never spoke, had a bandage on his arm. I'll bet he has a fresh burn under it to remove his tattoo.

The one that stood behind them had battle scars on his face with a medal from Stalingrad. Not a typical Wehrmacht soldier posted on guard duty."

The Major looked across at the medic. "This young man would seem to have delusions of grandeur dictating surrender terms, don't you think, Captain" announced the Major.

Roger froze, as he realised he had overstepped the mark. The adrenalin rush created by the whole event had taken him over.

"If it works out that is what they do, Gibson, I will personally see to it you get upgraded to Captain. On the other hand, if it goes belly up you will be on the lead tank on the next push!" scoffed the Major.

On the morning of the 15th April 1945, Allied troops, with as much medical assistance as they could gather, arrived at the outer perimeter fence. The soldiers stared at the inmates, trying to take in what they were witnessing. The inmates, stared back, eyes mixed with hope, uncertainty, fear, and degradation. The soldiers uncertain of what was next to come, the labour camp inmates, drained of all sense of anything.

The Allies passed through the outer fence and the area known as Camp One. It was full of new and recent arrivals gathered up from recent arrest, those who had not yet fallen to the horrors of labour camp disease and starvation. This was the view the outside world would see.

The scene that awaited them in Camp Two was unimaginable, unexplainable, and would live in the minds of those present for the rest of their lives, leaving scars in their brain as deep as lumps of shrapnel in flesh.

By the time Bergen Belsen was burnt down and bulldozed several weeks later, sixty thousand souls had perished. The Camp had been erased from the landscape. For the inmates, survivors and their liberators, the memories could not be erased as easily.

Chapter twenty-two

Loose ends

By June 1945 the war in Europe had ended. This time, unlike the Somme, all at Ballydrain had managed to pick up their lives and look to the future. Alec was progressing with his hip repair and his relationship with Gerri Muldoon had grown into an unlikely double act.

Roger was still out in Germany, his talents as an interpreter with Brigade support meant his return home was delayed with the process of surrender. He did not get leave until September.

Agnes, while relieved he had survived the war, spent the longest summer in life, waiting for him to return, She took on every extra shift she could get at the City Hospital just to keep her mind busy; fill the time. Every day he was not home was a day too long.

When the Heysham boat slid slowly to the dock and the gangways were lowered to the quayside, Roger leaned against the side of the boat looking at the crowd waiting for passengers to disembark. He couldn't see anyone he knew in the faces looking up. He spread his gaze wider towards Queens Square. He smiled when he could see a Rolls Royce parked beside Tedford's. He could see there was no one inside the front seats. "They are down at the dock side somewhere" he thought to himself in relief and satisfaction.

Roger stepped on to the corn strewn dockside, as he resisted the urge to get down on his knees to kiss the ground.

He breathed out and surveyed the crowd, too many to allow him to focus properly, before he began to walk out of the dock side hanger to Donegall Quay in the direction of the waiting Rolls Royce. At the same time he felt a tap on his shoulder, his first thought was Agnes, but he turned to find his mother, smiling at him as she leant forward to hug him. Davy was standing smiling at him from behind Anna.

He released his grip from his mother, his eyes searching, hoping Agnes was nearby. He did his best to hide his disappointment, but not well enough for Davy to not to notice.

As he stepped forward to his father, Davy gave him a slap on his shoulder. "What's with the Captain bit, son?" joked Davy, avoiding giving him the sort of hug Anna had planted on him. Davy, was old school.

"That's' a story for another day, Dad," sighed Roger, in almost a whisper, before he tried to discreetly, scan his eyes for Agnes.

All three turned side by side to walk along the quay side.

Davy gave Anna a look, lifting his eyebrows and nodding in the direction of the Rolls.

"Roger, you go ahead and stick your kit in the back of the motor. I've just seen someone your mother and me need to speak to. See you over there in a few minutes," suggested Davy, as they both released their grip from their son.

Roger walked to the Rolls, opened the back seat door, and threw his bag inside without looking into the car as he proceeded to lean against it, sadden by Agnes not being there to greet him.

The same door he had closed after dumping in the bag, opened slowly at his side before the kit bag dropped out on to the ground.

He turned to look into the open rear door. Agnes was sitting inside, smiling at him.

Neither spoke as they wrapped themselves in each other's arms.

The feeling of oneness said all that needed to be said.

When they finally released each other from their grips. Roger spoke.

"Nancy Miller, I do not want to ever be separated from you again," sighed Roger. Agnes smiled back and gave him one of those kisses that let him know exactly how she felt.

Roger could see through the rearview mirror that his mother and father were walking slowly arm in arm smiling between themselves.

Agnes grabbed her handkerchief, gave it a lick and wiped her lipstick off Roger's face. Roger stepped out of the car to greet his parents, giving Agnes the chance to fix her lips and adjust her best Sunday suit, before she stepped out of the car in a vain attempt to appear quite the proper 'butter wouldn't melt in my mouth" young lady.

Right, you two, back up for breakfast before Agnes and me get back up to the City and heal the sick. Right Agnes!" ordered Davy, as he noticed the telltale signs of red lipstick on his son's collar and laughed to himself.

That weekend Roger and Agnes had their first chance to have a day out together. They walked down the towpath to Shaws Bridge, trying to pick up where they left off, wrapped in their own cocoon of togetherness; but something was just not right.

Agnes had noticed that Roger, below the façade of a carefree youth, was not the same person he was before he left. He loved her, she had no doubt about that, but he was holding something back. He seemed distant at times, drifting off into his own thoughts. His manner was different. Something was bothering him, but he wasn't saying.

"Are you all right, Roger, you don't seem yourself. What's got you down in your boots. The war is over, there's nothing to be sad about, please tell me," asked Agnes, as she walked across him and stopped, placing both her hands in his, as she looked in concern into his eyes.

"It's nothing Agnes, My head is still a bit full of the war. It'll clear soon. I'm sorry I'm not being myself. Just give me a bit of time to adjust. Take in the fact that I'm with the loveliest girl in the whole world and nothing else matters. I don't want this to end Nancy Miller, ever," confided Roger, as they began a long embrace, standing on the edge of the river, only stopping as they saw an elderly couple walk arm in arm in their direction.

They passed Shaws Bridge and walked down to his grandfather's cottage and sat on the bench beside the lock gates.

"Three generations of Gibson's have sat at this bench; maybe there'll be a forth or a fifth for all I know," whispered Roger, face turned to the sky, as Agnes maintained a grip under his arm.

324

"I hope Granda Tom can see us sitting here. I hope he likes what he sees, Nancy Miller. I know he would approve," continued Roger, as he released his arm from Agnes's protective grip and placed it round her shoulder, caressing the side of her face.

They sat in silence, Agnes, just enjoying the moment, Roger still torn between the present and the past.

Then, without warning, Roger jumped to his feet and rushed to the side of the lock gate, hung over it and retched into the waters of the canal as he removed the contents of a good breakfast from his stomach.

Agnes, like any good nurse put her arms around his stomach, bent his head forward to help him get rid of any residue. She had already pulled her handkerchief from her pocket and begun to wipe his mouth.

"Come on Roger, take a seat and settle yourself," she cajoled.

"No let's just get out of here. Get me out of here Agnes!" he pleaded as he began to stagger away from the cottage and almost ran up the lane opposite, to the Milltown Road.

Agnes, with her much shorter legs had to run alongside him, as she gripped his arm.

When they got to the top of the lane , Agnes pulled him to a halt.

"What was that all about? Talk to me, Rodger. Get it out of your head, like you just got rid of that breakfast!" scolded Agnes.

Rodger, looked at her as he failed to hold back tears in his eyes.

"They burnt them, Agnes. They burnt them and I had to help them burn more. Thousands of them Agnes, thousands of them. I was one of the ones that entered the camp. The smell, Agnes, it was the same as the meat factory at Newforge down there. It just hit me. Should have remembered it was this day of the week. I'll know better than to go down there this day of the week.

Agnes gripped and soothed him like a patient in the City.

"Seems like your head needs a bit of nursing, Roger," assured Agnes.

Roger wiped his eyes with his forearm as they sat on the wall, giving him time to clear his thoughts.

"It might take a while, Agnes," replied Roger as he straightened himself.

"I'll be here for you, as long as it takes," assured Agnes.

"Could take a lifetime," mocked Roger, as he tried to regain his confident pretence.

"Might do," replied Agnes, refusing to be embarrassed by his wit.

"Walk me up to Edenderry and we can see if there's anyone to save from drowning. It's a form of therapy they say," smiled Agnes.

"Really, who says that?" replied Roger, as he began to rise from the bridge wall.

"Me, Nurse Miller, patient Gibson, and if you are a good patient you might get a bit of extra attention, for therapy purposed of course!" smiled Agnes.

"Lead on Nurse Miller. I am in your hands," replied Roger, as Agnes gave him a playful smack across his backside.

"It's over Roger, try and put it behind you."

"If it was only that easy, Agnes," sighed Roger. "I'll have to go back there soon; for the trials at Belsen and Nuremberg. I am down as a key witness. Some of those camp guards have to be punished," Roger shook his head ruefully, before he continued in almost a whisper.

"The Hyena," rasped Roger between gritted teeth.

"The Hyena. She's not much older than you, certainly no older than Gerri Muldoon. Pretty blonde girl too. She'd been a camp guard in Dachau and Auschwitz, both concentration camps, before the Russians liberated them. She was so good at her job she was sent to Belsen, a labour camp, to speed up the cremations of the dying and the dead. She enjoyed her work so much she laughed doing it. She wasn't the only one," sobbed Roger, as he fell back into the deep recesses of despair.

Agnes held him again as she stroked his head gently as if she was attending sick child.

"I have to go. That evil has to be exposed. My Dad fixed it that I could dodge the fighting. I will not be dodging this fight. Others have come back with physical injuries far worse than the damage it has done to my head," explained Roger. Agnes looked at him in silence while she thought of what best to say to lift his spirits.

"I think you need a picnic on Strangford. Go back to where we started. I loved that day," smiled Agnes. "Best day of my life."

By the end of the evening they had both regained a normality they had not experienced since Roger left for the war..

That night Agnes sank her head in her pillow, blissfully happy that they were so much more than just boyfriend and girlfriend and thinking of the first time she first saw him on the night of the Blitz.

Chapter twenty-three

The Proposal

A full year later, Roger, Agnes, Alec and Gerri were out on a day together. Roger had driven them up in his father's Ford to the North Coast. They travelled up the Antrim Coast Road through Glenarm, Cushendall, Ballycastle and Bushmills, to their destination at Portballintrae. The boys took the girls for a round of golf at Bushfoot. Gerri's camogie skills meant that she got the hang of it without much difficulty. Agnes, on the other hand, was terrible. Alec's description of her ability should really have been left in the Army barracks. Gerri threatened to do serious damage to him with a 'five iron'. To be fair, a set of clubs suitable for a six-foot man, being used by a girl barely stretching to five foot in her heels was an impossible task.

At the end of the day they walked to Runkerry Beach and sat on the sand dunes as they surveyed the horizon, the Causeway cliffs to the right and the Bush river entering the Atlantic to beckon the salmon home to their place of birth.

After they ran out of the opportunity to sling friendly insults at each other, they all fell silent, taking in the smell of the sea air and the sense of fulfilment of a wonderful day. Even the weather had not let them down.

Roger broke the silence.

"Alec, don't you think this is quite a romantic setting?" as he stared out across the Atlantic surf that rolled in great swells as it gouged into the sandy beach. Alec gave Roger a bit of a look out of the side of his eye, but remained silent,

"Mother of God, Roger. What are you asking him about romance. He wouldn't know about romance if it hit him up the face" laughed Gerri.

"Romance?" asked Alec. "Sure that's soft. Actions speak louder than words in my book."

Gerri and Agnes exchanged looks of despair, as they rolled their eyes.

"Ah, so all the times you have been wanting a bit of action that's your way of saying you love me, is it?" chided Gerri to Alec.

Alec was about to reply with one his standard responses.

"No Alec, Don't dig yourself a big hole in this sand. I want to be serious for a minute if you don't mind," demanded Roger.

"How would you two like to be best man and bridesmaid at a wedding?"

Gerri, Alec and Agnes held a stunned silence. Gerri looked at Alec. Agnes stared at the sand, smoothing it with her fingertips.

"Is there one coming up you know about, Roger. Is there a free bar?" bantered Alec, as Gerri gave him slap. "When is it?"

"I'll tell you in about ten minutes. Need to check if it's definitely happening," replied Roger, as he looked at Alec again.

Agnes sat motionless, staring at the sand, never lifting her head; afraid to make eye to eye contact with anyone.

Roger gave Agnes a nudge with his shoulder.

"Come on and we'll take a paddle in the sea."

Agnes had a heat in her body she had never encountered before.

Roger got up from the sand and offered his hand to walk Agnes to the water's edge.

Alec and Gerri, bit their tongues, both sensing this was a time best left for Roger and Agnes.

Gerri and Alec watched the pair walk hand in hand as the red sunset sank on the left side of the bay turning them into silhouettes.

Gerri and Alec both sat in silence, both without thinking, locked hands as they waited.

After an intimate head-to-head that seemed to go on forever. The silhouettes embraced. The larger silhouette lifted the smaller one into his arms and walked back up to Gerri and Alec to a sound of cheers.

"Easter Tuesday next year. Would you mind asking your neighbour if she would do the dresses. She worked wonders for that formal," announced Agnes, as she embraced, Gerri.

"Great stuff," roared Alec. "Well done the pair of you. It was always just a matter of time, but it was nice you chose to share it with us," said Alec, in a rare moment of sincerity devoid of his normal lack of subtilty.

The four talked in excitement of the day on their journey home. It was not until they reached Ballymena, before the fresh air of the North Coast began to dull their senses.

Agnes sat in the front with Roger, in a daze, thinking of her perfect day. Roger felt ten foot tall and couldn't wait until he got home to tell his mother and father.

Gerri and Alec, both became unusually silent, as they looked out of their rearview passenger windows; deep in their own thoughts.

By Templepatrick, Alec tried to discretely look at Gerri, as she stared out of her window. All he could see was her long jet-black hair

332

masking the side of her face. By Glengormley, Gerri had looked across at Alec who had been looking out of his window.

As they reached Carlisle Circus at the bottom of the Antrim Road in Belfast, less than a mile from Gerri's home in the Falls, both eyes finally met. Both looked each other in the face, both holding their stares.

Alec whispered. "We need to sort this!" Gerri, nodded and gripped his hand, saying nothing. At the bottom of Albert Street, she gave Alec a short kiss, stepped out of the car, and glanced back.

"Tuesday, the quadrangle, lunch time."

She walked back up to her house feeling the same as she did the day she walked home to tell her mother and father she was going to be a doctor. She had never allowed Alec to take her to her door. He had been the boy she was going out with that her parents never got to see or ever talked about. They thought she was ashamed to bring him home to a house in the Falls. The truth was to put off the moment that was now about to happen.

"Holy Mary, you don't half make life difficult for yourself, girl," she muttered to herself in despair."

On the following Tuesday lunch time Gerri left her lecture at Queens and walked over to the quadrangle, passing Sam Murray's porter's window giving him a wave and a smile as always.

As she walked onto the manicured lawn with the seats set along the pathway, she could see Alec. He wasn't sitting, leaning back, arms stretched, out across the back of the bench, as if he hadn't a care in the world. He was pacing up and down opposite the seat. Gerri, felt uncomfortable. Alec embraced her as she reached him, but it wasn't the usual cheeky clinch. It was uncharacteristically respectful. Gerri began to worry even more.

They both sat down as Alec put his hand in his jacket pocket and produced sandwiches Martha had made, lovingly wrapped in tinfoil and a linen napkin. Gerri's concerns lifted slightly.

He offered them to Gerri, expecting her to split them up to share and eat as usual.

"Let them be, Alec, I'm in no mood for eating," sighed Gerri, as she opened the bottom of her cardigan and leaned back in the seat, letting out a long gasp of air.

"Hardly took in a word of my lectures this morning. Do you want to start or will I?" asked Gerri, face looking at the gravel path, her voice, void of emotion, as much as she could manage.

"It might save a lot of bother if I start, Gerri," suggested Alec.

Geri's heart sank further. She did not like the way this conversation was going. Alec remained silent for a few seconds.

"I'd marry you in the furnaces of hell if I have to, so, wherever you want it, I'll run with it, girl. That is if you want an unromantic big 'peeler'[24] for a husband. I'm sure there's plenty of good Catholic lads that would have you. Don't think you'd go short."

Gerri sat silent, shaking her head slowly, face buried in her hands.

"That doesn't suit me, Alec," whispered Gerri, as she kept her head down, hands still across her face.

Alec, looked at her in surprise and disappointment. He thought that agreeing to marrying on her terms in a chapel, would solved everything. He leant back against the seat and looked at the sky; lost for words and empty in his soul, as the silence returned, only broken by Gerri's voice.

"Alec, I don't want you walking over any coals in hell or anywhere else for me. I don't want you sacrificing anything for me. I love you too much for that. The fact you would do it for me, is enough. I'm not having you paraded up the aisle of St Peter's like some prize trophy

---

just to please Father O'Rourke or my mother and father. I decide a while back that I would love nothing more than spend my life with you, but I couldn't say until I knew where you stood. I needed to know if you would do the same for me. Now I know," smiled Gerri, as she sat back in the seat alongside him.

"Hand me those sandwiches. I just got my appetite back."

By the end of eating their sandwiches, they got up to have a quick walk around the Tropical House in Botanic before Gerri had to return for a lecture.

"It's going to be fun telling my mother and father I'm not getting married in St Peter's. It'll be even more of a laugh telling them he's a Peeler," mused Gerri under her breath.

"Ah well, that's the other thing I was going to tell you. I'm not joining the RUC," advised Alec, in a manner that said it was not up for debate.

Geri looked at him in surprise.

"But you've wanted to be in the police since you were a kid. If it's what you want, don't let me stop you."

"No it's fine Gerri, I'll apply for the Harbour Police. It's still police, but I get round the politics, and it saves you any bother from your mother and father," laughed Alec.

"God you are a romantic big lad, after all," joked Gerri, as she pulled him in close, ignoring passersby on their lunch time stroll.

Chapter twenty-four

Time for change

Roger had to live with the memories of Bergen Belsen for years. It was not helped by the Nuremberg and other War Crime trials, he had to either give evidence or act as an interpreter. The Hyena sang Nazi anthems as the hangman's noose tightened round her neck.

It was 1952 by the time he was able to bury it so deep he could concentrate on his new life as a father of young William.

Agnes and he, had set up home down on the shores of Strangford Lough, as had quite as few of the large industrial dynasties of Belfast. It suited them both, Agnes worked as a District Nurse around the townland of Killinchy, Lisbane, Derryboye, Ballygowan and Killyleagh. She didn't need to work but all she had ever wanted was to be a nurse. She also liked to make a point.

Roger, did not have to be haunted by the meat factory every time he walked the Lagan towpath. The house they built near Sketrick

Island, Killinchy with its, stables and a few acres of land, looking over the Strangford Lough, they named Ballydrain.

Alec and Gerri, married, with only close family and friends, on the day she graduated as a Doctor of Medicine.

They had walked down from St Bridget's Chapel the few hundred yards down to the University. Gerri, with her robes over her wedding dress.

Alec received his own congratulations from some of the Police Band that provided the music as the graduates ate their traditional strawberries and cream. They were colleagues he knew. Gerri had not allowed him to change from the RUC to the Harbour Police.

Alec had convince her to let him marry her in St Bridget's. It satisfied Gerri's family and avoided a St Peter's victory parade. Canon Rab Tate had shared a pint with the priest of St Bridget's in the Eglantine Inn and came to an amicable agreement as they often did. Being in a middle-class Protestant area of Belfast, obliged to have a more liberal stance on the Vatican's rule book, St Bridget's never put them under any pressure to take the sacrament after the wedding. Gerri and Alec were able get on with their lives without complications.

In 1960 Davy and Anna, both retired, sat on the veranda looking over the estate they had been so fortunate to have shared. They had returned from Malone Golf Club after a Captain's Day event. Davy and John Clarke had both played poorly and had both decided their golf handicaps would likely be raised to the 'hackers' level. Anna, planning the work needing done to 'Roger's Roses' as she still called them.

Anna broke the relaxed silence, unannounced.

"All good things have to come to an end, at some point," she announced in subdued resignation.

Davy raised his eyebrows, confused by the announcement.

"It's time for change, Davy. It was always going to happen. Can't put it off any longer. Decisions have to be made," sighed Anna.

"What changes, Anna, explain? My brain isn't all that great after eighteen holes of golf, a big meal, John Clarke's speech, and a few beverages too many. I'm not like you, wafting around with your glass of wine, that no one noticed you had in your hand most of the evening, without ever topping it up," he asked, as he put his hand behind her shoulder and rubbed his fingers behind her ear in an attempt to reassure her unknown dilemma.

"Ballydrain," sighed Anna. "We have decisions to make."

Davy, looked at her, still not exactly sure what she was talking about.

"We've had our day in it, I've loved every day of it," continued Anna.

Davy, held his silence, as he thought, before he replied.

"Anna I'm not sure where you are leading with this. Ballydrain is yours. It's for you to make decisions about it. None of my business," replied Davy, not wanting to heap pressure on the issue that clearly meant something to Anna.

"This place needs a lot of work done to it. Roger and Agnes are enjoying life down at Killinchy. Joseph is up the road in his own place at Drumbo, following in your footsteps down at the City Hospital. Kathleen is well settled in her Veterinary practice at Boardmills. Any amount of horses and ponies to attend to around there. This place is far too big for us. It's time we moved on."

Davy looked at her with more than a certain level of surprise. He had not seen this coming. The house was becoming a bit tired and in need of renovation but having spent his first twenty years in the lockkeepers cottage it was still a palace to him.

Anna stared over the lake as she continued.

341

"Winter in our place in Villefranche, and somewhere a bit more manageable nearby in the warmer months. would be the best solution. My hip gave me a lot of pain last winter with the cold and damp," explained Anna, with an assurance that Davy realised she had been mulling this in her brain for quite some time.

"Where you go, I go. The lockkeepers cottage would do me, as long as you are there. Do whatever you want. I'm with you on whatever you decide, girl," consoled Davy, trying to make it easier for Anna.

"I'm getting nowhere with the solution. I need your help, Davy," stressed Anna.

"Is it not simple? Put it up for sale, and we'll go house hunting. I've loved every minute of this place, but if it's what you want; work away. I'm right behind you, girl," replied Davy, again.

"Wish it was that simple, Davy," sighed Anna, "I don't want what has been happening to other beautiful houses like Ballydrain around Belfast. Bulldozed in the name of progress, covered in tarmac and concrete. I know only too well that people have to have houses, but" as she buried her head in her hands, elbows resting on the small table in front of her, "Not Roger's gardens, Father's wood, the lake. Mother's view from the drawing room. Davy I cannot allow that to be erased. I don't care if I am being selfish. It is how I feel," stressed Anna, her fingers gripped in her delicate hands before she continued.

"I have already received letters from Stormont about redevelopment in the area. We are on their target list for a large housing estate," explained Anna, as she fell silent, relieved she had finally brought her hidden dilemma out in the open.

Davy, sat thinking of a reply, from his misted brain.

"Would you take less money if it solved you problem?" asked Davy.

"The money isn't an issue. We have more than enough to do us. The children are all well set up. Good rents come in from the Belfast property rentals and premises in the city centre. With Roger moving the factories to the Far East and South America; the dividends are flowing nicely to us all. Father would be proud of him."

She took a sip of tea before she continued.

"We could just close it down, but it would fall into ruin and the Government would have reason to vest it. It needs someone to look after it and keep it the same," explained Anna.

Davy's mind began to focus, as if it had been alerted about an emergency operation.

"Suppose there was a buyer, who would give you a decent amount. It would be nothing like the government would pay, but you would have the satisfaction of Ballydrain staying much the same," asked Davy.

"It would be perfect, but it is a pipe dream, let's be serious, Davy," replied Anna, as she raised her head from the table and looked wearily at him.

Davy looked at her confused expression, while the beauty and compassion in her face shone through. He looked at her, devoted to the posh girl. who rode her horse to the edge of her field and give him the eye.

"I might just have the answer," consoled Davy.

"Queens University are itching to take over Malone Golf Club down at Barnetts Park, but the Committee won't consider it without somewhere else to move to in the area," smiled Davy, "They are stuck for options."

Anna looked over the lake, as Davy continued.

"John Clarke is the Club President, Gerri Price is Lady Captain. They are both on the Committee. Leave it with me, Anna. Maybe time to have a few favours returned," winked Davy to Anna.

Long after Anna and Davy had passed away and joined Joe and Kitty, Ballydrain has remained as it was in the days that they ran through the meadows, excited and innocent fourteen-year-olds.

It is still a place of beauty and heritage, courtesy of the green keeping staff of the Golf Club. A small inclusion in the deeds confirmed that, given the below market price, it could not be used for anything other than recreational purposes.

Their children and grandchildren continued the line of the Arthur-Gibson family. Roger, Joseph and Kathleen all told their children the stories of Granda David and Grandma Anna.

Little did they know that the next generation would have their own experiences, of danger, love and understanding in the years that lay ahead.

That, as they say, is another story.

Printed in Great Britain
by Amazon